Richard Dee is a native of Brixham in Devon, England. He left Devon in his teens and travelled the world in the Merchant Navy, qualifying as a Master Mariner in 1986. Coming ashore to be with his growing family, he flirted with various jobs, including Dockmaster, Marine Insurance Surveyor and Port Control Officer, finally becoming a Thames Pilot over twenty years ago.

He regularly took vessels of all sizes through the Thames Barrier and upriver as far as London Bridge. He has returned to live in Brixham, where he has taken up food writing and blogging. He retired from pilotage in 2015.

Myra is his fourth Science Fiction novel; his other titles, *Freefall*, *Ribbonworld* and *The Rocks of Aserol* are available in paperback and electronically. He is married with three adult children and two grandchildren.

MYRA

Richard Dee

4Star Scifi

For Tom

Chapter 1, Now

I could see the feet sticking out from under the auxiliary generator; they were small and very pink, the nails painted with rainbow glitter. They looked incongruous against the machinery, delicate and unprotected.

There was a muffled hammering noise from the bowels of the machine, and a few choice words punctuated the clanging as some part of the workings was persuaded to behave. The sounds echoed in the confined space. It sounded wrong to hear the crude curses uttered with a soft feminine voice. Hearing the Navy slang took me back to a time before the madness of the last month. I was poised to shout a response when I felt a hand on my sleeve.

"Come on, boy, keep up," my mentor boomed, his hand on my shoulder dragging me away. "There's plenty of time to meet the engineer later, right now the captain wants to see you." He ducked his head under a low pipe and walked off. Shrugging, I followed.

The engine casing was spotless and well maintained, as was everywhere that I had been shown so far. The equipment was all painted in the familiar light green that the Navy used; apparently the colour made spotting oil leaks and overheating easier in dim lighting. Apart from the feet, and the swearing, the compartment was deserted. After the bustle of the *Moth*, it felt wrong somehow, like part of the ship's heart was missing. I stopped for a second and closed my eyes, I could still see the faces of my old shipmates, I could feel them brushing past me.

We moved deeper into the ship, an old decommissioned Atlon class cruiser, but as we progressed I could see that it had been severely modified from the one I had spent the best part of the last two years serving on. From a distance my new home hadn't looked pretty, the hull was worn and battered, but close up I could see that the exhausts were clean and all the fittings on the stern ramp looked new and were well greased. The armament appeared to have been kept, so there was firepower to spare if it was needed.

Of course I was the new boy here and was being given the full tour, despite the fact that I probably knew the basics of the ship as well as my guide. But I was constantly surprised by the differences; mainly in the automation required to compensate for reduced manning. Money had clearly been no object in the conversion, and in the long run was cheaper, after all the Navy used lots of men because it didn't have to make a profit, out in the real world wages needed to be paid on a regular basis and machines didn't need pay cheques.

Oh yes, things were going to be different and I was going to have to adjust. Fast.

We left the engine room and climbed up the stairway on the side of the hull, arriving on the catwalk. This open walkway ran athwart the ship and gave us a bird's-eye view of the cargo hold.

This Atlon had a much larger cargo space than that on the *Moth*; of course the conversion had removed all the troop accommodation and military stores. As we walked to the central passageway I could see a hive of activity below us, crates and trailers were being unloaded by a fleet of stevedores on lift trucks. The addition of a bigger stern ramp had made for easier access and had turned the warship into a versatile cargo vessel. The bulges of the four boat stations were visible, distorting the hold's shape and if they were all filled, that would add to the ship's flexibility.

All the familiar plans and safety gear were in place as we left the hold behind us and walked down the crew alleyway, our boots ringing on the painted steel deck. In the Navy, there would be people hurrying round, speaker messages and an air of industry. I wasn't used to the quiet; it felt weird and reinforced my feeling that the heart of the ship was missing.

The outward look may have been of a slightly worn, innocuous craft, but inside all was clean and tidy, maybe not up to Navy standards, but well cared for and capable of more than it appeared to be. Perhaps it wouldn't be so bad after all.

We passed the mess room and communal spaces and went up a deck; this was the officers' accommodation. I recognised my cabin. "You'll be in there," said my guide as we passed it. Another flight of stairs and we were in the senior officers' sanctum, at the end of the alleyway was the wheelhouse door, to starboard the captain's cabin. A haze of tobacco smoke drifted through the doorway, and I could hear the chink of glass and party noises from inside. My guide pushed his head around the doorway, after pulling the beaded curtain to one side.

"Hey, Rixon, I got the new navigator here to say hello."

"Well, Griff, wheel him in." The voice of my new boss, it didn't sound much older than mine, Griff turned to me, "Good luck, boy, off you go," he stepped aside to let me pass, then gave me a slap on the back. I tripped over the coaming and sprawled on the carpeted deck of the suite. "Send us a card from your next trip!" he shouted over his shoulder as he departed, the last thing I heard from him was his roar of laughter as he walked away. To him it was probably just a friendly pat on the back, thanks to my nervousness and the steel coaming it had become an embarrassment.

"Get up, lad, pay no attention," Rixon was grinning, and his companions, an assortment of tough looking men and attractive young ladies, regarded me with laughing eyes. "Griff doesn't know his strength, one day he's gonna find someone his own size."

Since Griff was about two metres of solid muscle, I suspected that there would be a few more victims before that day. How had I got myself into this?

As my eyes adjusted to the subdued main lighting, I saw comfortable leather covered seats, the deep piled carpet which I had already inspected and dark curtains covering the ports along one bulkhead. The spotlights along the bulkheads were dimmed and were shining in red and blue shades, giving the room the feel of a cellar or cheap club. Conversation stopped. In the silence I looked around at all the faces, trying to spot my new shipmates.

There were two distinct groups spread out on the seats, the first had three members, shaved heads and worn but clean jeans and shirts. Their look screamed soldiers, and they held cans of beer as they all faced the door. The other group was a lot larger and were more interesting to look at. All female, they had hair in various styles and amounts, and more outlandish clothes. A lot of toned flesh was on display and my day got brighter. It felt like everyone in the room was poised, waiting to see if I would be interesting, hopefully I wouldn't disappoint them.

Rixon was still talking. "Hey everyone, welcome our latest defector. Meet the new Nav; Dave Travise." The name still sounded strange to me, I had to remember that I was being addressed as everyone muttered 'welcome Dave' and 'good to see you'.

Dave Travise, Rixon had chosen the name and his tame forger on Basilan had set up the fake ID. It looked just the same as my old one, now languishing somewhere in electronic limbo. And it certainly worked; all my credits and accounts were still there in my new name, less the loan that I had been having trouble paying off, which was a bonus. So I was now Dave Travise, whatever my brain told me. And I probably didn't want to enquire too deeply about the original holder of the name. I would get used to it, in the end. That was the least of my worries, until a month ago; I had never considered that my life could turn out this way.

At least the change of name should keep me out of prison, or worse, the theoretical punishment for desertion from the Navy was still death. And depending on your point of view, I was at best a deserter; it would certainly be difficult to prove otherwise.

My father would have nodded wisely and considered that he had been right all along; at least he wasn't here to say 'I told you so', although I could hear it in my head as I stood there. I hadn't thought about him for a long while, now I felt his gaze.

He used to despair of me ever making a success of my life; he of course was at the top of his game, trading in cargo space on the freighters our family business owned. He had done military service during the Holy Wars, although I never knew exactly what.

I had been a late arrival in his life; his other sons, my brothers, were grown adults when I appeared, they were too old to be interested in me and all sickeningly successful in their own right. I idolised them and their stories and they ignored me. And I never knew my mother, I suspect my father suffered from referred guilt and that made him treat me the way he did. I had a sister, but again she was older and too preoccupied with her own life to take much interest in the new arrival. The impression she gave was of disapproval of my father, siring me when he should have been old enough to know better. And with someone who she told me was not much older than she was.

So he was a respected ex-Navy man and ship's Captain; large in both body and attitude, he dominated any gathering, his pointed beard forcing its way into the centre of things, his self-confidence and volume making everyone listen. To make matters worse, he lavished praise on my siblings, whilst telling me that I needed to try harder to gain his approval. It made me determined to show him that I was a worthy son, but somehow he kept the approval dangling, just out of my grasp.

In a last attempt to gain it, and prove it to myself as much as to him, I enlisted in the Navy on my sixteenth birthday, just as fast as I could get away. His response was to tell me that it wouldn't last and if or more likely when I failed, not to bother coming back to him.

I had stuck three years of training, all the casual brutality and the unflattering comparisons to my father's achievements, thinking that every day was one day closer to proving him wrong. I got through it all; then I was qualified and could start working my way up the slippery ladder to a command of my own.

When I made Navigator, just short of my twenty-first birthday and one of the youngest in the service, I sent him a message, but he never replied. Neither did any of my siblings, all contact having been severed; sometimes I wondered if it had been on his instructions.

When this all started I was three years out from the Navy Academy on Bleese. I was a Second Class Navigator in the Colonial Support Corps, assigned to the Atlon class cruiser, *Moth*. We were patrolling the edge of Federation influence, keeping an eye on miners and planetary surveyors and colonists. Generally protecting the honest settlers of the Rim against the assorted criminals, scavengers and other lowlifes that lived and preyed on the edge of civilisation. With that, and the threats posed by space and by nature itself, we were kept pretty busy. We were a kind of cross between the police, a lifeboat and about a hundred other things. But it made for an interesting life; one day we could be setting up a colony, the next rescuing the crew from a drifting ship. We stopped a few fights but had never fired a shot in anger.

The *Moth* was commanded by Captain Hermann Dror, a relic from the old days, and a man with a reputation. In his youth he had been one of the rebel captains involved in the uprising that had led to the Holy Wars, and he should have been retired years ago. His knowledge of the old religious government was probably part of the reason he was still around. And maybe he knew enough secrets to be kept where he could be controlled. The mess deck version was that no one was brave enough to tell him to quit. He was a hard taskmaster with a withering tongue, but nothing that I couldn't handle. And it was just nice to be out of the classroom and doing something. I could put up with a cantankerous old man, my father had been one. He must have known my father, but he never let on, and my treatment was no different to any other junior officer, so in some ways that was a good thing. I never knew if they kept in touch and wasn't likely to find out.

The *Moth* wasn't the biggest or newest ship in the fleet, but the

Atlon class were still quite impressive. Just over a hundred metres long, with twin engines aft and stub wings forward, they carried a crew of around fifty, plus a detachment of twenty marines in two groups, each with a drop ship in its own hangar. They had two shuttle runabouts as well and with their manoeuvring thrusters they were handy craft for the role, and big enough to carry the equipment needed to make a difference. They had reasonable armament and defences, although it was rarely used in anger. Test firing was about as exciting as it had got.

Of course, the people of the Rim viewed us in slightly different ways; depending on their activities we were saints or sinners, the welcome face when all is collapsing around you, or the nuisance who always appears when least wanted.

Rixon coughed, and I realised that I had been stood there lost in thought when I should have been talking. I snapped back to the present.

"I wouldn't say defector," I answered, looking him straight in the eye. "I like to think that they left me, if you don't mind."

I might have been the new boy here, but I was going to start as I meant to go on. I looked away from Rixon, and could see sympathetic nods from the group I had decided were crew; the rest just watched me and carried on drinking.

"Sure, no offence meant." He stood and put out his hand, still grinning. "I'm Rixon, just Rixon. It's good to have you aboard, various people speak highly of you and that's enough for me. And I understand your change of heart regarding the Federation; most of us have been there. Do you want to tell us all about it?"

He was a big man, just slightly taller than me, with a tanned, honest face and blond stubble on his scalp. Wide shouldered with a fluid agility as he moved, he exuded calm confidence and honesty through clear blue eyes. I instantly liked him.

"Not just at the moment," I answered, "if that's alright with you. I'm still reeling from the turn of events; let me get it straight in my head first."

"Sure," he replied, he waved his arm around the room. "I'll introduce you to the crew, over there is Tan. She's the mate and those are some of her cronies," a striking woman in the group of striking women raised her glass and nodded. They were the ones I had dismissed as 'others'.

"You've met Griff, he's got no official title, just think of him as the fixer, he's worth his weight in gold, he knows everyone and everything. Myra the engineer is around here somewhere, and those three," he pointed to the shaven denim-clad group, two men and a woman, "are the crew. They love to think of themselves as guns for hire, Stu, Mitch and Ardullah. They sit watching the door. Anyone else is just here for the party."

They all nodded at me, and raised cans and glasses, then went back to their conversations and drinking. I realised that Mitch was very female, but unlike Tan she had shaved her head. I knew that it made it a lot more comfortable to wear the helmets of pressure suits for long periods, although not everyone bothered, preferring looks to comfort.

Rixon was still talking as I scanned my new shipmates. Now I had spoken, they had lost interest in me, but I supposed that was only to be expected.

"It must be a shock to find out that we're human." Again there was the mocking grin.

"It's true that the Federation don't see you as anything more than a nuisance," I told him, "but they aren't so perfect themselves." I had learnt that the hard way and after all it was the biggest bit of the reason for my being here in the first place. The events that had led me here still gave me sleepless nights, and whatever Rixon and his bunch got up to, it could hardly be worse.

Rixon was looking past me, over my shoulder at the doorway. I heard the swish as the curtains parted. "Well our engineer has chosen to join us," he said. Again his tone was one of gently mocking affection, it seemed to be his default setting, but it was so warm and without obvious malice that it would be difficult to get upset at his comments.

"Hey, Myra, I thought that would get you away from the engine room, have you come to check out the new Nav?"

I turned, and even though I didn't immediately realise it, it was then that I fell in love.

She was about a head shorter than me, well curved with delicate features. Even though it was a patronising assumption, I couldn't imagine how she had the strength for the manual work that went with the engineer's job. She thrust out a hand, the motion strangely masculine, her grip was strong, very strong, and I banished that thought from my mind.

She was dressed in a faded brown boiler suit, which looked like it had been altered to show her shape. She had kept her hair, which was brown and piled on top of her head, where it was fixed with a metal pin. Wisps of hair had escaped and floated around her face. Her eyes were easily her best feature; sparkling in the reflected lights they were large and very blue, the sort of eyes you could get lost in. The painted toes now peeked through leather sandals.

Overall, she had a quiet air about her, as if deep in thought about the secrets of the universe. She looked at me and blushed, as if she could read my mind, and then her face cracked into the broadest grin you could imagine. Her teeth were white and even, and a small pink tongue waggled furiously as words came out in a rush.

"Hello, you must be Dave, I'm Myra, the engineer on this bucket, don't take notice of Rixon, well I suppose you must as he's the boss, but just ignore his sarcasm, and you'll be alright." She stopped for breath and I saw Rixon grin.

"Myra, you're gabbling again," he said, in that gently mocking tone, "you always do that when you get a man in front of you."

"Well it never happens with you, does it, Skipper?" She raised an eyebrow. "Now where's the beer, I've had my head stuck in the Inverter for half a day and I need hydrating. And why is Dave not drinking?"

Rixon lent over behind his desk and produced two cans of beer;

Myra took them and led me to a vacant seat. I sat and she wriggled herself in beside me and passed me a can; I clicked the bottom, hearing the hiss of the chemical reaction that instantly frosted the metal. We opened the tabs and knocked our cans together in a toast and I took a long drink, it hit the spot straight away.

"So, Dave Travise," she said, sounding genuinely interested, "tell me all about how you ended up here."

Myra was touching me as we sat, wedged into a space really only big enough for one of us, and I realised that she was leaning into me as she spoke.

And the warmth of her body, the tone of her voice, and her huge eyes gazing at me, made me open up and give her the full story.

Chapter 2, Then

It was a long story; it had all started out as a mission of mercy. The local Navy Commander had received a call for help from the settlement on Oonal, a recently incorporated world in the vastness of the Rim. It had been settled after the Holy Wars by a fundamentalist religious sect that wanted a bit of peace and quiet.

In the aftermath of the Wars, there were a lot of groups like theirs, the losers who had slunk off and now kept out of the way, or those who had used the peace as an excuse to wipe the slate and start again.

This particular bunch had called in desperation; they were complaining about harassment from some criminals, although they actually used the term pirates, a catch-all for criminals on the Rim. Apparently they had been turning up on a semi-regular basis and were giving them grief over their way of life. Despite the wish that they had for seclusion and their lack of admiration for the Federation, they had had enough and needed some help. Things were apparently getting more violent each time they appeared; they said that this time some women had been taken hostage and crops and equipment had been stolen.

The uneasy peace that held between the Federation and the remains of the Blessed, the collective name for the old order, meant that we had to help, but we didn't have to enjoy it. As most of the Blessed had set up their own federation, which they called the Independent Worlds, a lot of people thought that they should assume responsibility for these splinters, but they were in 'our' space so it was down to us.

When we received the call, we were up to our eyes in disaster relief, a meteor storm had wreaked havoc on a settlement called Michael's Hollow, and we had been one of the ships sent to assist in any way we could. When we had arrived with a full load of emergency supplies, we had found ourselves a small part of a multi-ship rescue operation. We were one of three naval vessels, there were ships from charities and chartered traders as well, all doing their bit to help. Between us we had spent a week burying the dead, repairing the power grid, and were setting up some the last of the prefabricated shelters from our hold when Captain Dror had got the orders.

We were the last ship left on the planet, the others had left on other missions as the amount of work that needed doing had decreased. There was always another crisis somewhere that needed attention. At the time we didn't know what was happening, just that new orders had been received. Obviously that never stopped the on-board rumour mill, which swung into immediate operation.

Depending on who was talking, the Holy Wars had started again with all that entailed or we were off on a rescue and it might involve a bit of excitement. The marines were buzzing at the thought of something different. There was always tension on board because none of us ever really knew what Dror would do next and twenty pumped-up marines itching for action added to the mix. The chance of a real fight and we were all raring to go. But Dror said nothing.

The first I knew about it officially was about half a day after the rumours started, when Dror came onto the bridge. I was using a bit of my time away from building shelters to catch up on some of the never-ending paperwork. He handed me a copy of the signal and stood behind me whilst I read it. I could feel his anger; it was like an aura surrounding him, radiating energy in all directions.

"Bloody religious fanatics, eh," Dror muttered when I handed the signal back to him. "They bitch about us until the turds hit the turbine, then they want us to ride to the rescue." He warmed to his theme. "They're probably claiming to be pacifists. Well, they're meeting the real world now and you know what that means don't you, Nav?"

It was time for me to reply and his pointed beard twitched in anticipation of the expected response. His beard was the same style as my father's and at times the resemblance was uncanny. If I closed my eyes, it could almost have been him speaking, the sentiments were the same. But then they were both from the same place.

"Even pacifists need a pulse cannon sometimes, sir," it was a straight repeat of both of their views; I had learnt the hard way that anything else would not be tolerated. He nodded his approval.

"Quite right, Nav. It's good to see that you're coming round to my way of thinking."

He paused, as if considering things although I was sure he had already made up his mind.

"I suppose we should go and help them, but let's not rush, eh; plenty of time. We'll go over all the details when I've briefed the marines and the tactical team, in the meantime just carry on with your duties."

Dror's lack of urgency and bias annoyed me, but having been on board a while, it was no longer a surprise. It seemed to me to be a dereliction of our duty, but hey! he was the captain.

He was very anti Blessed, and would fly into a rage at any mention of them. Given his history it was understandable that he had no room on his ship for anyone even slightly religious. Whereas I understood from my training, and indeed had sworn at my passing out that I would protect and serve all the peoples of the Federation, without fear or favour.

It also seemed a little strange that we were going, after all there were other ships, and we were busy here, why pick out the one with the most unsuitable skipper for the job, but then the Navy worked in mysterious ways and orders were orders.

I wondered if there would ever be a closure until all his

generation were put out to grass. People of my age had only vague recollections of the conflict, and none of the times before it, so in general bore the Blessed no ill will. And surely anybody, whatever their allegiance or beliefs, deserved a quiet life. Despite his words, I started planning out a few things in my head, the sort of arrival that he would want and how to do it.

Later, in the mess room, over a plate of the unappetising and unidentifiable things that passed for food, I was talking to Leonie, the officer in charge of the marine's on board, and the intended object of my affections. Officially fraternisation was frowned upon but with the amount of adrenaline and other hormones on-board it was inevitable. While a blind eye was turned to nocturnal events, the antics of jealous ex partners were not; as far as I knew (and I had looked) Leonie was currently unattached. And she was something to behold as a result of all the fitness training.

The layout of the space in the mess meant that we were pressed close together at the table, good for a budding romance but she didn't seem to notice the contact as much as I did. She was fresh from Dror's briefing and her eyes shone with excitement. She seemed to glow with a desire to shoot something as I told her my feelings about the delay. I already knew that Oonal was not exactly next door, it would take us a while to get there.

"So the disillusionment is setting in?" she laughed. "It doesn't normally take this long, but you're unlucky here, Finn."

"How's that, then?" I asked her, at the academy I thought that I had been envied for my posting to the *Moth*, but maybe that was just for the excitement of working the Rim. It was definitely the juiciest posting, better than the ceremonial duties that seemed to be the function of the rest of the fleet.

"Well Dror is old school," she said, pushing her food around the plate. "If you cut him in half it would say Federation right through him, but he's got the religious intolerance as well. It comes from his generation, they remember the overbearing Holy governments and it colours their thinking." She stopped talking and ate a few mouthfuls, grimacing at the taste.

"So if the call was not from a religious group he would go quicker?"

"Probably," she nodded, pushing her half-eaten food away. "Trouble is he's torn, he hates criminals and bullies, but he hates zealots as well, and any reminder of the old order, so it sets up a paradox in his brain."

"It seems to me though, that all we've done is exchanged the Holy governments for the Federation, and in a way it's just as bad but without the religion."

Leonie looked around to see who was close enough to hear; she lowered her voice, "Watch it there, Finn. There's a lot will agree with you, but it's better to keep talk like that to your close friends."

The fact that she had said close friends was promising. I was just about to bring the conversation round to getting to know Leonie better, when Dror pushed the mess room door open. All conversation stopped and we stood.

"Carry on, gentlemen and ladies," said Dror. He scanned the room and spotted me. "There you are, Nav," he called. "I suppose you'd better get organised and sort out a route. And you know our destination, I'll be up to the bridge in a few minutes to discuss tactics, but finish your meal first." He nodded to Leonie then turned and left. The room collectively let out a breath; everyone else was relieved that Dror had spoken to me and appeared to be in a good mood. They regarded me with jealous eyes; I would know where we were going before them.

"That was close," Leonie said, with a worried tone that gave me hope. "Remember, Finn, close friends."

Dror had said 'finish your meal first', but I had choked down as much as I could.

As navigator, it would be my job to plot the approach, so when I got to the wheelhouse I fired up the ship's chart computer. There was the usual frustrating wait whilst it initiated and checked the secure link for updates, the technology was about ten years old, in other words obsolete, but it would not be replaced until spares were no longer available.

Unlike on newer ships there was no voice interface, all the route planning was keyboard based and there wasn't even a calculation mode, the chart computer linked to a separate computer for that, with all the attendant potential for error and malfunction.

The standing joke was that the bad guys had better gear, and in border disputes were more aware of their position than we were.

The machine finally bleeped and I pulled the keyboard towards me. I typed in Oonal and the 3D screen built into the chart table showed it as a red dot. I zoomed in and rotated the picture until I had it centred; it was on the Rim at least sixty degrees away from our blue dot.

I adjusted the picture until I had both dots on opposite edges of the screen and using the menu illuminated the gravity field overlay.

Yellow spheres surrounded each star, showing the extent of the gravitational influence that would prevent our use of trans-light speed. As long as I plotted a course that kept out of the yellow, we could ignore Einstein and use the Padget Inverter to create a field that enabled what we called C+, faster than light travel.

After an hour's steady work I had produced a route and plotted a series of course alteration waypoints, they all needed joining up and that was where the number crunching started.

I saved the route and transferred the points to the computer, which calculated course, speed and engine settings before passing it back to the chart. As it worked, each point was joined by a green line. Finally I had a route, which I saved in my files and the ship's.

Dror had not appeared, so I took a look at our destination.

Chapter 3, Now

I paused for a drink; it took me a while to come back to the present. In my mind I was still on the *Moth*. I could see that all the people had crowded round me and the music had stopped. I had been so involved in telling the story that I hadn't noticed. It was a surprise to see that they weren't my old shipmates. There was an air of expectation about them though, you could feel the interest. Myra had put her arm around my shoulders and was obviously comfortable squeezed in next to me. I was enjoying the contact.

"Oonal is some place," said Tan wistfully. "My first voyage was on a boat running supplies for the settlers, and well, it's some place." There was nodding and murmurs of agreement.

"Go on, Dave," someone else urged, "tell us more, you can't stop now."

Taking a long drink from my can, I continued. So far the story had been boring, now it was going to get a bit more interesting. I took a deep breath.

Chapter 4, Then

There wasn't a lot of information in our system; the latest updates said that Oonal was a medium sized world with a young star. According to the notes attached to the surveys the star had not really settled and was prone to phasing, the analysts term for hot and cold periods. There was no clue to the duration, or severity of these, so it could warm up tomorrow, or cool down come to that. It didn't sound like an attractive prospect, but maybe it would be stable for thousands of years.

The reports said that it had recently entered a cooler phase. As I scrolled through the charts and pictures that we had, and there weren't many, I could see that most of the planet's surface showed signs of severe heat damage. There was scorched and blackened rock and evidence of lava flows. Somehow the life that had existed before the planet had warmed had clung on in the only possible place, the deep valleys that ran for thousands of miles across the low latitudes.

The result of erosion or seismic activity, any water that had once formed or ran in them had long since gone. Such moisture that existed was partly held in the tough vegetation and partly condensed in the cold night air, before evaporating with the dawn. The notes said that the settlers collected this water and stored it in the caves that honeycombed the valleys. A lot of water had found its way there, because of that and the shelter from the heat, plants and small animals had survived.

Now that the surface had cooled to a more conducive temperature the plant life, with natures amazing power of survival had started to spread back onto the surface. The increasing plant life had boosted the oxygen levels to a reasonable twenty per cent; the planet was listed as having been inhabited for the last thirty years, with a question mark.

The information we had suggested that there was only one settlement on the planet. It was built on flat ground in one of the larger valleys and consisted of a cluster of prefabricated huts surrounding a large open space. The dwellings were surrounded by fields in which the settlers were growing crops and grazing animals for food. At that point the valley was over a mile wide and naturally terraced, with the settlement on the higher ledge. Power was supplied from solar panels and wind turbines on the surface, microwave linked to a utility suite on the edge of the settlement.

Looking at the buildings and gear, which was all the best quality; money appeared to have been no object when constructing the settlement. That fitted in with the story, obvious wealth would have made them a target. Anyone seeing the place would have thought that there might well be some loot from their days in the last of the Holy governments around. Or maybe they just weren't liked for the way they had behaved when their kind were in charge.

A dry river bed ran through the middle of the settlement, splitting the buildings from the fields and there were several metal bridges connecting the two halves. Off to one side was a small landing strip with room for a couple of transports. Behind them were cliffs and in front a drop of several hundred metres to the next terrace. According to the last estimate there were up to two thousand people living in the settlement.

There was a beacon on the utility transmitter that we could use to home in on, assuming the intruders hadn't turned it off. Of course, they may have left their own beacons in orbit to detect our arrival, giving them the chance of a quick getaway.

"Right, Nav." Dror had come into the chart space while I had been working and now leant over my shoulder. "What do we have?"

I gave him the gist of what I had read, about the valley and the layout. We discussed tactics and my rough plan to surprise the pirates, assuming they were still there. Dror was pleased with what I had in mind and grunted his approval. "Set it up," he ordered. "You can brief everyone on the way."

Then we packed up our relief effort and headed for Oonal.

It would take us three days to get to Oonal. Dror and his Tactical Officer spent the time preparing for a show of force. I presented my plan for our arrival over the settlement but was excluded from the warfare meetings. Leonie's troops set up and checked their gear time and again, and we rehearsed dropping out of orbit and deploying the troopships on the *Moth*'s simulator.

I was excited in a strange way, this was my first combat mission, apart from the disaster relief work and a few rescues, all we had done up to now was patrol, survey and show the flag. Contrary to popular opinion, there was no longer a continual battle on the Rim, and apart from drills we had not fired our cannon in all the time that I had been on board. The senior officers were always complaining that the Galaxy was getting too civilised.

The night before our arrival, I was again in the mess with Leonie and her second in command, a big marine called Tanner. They were fresh from a training session and wound up as tight as coiled springs. Over our meal I tried to talk to Leonie but she was impervious to my attempts at conversation, all she could say was that she would be leading her boys into combat in the morning. Her eagerness to shoot something unsettled me, particularly as we didn't know what we would find, but maybe that was just her way of dealing with the anticipation. Tanner was a lot calmer, a long service veteran, he had seen most things and survived them all.

"I reckon they'll be long gone," he said, "we shouldn't have waited before we left."

"I do hope not," said Leonie and I could see the sadness in Tanner's eyes as he contemplated her passion for action. He had clearly seen some and had realised, as all survivors did, that it wasn't as glamourous as you expected.

~~~~

Next day, I was called to the bridge as we dropped out of trans-light speed. We were still quite a distance from the planet but the gravitational influence of Oonal's star had increased and we could not maintain the C+ field. From here on in, our maximum speed would be ninety-five per cent C, the maximum our engines could make. To confuse any hostile beacons we approached across the planetary plane, it made for a less efficient route but one more likely to escape detection. Our electronics were primed, ready to jam any signals that we found.

My plan, which Dror had accepted, was to approach the settlement along the line of the sunrise, dropping into the valley at the last minute, giving us room to catch any escapees. We would appear at the same time as daylight whilst hiding in the shadow. Our troop shuttles would be flying free, one with us and one which would approach from the opposite side of the valley. If any of the pirates were left on the ground one or both could deploy troops, whilst we covered them from above. After a three hour flight, we arrived high above the dark side of the planet, ready to enter the atmosphere. Dror was seated in his command chair, yeoman at his side, ready to control the operation.

There were no clouds in the atmosphere, and the lights of the power station and utility transmitter could be seen far away and below in the darkness. The beacon was working normally and scans revealed no others in orbit. I matched the view below with the mapping on the chart; we were where I had wanted to be in relation to the power station. This was my aim point to drop onto the settlement, now we just had to wait for the planet to rotate beneath us. With everything set and computed, I was done and I reported to Dror.

"Well done, Nav," he gruffly acknowledged. "You have control. Count us down."

I checked the computer for local time. "Ten minutes fifteen seconds to sunrise at the settlement, Captain, so we need to commence our descent in four minutes and thirty seconds."

I watched the clock. "Mark," I called as the seconds ticked by.

"All yours then, Nav." Dror turned to the Yeoman beside him. "Call Leonie and Tanner, load up and stand by to deploy on my command." The yeoman repeated the order and received a reply from the troop carriers. "Standing by, sir," he confirmed.

I watched the numbers count back and issued the orders as the seconds hit zero. "Helm down angle twenty degrees, slow ahead two, and steer for the lights." There was a jolt as the engines fired and we dropped into the atmosphere as my orders were acknowledged.

The re-entry was smooth, the thinner atmosphere meant less buffeting and we dropped into a clear sky at fifty thousand metres, still several hundred miles short of the valley. I took the *Moth* down to just under a hundred metres and flew slowly over the featureless plain, occasionally passing over deep valleys. I knew that in the shadows they were lush and green, a contrast to the arid surface, the only features on the plain were solidified lava flows and an occasional patch of lichen. At fifty miles out Leonie and her troops were launched, they sped off in a long curving track that would bring us back together from opposite directions. The second troop carrier launched and stayed with us.

Thirty miles out and two minutes to sunrise, we adjusted course to pass close by the red lights on the wind turbines, I slowed us down a touch, reducing the engine noise, keeping in the dark shadow that marched across the plain in front of us. Our detector showed Leonie on the other side of the canyon, radio silence meant that we couldn't be sure she was ready, but we had planned enough, and she could see us.

Fifteen seconds to go and the line of light cleared the canyon rim, I followed it over the edge and looking through the belly camera saw the settlement below, it looked quiet. Ahead, Leonie appeared over the other rim and dropped towards us, breaking radio silence she reported all quiet. Together we fell on the buildings.

Surprise was complete, and we arrived over the settlement at the same time as the shadows raced away in the sunrise. I put the *Moth* into a slow circle over the buildings; I saw that there were two transports on the ground. The troop carrier landed and Leonie and her squad leapt out and formed a skirmish line, facing the buildings. I was busy keeping station and lost track of what was happening but I could hear Dror's voice as he announced our arrival on the hailer.

"Oonal settlement, this is Captain Dror of the *Moth*, please show yourselves, do not be alarmed, my marines will secure the area, please cooperate."

There was movement, people came rushing out of the huts, waving and jostling, their clothing blown about by our thrusters' wake. Leonie and the marines moved towards them, poised for action, but they stayed passive and allowed themselves to be searched.

"All clear, Captain," Leonie reported over the radio. She sounded cheated, as if something had been taken away from her.

"Thank you, take us down, Nav," ordered Dror and I started the landing sequence.

The settlers had been assembled on one of the bridges over the river bed when Captain Dror stepped down the stern ramp onto the surface. The second shuttle containing the rest of the marines was hanging overhead, ready for action. Leonie had separated the men from the women and children; they were lined up on each side of the structure. Marines guarded each end. I was standing close to Dror as he stood in front of the bridge. It was a fine morning and the air smelt fresh after the *Moth*. Every planet smelt different, this one had the aroma of freshly tilled earth and honey.

The settlers looked like a pretty average bunch to me, there were lots of women, at least twice as many as men and I wondered at the form their 'religion' took. There were plenty of stories about weird sects and cults, perhaps this was one. Small children ran around, oblivious to the adults and the presence of armed marines. The men were mostly older, dressed in dirty white robes with sashes of various colour. Just about everyone looked hungry.

Someone who I took to be the leader of the settlers came forward; he was a large man with long hair, a bushy beard and a wild look. Dressed in the stained robes of a Priest of the Blessed, he looked around himself nervously as he spoke, watching the reactions of his fellows. He was closely attended by two acolytes, similarly dressed and younger looking, their robes cleaner. I got the impression that they were the real power.

"Where have you been, Captain?" the priest demanded, his tone indignant. This was probably the worst way to speak to Dror. I was standing slightly behind him and could see his neck redden as he listened. "We called for your help five days ago." He spat on the ground, close enough to Dror to be insulting but far enough away to avoid comment. "The pirates have only just gone, and they have taken a large amount of our crops and some of our women. You must get after them straight away, they are headed for Mistiq."

Dror looked around him, his gaze icy. After a long pause, in which you could see that he was not impressed with the lecture, or the suggestion that he fly halfway round the Federation, he replied, "Sir, you are not the only place on the Rim that needs our help, are any of your people injured?"

"No," the priest replied. "We have three dead, but have buried them already, as is our custom, apart from the hostages taken we are all in good health."

"Well then," said Dror, "it seems to me that we have come to you from aiding people who NEEDED our help, we have had to leave them with little shelter and food, you might at least show some gratitude."

The priest was unimpressed. "Captain, we are as much entitled to your service as anyone else, I have no control over who is sent, or from where and it's not my fault," he paused and waved at the heavily armed marines, "that there is no one left for your soldiers to shoot at. I have told you where they were headed," again he looked around, "now perhaps you could leave us and chase after them. I can give you their ship's signature, you can alert other ships to join in the chase."

It seemed to me that if we did what the priest was suggesting then most of the Rim fleet would be removed from the area. Dror must have come to the same conclusion.

"Well, sir," said Dror, somehow keeping his voice neutral, "you seem to have a good idea of how I should conduct Federation business. I will not send half the fleet chasing a single ship on a whim. May I remind you that you and your ilk are no longer in any position of authority, I am now the law here, and I will decide how I investigate and where I go."

Turning to address the rest of the settlers, he continued, "I think that my first job should be to search for any evidence that these people you call pirates may have left. We will have a look around your settlement to see what we can find. Tell me, are these your craft?" He pointed to the two transports.

"Yes," replied the priest. "But the pirates have immobilised them, their Inverters have been removed."

Dror took the priest by the shoulder and started to walk towards the largest of the huts, he motioned me to follow him and I took a position just behind them. He and the priest were talking in low tones. The acolytes moved to follow. "Leonie," snapped Dror, "I would talk alone to this man." She waved her hand and two of the marines stood in front of the pair. They stopped and glared, obviously uncomfortable.

We moved twenty metres away. "Tell me, sir," said Dror to the priest, "you seem to be putting on a show for the benefit of your men, trying to convince me to leave, is there something you wish to tell me, now that we have some privacy?"

"Yes, Captain," replied the priest, in a relieved tone, his hands were shaking and sweat ran down his face. "I apologise for my conduct but I think that some of my group are not all they seem.

I'm not sure but I have come to believe that my two acolytes are connected to the pirates. I was told to make sure that you set off as quickly as possible, and I think that they are still in contact with them."

"Thank you for the information," said Dror. "I assume some dire warning was given."

The priest nodded. "Yes, I heard one of them saying that they had business that required privacy, he was told to be quiet very quickly."

Dror nodded. "I'm sure they also said that they would be back."

"That's right," nodded the Priest, still shaking, "as soon as they had finished, they promised to return the hostages." He looked miserable. "I'm concerned for the safety of the people here."

"Thank you for your honesty," said Dror. "Don't worry, we will sort all this out for you. Here's what will happen, we will go and do what they want, or at least make it appear so, follow my lead in the conversation."

We turned and walked back to the group. Dror started talking in a raised voice for everyone to hear, "We will chase them, Priest, but we will leave some troops to search the area." He called across to the troops. "Leonie, walk with me. Nav, get back on board and set up for a trip to Mistiq, quick as you like."

Chapter 5, Now

I paused again, Myra was hanging on my words, but my can was empty. She took it, rose and walked over to Rixon. I had been so engrossed in my tale and Myra's closeness that I hadn't been aware of anything else.

Rixon noticed that I had stopped talking and shouted across, "Don't stop, Dave, what happened next?" There was a murmur from the others, everyone seemed interested. Rixon took the empty cans from Myra and passed her two full ones.

"Okay," I said, "but I need another drink first." Myra passed me a fresh can and I took a mouthful, it was ice cold and went down a treat. Myra squeezed back into the seat beside me and I continued.

Chapter 6, Then

Dror and Leonie must have had a long and detailed conversation while I went to the wheelhouse and set up the route for our run to Mistiq. Although I didn't think we would be actually going, I did it anyway. Dror could change his mind and then I would need it.

I had the time anyway; Dror could always stop me when he came back on board. It turned out to be quite a complicated route to plan. Mistiq was deeper in Federation territory and the overlapping gravity fields meant a lot of calculation. I lost myself in the work. I was surprised to find that it was more than two hours later when I heard the hiss as the stern ramp closed. A moment later Dror arrived on the bridge and settled himself into his chair. The Tactical Mate had the bridge watch and Dror explained his intentions to him.

"I've briefed Leonie and left her and her squad behind to secure the settlement and watch for hostile action," he said. "We're going to pretend to leave and then hang around; I get the feeling that here's where the action will be."

It was logical, based on what the priest had said; I only hoped that he had told Leonie about the priest's warning that there were at least two of the gang in the group and his suspicions. He turned to me.

"Okay, Nav, take us up and pick up Tanner's men." I gave the orders and *Moth* took off, when we were at two hundred and fifty metres, the second troop ship was recovered. Then we climbed into the sky, apparently on the way to Mistiq.

But we never went into orbit; instead we circled around when we were out of sight and sound of the settlement. We landed again in the shadow of a range of low lava cliffs. Dror called an officers' meeting where he explained his strategy.

Dror repeated what I had heard the priest say; he added that he thought that the pirates had never really left, just tried to get us out of the way for some unknown purpose. He had decided to lay in wait, he said, after pretending to leave. Leonie was to set up a camp, keep her eyes open and report to us.

"You take command of the second troop shuttle, Nav," Dror told me. "You're a better pilot than Tanner; he can leave one of his squad here. No offence meant, Mr Tanner."

Tanner and I had been competing for honours on the simulator, flying all sorts of challenges; so far I was ahead and even though it had been unofficial Dror had known, like all good captains.

"Yes, sir," I acknowledged.

Tanner grinned and punched me on the shoulder. "Understood, Captain," he said. "Looks like you'll get a chance for some fancy flying, Finn," he grinned.

"Thank you, gentlemen," said Dror. "You will standby for deployment. If we detect a craft we will capture it. Then if we have some prisoners, perhaps we can find out what's really going on here."

So we waited and we waited, all sensors scanning. Dror paced the wheelhouse, muttering to himself and as day turned into night, we all began to doubt his decision. I was stuck in the cramped shuttle with Tanner and eight sweaty marines, the air-con was struggling and the temperature rose. We all dozed, despite the heat and the snoring.

Then, just after sunrise there was the distinct 'ping' from the detector, it had picked up a ship's drive starting. "Contact," the detector chief called from the tactical space. "Repeat, contact, vessel taking off, range is 125,000 metres, bearing green 045." We had a remote video feed from the bridge in the shuttle so could follow what was going on. The launch was nowhere near the settlement, it was in another valley altogether.

"Wait till it clears the canyon and follow it," ordered Dror. "Stand by to deploy, Nav. If it goes into thick cover you can take over the chase." The viewer was swung to focus on the bearing and the zoom activated. *Moth* lifted into a hover and swung its bow towards the craft.

Tension mounted as we waited, the picture was distorted by the magnification and the haze of morning, but we all saw the craft appear from behind the rocks, gaining altitude quickly as its room to manoeuvre increased. It swung and tilted, obviously preparing to leave the atmosphere when Dror quietly said, "Weapons officer, arm missiles and prepare firing solutions."

They must have detected us at that point, because the craft suddenly tilted down and disappeared back into the canyon. There was a flurry of orders and a rush of acceleration as we followed. Dror had taken control, he was probably the best pilot in the Rim fleet and maybe that was why he had been sent to this place.

"Nav," Dror called, "we will follow as far as we can and attempt to keep up, if it gets too tight to manoeuvre, you deploy and take over while we wait above in clearer space."

Moth dove over the canyon edge and closed on the other craft. It dropped down and we followed. Dror threw the *Moth* around in the confined space as the chase continued. He stayed above the smaller ship; even so there was a lack of room for us. The pirate craft was smaller and more agile and was using the deeper, narrower levels and all the natural cover to keep ahead, all the time trying to lure Dror into an error. We slid sideways into a branch, and the walls closed in as the canyon suddenly narrowed. "Running out of room," muttered Dror. "We'd better get clear."

He shouted orders and *Moth* shot up above the Rim into clear air and Dror called down to me, "Deploy, Nav, and good hunting; we will be on station above you."

I punched the controls and we dropped away, the engines started up as we cleared and we were off. I was flying this one myself, whilst behind me the marines, all strapped in, watched the screens as we entered the narrow lower part of the canyon. Some slept.

The other ship was a red dot on my detector screen, reflected onto the port in front of me. Fortunately the detector didn't show the terrain, at my speed it would have been a blur anyway and I needed to concentrate on what I could see. I put speed on, trying to get closer as trees and rocks flashed past, inches from our heads behind a thin skin of metal. Pursuit was easier in this small craft, *Moth* would have been jammed in some of the gaps and for them, anything more than slow speed would have been impossible.

I felt exhilarated as I concentrated on the pursuit; this was why I was here, chasing the bad guys and protecting the Federation. I coaxed power from the engines as we caught up to the fleeing craft. We had the edge in speed, but they knew the area, it evened things out as I had to slow for the twists of the canyon, rolling us through ninety degrees to change our profile for the tight bits.

I clipped a rock, the whole craft shook and there were mumblings from behind me. "You woke me up," someone called, "now I'm getting angry." There was a nervous laugh.

I had the other ship locked on my targeting system and several times got a firing solution, but keeping to my orders, concentrated on getting closer. Their pilot was good, and there were times when I felt respect for their abilities, but I felt more determined to prove that I was better.

The canyon was still narrowing significantly, trees now grew above us as the walls arched overhead, blocking out the light, when suddenly we plunged into total darkness; we had entered a cave. The pirate craft still proceeded at full speed. There was no illumination so he must have had some sort of night vision; I didn't, so I had to turn on the searchlights to see where I was going.

I wished I hadn't as they revealed just how close we were to solid matter, the walls were a blur and I knew that one outcrop would mean an end to our pursuit. Large lumps of rock hung down from the ceiling, giving me something else to think about. I had turned the proximity alarm off because by now it would have been continuous. It was better not to think about anything but the target, my ship was smaller; if he could fit then so could I.

Behind me I heard more mutterings of interest from the marines, tough as they were, they could appreciate our situation and at the moment they had no control over it. Like it or not they had to trust me.

Suddenly the cave opened out into a huge space, beams of light shone down, looking like pillars of rock in the gloom, and my room to manoeuvre increased. I could see light in the distance ahead from where the cavern opened out into another valley as I cranked up the speed and got up alongside the speeding pirate craft.

Chapter 7, Now

"Okay, people," Rixon's voice cut over my story, jolting me back to reality. "Time to go to bed, we have a busy day tomorrow."

"Aww thanks, Skipper," said Myra sarcastically, echoing the groans from everyone else. "You can't stop him there. We all want to know how it ends."

I glanced around, I had been back in the shuttle and it took a while to realise where I was. In a way I was relieved to have been stopped, I was coming to the part of the story that I didn't want to remember.

People got up and started to drift away, they all talked to me on their way out, either to welcome me on board or ask about what had happened next. As I turned to leave, Rixon stopped me. "That's some tale, Dave," he said, "but that's a good place to leave it for now. You can finish it later, I hate to break it all up but it's getting late. There's a big day for you tomorrow so get some rest, you're going to show us what you can do."

Myra was waiting in the alleyway and walked with me, trying to get me to tell her more of the story. I didn't want to have to say it more than once so I just told her that the next bit wasn't pleasant, it involved a lot of death and destruction.

"Oh," exclaimed Myra, her eyes as big as saucers. "It just sounds like an exciting adventure so far, our lives are pretty boring in comparison, I've been here two years now and we haven't chased anyone yet."

"That's not what the Federation propaganda tells us," I said, "or what Dror used to say. As far as we know you're all practically biting the heads off babies, when you're not drunk or high and zooming round terrorising people."

She laughed at that, a full throttle explosion of mirth that made her shake. "Are you crazy, do you really think I would go into the engine room and run machinery when I was drunk, or that Rixon would fly in atmosphere stoned? We wouldn't last long like that. We may be having a few drinks now, but as soon as we decide to get moving it's all locked away. And there's no drugs on here, believe me."

We reached her cabin and she opened the door. "Goodnight, Dave," she threw over her shoulder as the door closed behind her. "See you in the morning."

Griff had told me that my cabin was the same one as it would have been on the *Moth*, but of course it had none of my gear in it. And I had it to myself. There was a lot of space from when I had been forced to share with two others, the extra bunks had been taken out and replaced with a pair of armchairs. There was a large pile of random objects in the corner which I presumed had belonged to my predecessor. Hopefully there would be something there that fit me because apart from what I stood up in I had nothing.

Closing the door behind me, I noticed that there was no lock, but by that point I was too tired to care. There was a pile of clean bedding on the mattress and after I had made the bunk up I stretched out on top of it and fell asleep.

I had the dream again, I'd had it every night since the events on Oonal and it always made me wake sweating and shaking. It was the part of the story that I hadn't told Rixon and the crew yet. Although Rixon probably knew it as well as I did. Maybe that and the presence of non-crew on board was why he had stopped me when he did.

Chapter 8, Then

As I pulled alongside the fleeing craft in the dark I tried to crowd it into the cave wall. The other pilot was too clever for that though and had rolled over me, the wing passing barely a metre above my head. Now we were on the inside and they tried the same manoeuvre on me. I wasn't sure how much room I had above so I elected to slow down. I dropped the flaps and cut the engine. They weren't expecting that and shot ahead. I followed, piling the power back on and sitting in their wake.

I got level again and did the same, but as they started to roll I lifted the shuttle up, reducing the room. Our wings clashed and I peeled away. The clash had caused a momentary lapse in the other pilot's flying. As they tried to correct they touched the cave wall and turned in towards it.

Tanner had been watching, he cheered, "Well done, Finn," he shouted and the marines joined in.

Somehow the other pilot had slid along the rocks without major damage and incredibly had regained control but as we both shot out into bright sunlight I could see smoke pouring from one of their engines. They were in no state to fly and pancaked onto the ground, sliding over the grass. Their passage left a long gouge in the earth, in the end one wing hit a tree and they spun around a few times and came to a stop.

I landed the troop carrier beside the smoking wreckage of the pirate craft and Tanner and the marines jumped out with their weapons at the ready and surrounded it.

I took my hands off the controls; they were shaking as the adrenaline surged through my veins. My vision felt clearer than it had ever been and everything was sharply focused.

I followed the marines, moving more slowly, my legs strangely reluctant to obey the orders of my brain. I had grabbed a pulse rifle from the rack by the door but didn't trust myself to point it at anyone, it hung by my side.

We were sat on a grassy plain, dotted with strangely shaped trees, on a terrace not unlike the one that the settlement was built on. Behind us in the cliff face was the cavern we had just emerged from. The sun was bright in the sky and a few insects buzzed around. There was a rumble from the sky, like distant thunder, *Moth* had been following our progress and now hung in the sky above us.

The hatch of the wrecked craft opened and two people staggered out coughing and spluttering, surrounded by smoke. The smell of burning insulation drifted on the breeze. To my surprise, one of them was the priest from the settlement and when he saw me he shrank back and tried to hide behind his companion, who I did not recognise. Tanner waved his left arm and two of his men detached and moved towards them. Pulling their hands behind them, they tied their arms together with zip ties and we marched them into our shuttle.

I called Dror. "Sir, we have two men on board from the wreck, one of them is the priest from the settlement. I will leave troops behind guarding the wreck and bring them up to you."

"Roger, Nav," said Dror. "Make it sharp, we can secure the wreck later. Don't bother guarding it; just get everyone back up on board as quickly as possible."

We made two runs to the hovering *Moth*, transferring the prisoners first then returning to pick up the rest of the marines. There was a body in the wreck, strapped into the pilot seat. Her neck was broken, the head lolled sideways and she was very dead. She had been a good pilot and looked to be only about fifteen years old. I felt tremendously sad as we left her there. When my shuttle was secured, *Moth* set off back towards the settlement and

I went to the bridge to report.

As I entered the wheelhouse there was a sombre atmosphere. Dror greeted me with a grim face. "We've just lost contact with Leonie," he told me. "Are your prisoners secure?"

"Yes, Captain, they have been taken to the brig. The shuttle and the marines are ready to redeploy on your command."

"Thank you, Nav," said Dror. "That was good flying; you'll have to tell me all about it later. Right now I'm more concerned about the status back at the settlement, all comms are down, even the individual headsets and I don't know why. We're heading back now to see what's going on." He gave orders and we spun around and picked up speed.

It took us a few moments to arrive over the settlement; we were guided to it by a plume of oily smoke that was rising into the clear sky. When we dropped over the Rim we could see several fires burning and as we got closer we saw a lot of bodies on the ground. There was no sign of the other craft on the ground; our troop carrier was the source of the oily smoke. There was no sign of any living person.

"Tactical," called Dror, "please scan for life-signs from the marines on the ground."

All of us had bio-transmitters implanted as well as our ID chips. They worked over short ranges only, but enabled bio-monitoring when in close proximity. We waited in anticipation. The speaker crackled:

"Captain, Tactical, all chips responding, but no life-signs." There was a pause. "I'm sorry, sir, but they've all gone." There was a noticeable change in the mood, like a sudden intake of breath and conversation stopped. Although that was the business we were in, the emotion was almost solid. I thought of Leonie, so alive and itching for action only hours ago; it brought a lump to my throat. How could she be gone? What WAS going on here?

"Get the prisoners up here right away," commanded Dror and they were brought up from the brig with their arms still tied behind them. Dror was in full unpredictable mode, he muttered to himself and his eye twitched, sure signs of some sort of impending action.

Dror turned to the priest. "Well, sir, what is your explanation for this and don't try and give me any more lies, what has happened to my marines and what is going on?"

The priest gazed at him with a stubborn expression, saying nothing. Dror turned to Tanner, who had escorted the prisoners. "Mr Tanner, would you care to shoot the priest's companion if he will not answer my questions a second time."

Tanner drew his pistol and placed it against the side of the man's skull. "With pleasure, sir, just give me the order." He was as shocked as the rest of us, but his training had taken over.

"Now then, Priest, if you even are a priest; give me the information I seek. What has happened here?"

"Very well," said the priest, "you do not need to shoot my companion, I will tell you." His manner was smug, almost triumphant; there was a gleam in his eye.

"The offer still stands, sir," said Dror. "If I don't like your answers he will be shot."

"I understand," said the priest. "We are not solely a religious community, although some of us still follow the Holy path. And I am ordained, since you ask. We were not attacked by pirates; there are a group who you would describe as such who live amongst us. Since the end of the Holy governments we do not recognise the authority of the Federation, and wish to carry on our lives without your interference."

"Then why not go and live among the Independent Worlds?" asked Dror. "After all, every planet had its choice at the end of the Wars."

The priest shrugged his shoulders and continued, "The people voted the way they did. Most of us weren't even there at the time. It is what it is. Collectively we make a fair living smuggling and trading in things that others want. There are a lot of things one side allows and the other does not. And again there are things that neither government approves of that the people desire. There were dealings in progress for which we wanted no witnesses." He paused for a moment, licking his lips.

Dror had gone red and was clearly having trouble keeping his emotions in check. The priest carried on talking. "Your presence at Michael's Hollow was too close to our intended operation for comfort so we decided to distract you by sending you off to Mistiq. If we could get you and some other ships out of the way for a few days we could do our business without fear of your interference. You leaving the troops behind was a nuisance but my men had instructions to deal with them should they find anything incriminating." Still the priest had the smug look on his face.

Dror was beside himself with rage, he screamed at the priest, spittle flecking his face, "Those troops were under my command, they were my friends as well as my crew. How dare you behave in this way?" Suddenly it was as if his rigid military bearing collapsed and his shoulders slumped. It made him as human as the rest of us, at last.

Crossing to Tanner, he took the pistol from his hand. He turned and shot the priest in the knee. The man fell to the floor screaming; his hands clutched to the wound, blood pumping through his fingers. The sound echoed around the wheelhouse, the watch-keepers were frozen, disbelieving. At that range, the bullet passed straight through his knee and ricocheted away with a twang; everyone flinched as it bounced around, like a skimmed stone.

Scarcely believing what I was doing, I went to Dror and snatched the pistol from his hand. "Captain, this is not the correct procedure," I said. "These two are prisoners and should be properly treated."

There was more stunned silence, and then Dror raised his arm and struck me backhanded. The force of the blow sent me sprawling into the bulkhead by the feet of a signaller, where I sat dazed. The pistol fell from my grip.

"Tactical Officer," said Dror, "I want that settlement wiped out. Concentrate fire on the buildings. I don't want to see them standing when you have finished."

He turned to me. "Nav, you may have a certain idealistic zeal, but be careful not to cross me or presume to lecture me on the finer points of the law. Remember that out here I am the law. In the heat of the moment I am prepared to overlook your actions, but first I have a job for you. Take Tanner and the rest of the troops; when the firing is finished deploy to the ground and seek out any survivors. Take these two with you, kill them all, we will take this place off the map."

Moth shuddered as the cannon started firing. On the forward view-screen I could see the settlement being reduced to twisted metal and shattered plastic. People must have been hiding in the huts. As the firing started they broke cover and ran, the lighter pulse cannons firing continuously were mowing them down like ripe wheat.

I had to speak out. "Captain, what about the law, surely we must..."

Dror overrode me. "Do NOT question me or push your luck, unless you wish to be in the brig; now follow your orders."

Tanner and I left, taking the priest and his companion with us. The priest left a trail of blood from his shattered knee as he dragged his useless leg behind him, supported by the other prisoner.

We embarked the shuttle; the two prisoners were secured into seats. "Dror has lost it this time," said Tanner, "and you must be careful, Finn. Leonie told me that you were liable to open your mouth a bit too far."

"But, Tanner, it's wrong, we can't just wipe them all out, there are women and children down there, I've seen them."

"I know, lad, but orders are orders, and those marines were good friends of yours and mine."

We cleared the *Moth* and dropped quickly towards the ground, we were heavily overloaded but I hadn't dared mention it. The troops were grim faced and ready for action. They hadn't bothered strapping in and stood, ready to deploy as we touched down.

Tanner addressed them, "Lads, Leonie and her squad are gone, and these bastards," he pointed at our two captives, "are responsible. Captain wants everyone dead, to send a message." There were nods and agreement.

The priest looked calm, despite the pain from his knee. "Do you think I told you all this so you can go and report back to anyone?" he said triumphantly. "You are about to be surprised. Look!"

The thrusters howled as I tried to slow us down to land softly. I saw a section of the cliff drop away, and realised that it was only fabric, a piece of camouflage. Behind it was a heavy calibre missile launcher, already pointed towards the *Moth*. At that range it couldn't miss, and there was no time to give a warning. With a spurt of flame four missiles were launched; they raced across the gap and slammed into the *Moth*, which shuddered as they exploded. It split in two as it fell from the sky; flames boiling from the rents in its hull. There were more explosions as the pieces hit the ground, each a ball of fire. The shock waves tumbled our shuttle over and over; I had no reserve power to attempt to control our motion. The troops fell into each other, bones snapping, as we bounced across the ground and into the cliffs. I remember shouting, then one of the falling bodies crashed into me and everything went black.

Chapter 9, Now

I woke; I was covered in sweat and felt drained. As I stood, the cabin lights came on and I went into the washroom and splashed some water on my face. Looking at my watch I saw that it was just about six in the morning, time to get up and see what my new life was all about. I put yesterday's clothes back on; I would have to do something about that later.

I wasn't the first into the mess room. Tan was there and she muttered a greeting through a mouthful of something. The three that Rixon had described as guns for hire were sat in a close group in the corner facing the door, old habits I guessed. They waved greetings as I looked around. The smell of bacon and coffee made me feel better immediately, and there was another odour that I hadn't expected this early. Tracking down its source, it gave me a clue as to why the man was called Stu. And I had thought that it was short for Stuart.

Ardullah saw my gaze and grinned. "It's all he ever eats," he explained as Stu shovelled the food in, arm like a metronome. "He got the taste for it in a mining camp; it's a nightmare because now we have to get the same brand, tonnes of it in ration packs to keep him happy."

Stu raised his head and stopped shovelling. "Mornin', lad, want some?" He waved at his plate. The sight reminded me of Navy food, it had the same consistency but the smell was slightly more appetising. Seeing my expression, he roared with laughter, "Well you can't have any and don't let me catch you sneaking a…"

Mitch slapped him round the head. "He's new here, don't tease him."

"I'll stick to the eggs, thanks," I replied with a straight face, I wasn't going to get drawn in.

Just then, Rixon and Myra arrived, deep in conversation. Myra was in dirty overalls and had obviously been up and working on something long before I had awoken.

Rixon called across to me, "Morning, Dave, leave those three for a minute and get over here, we've got a day to plan, grab me a coffee on your way."

"And me," said Myra.

"Make that three," shouted Tan.

I pushed buttons on the dispenser and carried the coffee over, the square recycled paper cups making the job of holding four a lot easier.

"Thanks, Dave," said Rixon, and the others murmured the same, sugar and creamer were added and stirred, and then we got down to business.

"Right," said Rixon, "Griff has found us a job, and as it happens it's a legal one, he's off getting us clearance."

I sipped my coffee, it was good, real coffee not instant, and better than Navy stores. And the food in front of Tan smelt and looked better than what I had been used to.

"We do get them sometimes," said Tan, spearing what looked like a fried mushroom with her fork. Putting it in her mouth, she spoke as she chewed. "Where are we off to then, Boss?"

Rixon handed her a sheaf of papers. "Here's the lashing spec, we're picking up a load of equipment on Wishart, for a mining job somewhere out on the Rim, we don't get the destination till we're loaded and away, you know how paranoid the corporations are. Anyhow, we got a few days to get to Wishart, so Dave here can do his Navy thing, plot our route and fly us there."

"Sounds okay to me, sir," I answered. "I'll get the charts and get started." I stood up, resisting the automatic urge to salute.

"Two things, Dave," Rixon spoke in that lazy, gentle tone. "Firstly, you're not in the Navy now, so Boss is fine, or Skipper, and second, there's not the rushing and leaping about here, sit down and have a good meal first, you'll work better on a full stomach. Now then, Myra, how's the work going, when will we have engines?"

He turned his attention away from me and I sipped my coffee as they talked about engines, Tan got up and went off clutching the papers, she called the GFH and they finished up and followed her. I realised I was hungry and went to check out the food situation, apart from the boxes of stew, with a label on the top of the pile reminding everyone that it was spoken for, there was a good selection of ready meals, better than I had expected. I chose one that, according to the box, was a 'Full Breakfast' and put it in the microwave. The auto-sensor read the chip on the packet and worked out the cooking time.

Two minutes later I was tucking in to eggs and bacon with mushrooms and various other fried things. It was hotel quality, and I wondered how Rixon managed to afford this sort of stuff when the Navy, with its vast resources and buying power, ended up with slop.

By the time I had finished, I was alone in the mess, so I tidied my things away, got a fresh coffee and went to the bridge.

It might have been the same basic shape as the *Moth*'s but that was where the similarity ended. The equipment was more up to date, and there were several things that I didn't recognise. It was still split by a half height transverse bulkhead into a wheel-space with a chartroom behind it though, and it was here where I sat.

I looked for ages for the controls for the chart computer; I couldn't see anything like it, although the chart table was familiar. I hoped that I wouldn't have to go and ask; that wouldn't look too clever on my first day.

"Where is the bloody thing," I muttered and to my surprise a female voice came out of the overhead speaker.

"Good morning," it said. "I'm Nancy, how may I assist you?"

The Navy had no voice activated computers; after all they had the manpower to spare, and they were still a new toy, so I was not used to dealing with one.

I cleared my throat. "Good morning, Nancy," I answered. "I'm Dave." I felt silly introducing myself, but didn't know how else to begin. I was glad that no one could hear me. They probably wouldn't have noticed though.

"I know, Dave," said the voice. "I can read your chip, but you are not the Dave that used to be here, where is that Dave, please?"

So that explained a few things, Griff's choice of name, and the pile of things in the cabin, I was in a dead man's shoes, or at least a departed man's. The list of questions I had for Rixon was growing longer.

"I can't answer that, Nancy," I continued. "Today is my first day on board, and I need to plot and store a route to Wishart."

"I can do that for you, Dave," she replied. "Any special requirements or just the best path?"

I didn't really know; Rixon had not mentioned anything apart from that we had time. "Nothing special, just the most economical, like you usually do." I waited, expecting a window to open on the chart table so that I could start work. Hopefully the system wouldn't be too unfamiliar; surely it must be better than I was used to.

Nothing happened and there was silence for a minute or so, then Nancy spoke again. "All done, Dave. The route is saved as Dave Route One in my memory, to activate it just ask me to execute the route name once we are in orbit."

Feeling a little surprised, as I had been expecting a bit more effort to have been required, I wandered around the bridge, inspecting the various bits of equipment. I was surprised at the sophistication of the gear; clearly money had been well spent when the ship had been converted. Unlike on the *Moth*, where things had been placed for multiple operators, all reporting to an officer of the watch, here things were grouped for single man operation. There was a chair which moved on rails along the front of the console so you could sit and move from one panel to the next.

Looking out from the wheelhouse, I could see along the top of the hull, with the stub wings on the bow at each side. The engine pods were just level with me with the landing gear on the main wings keeping us balanced as the hull lay flat to the ground.

I felt a vibration and flipped through the cameras. I could see the stern ramp closing, the pressure seal locking in place. We were now air-tight.

There was a familiar vibration, and a low whine, which increased in pitch until it was inaudible; the main engines were firing up. I could see lights glowing on the various panels all along the console, and flow charts on the screens showed that power was available. I found myself going through the drill of checking all the read-outs automatically.

The engine room intercom buzzed and I turned without looking and pushed the pickup. Myra's voice filled the room, "Hello, Dave. How you settling in? Rixon's on his way to you, you can tell him that we're ready to launch."

Rixon walked into the bridge with Griff and strode over to the console.

"Hello, Dave," said Griff and handed me a piece of paper. "Here's the clearance." He slapped me on the back, gently for him although it still felt like being hit with a tree trunk. I grabbed the handrail on the console for support.

"It's good to have you aboard," he said. It felt like a peace offering.

"Good to be here," I replied.

Rixon was watching my reaction. "She's all yours then, Dave," he said. "Take us out."

I slid the chair along to the end of the console, out of my way and stepped to the comms panel. I selected the calling channel given on the clearance and pressed the transmit switch on the handset.

"Control, this is the…" I was just about to say *Moth* when I stopped; I was sweating, that had nearly blown it. I realised that I had forgotten the name of the ship I was on. I looked wildly around till I saw it.

I tried again. "Control, this is the *Orca*, permission to lift off please." At their request I passed them the clearance number that Griff had given me, and was given permission to depart. I crossed to turn on the local control but Rixon was there before me. He held his hand over the switch and shook his head.

"Not this time, Dave. Let's see if my sources were right about you."

I was just going to have to do it the hard way. I opened the manual control panel, revealing the manoeuvring levers below.

"Engine room," I used the intercom, "please give me main engine and thrust control."

The lights on the status panel turned from red to green as Myra transferred control to the buttons and levers below my fingers.

Without looking down, my hands moved across the panel and the forward thrusters rotated and fired. As I watched through the port, the nose lifted as the weight of the craft pivoted on the main landing gear. As the angle increased and before the stern could scrape on the ground, I rotated the thrust deflectors on the main engines, and set the flaps on the wings to maximum. Putting the main engine power to five per cent made the body of the ship lift slowly into the air, with minimum forward movement. The nose was still swinging upward under the influence of the thruster as I slowly decreased the angle of the deflectors. The upward movement reduced and forward motion started, slowly at first as we rose into the sky, skimming over the blast walls.

As I increased the power we started to move faster. The gauges showed a positive increase in altitude along with the forward motion and I closed down the thrusters. They would be useless at this speed anyway. Now that we were gaining altitude I rotated the deflectors back to normal running position and levelled the flaps. The landing gear retracted with a thump, and I realised that I had pushed the button without thinking.

I called the tower and reported that we were airborne, they replied with a course and a rate of climb for me to follow to clear into orbit. I set these on the control panel and looked at Rixon, he nodded so I finally engaged the local control; it would do a much better job of keeping to our assigned path than I ever could. And the tower could now take over remotely if it didn't like the way we were flying. In manual control that would be embarrassing and would mean a fine, probably from my wages. That was another thing I had to discuss.

We banked gently as we settled onto the new course. As we passed through 10,000 metres the safety locks came off and there was a jolt as the boosters fired.

"Nicely done," said Rixon, as the sky turned black and the stars came out.

Relenting at last, Rixon turned on the Nav and Nancy's voice filled the bridge, quite surprisingly, at least to me, she sounded hurt.

"Rixon, we are clearing atmosphere, don't you trust me?"

"It's not that, Nance," said Rixon. "I wanted to see how Dave did."

Nancy replied, "He's not Dave, I know his chip says that he is but you can't fool old Nancy, where is Dave?"

To my surprise, Rixon said, "Mode 101."

Nancy now spoke in a flat mechanical voice, "Command."

"Delete all references to Dave Travise before today's date," he continued.

"Complied," said the metallic voice.

"Mode 101 off. Nancy, who is the navigator on board?"

"Dave Travise," she said, back in her normal voice. "He's new here, I think, I haven't talked to him before today, he has one route stored in my memory."

"Execute Dave Route One," I said, and we set off for Wishart.

Chapter 10

After lunch, which was another excellent meal, Rixon asked me to come to his cabin, and as I sat in the same seat that I had with Myra, I reflected on the last eighteen hours. Now I was truly free, free of my father's dead hand, free from the Navy, free to do whatever I wanted, and right now what I wanted was to be here.

Rixon passed me a glass of juice. "Don't look surprised, Dave. All the booze is locked up, and will be until we get free time on the ground. Now then, we have some formalities to go through." He lifted a pile of trans-papers. "But first, can you tell me why you were shouting this morning; was it to do with what happened on Oonal?"

"How much do you know about Oonal?" I blurted out in surprise, although I suppose I shouldn't have been. Griff had been waiting for me in that bar, so he must have known I was coming. I wondered who else had heard me shout.

Rixon smiled again, that relaxing grin, he spoke softly, "Dolmen is a good mate of mine, he called me when they captured you, after the *Moth* was destroyed. We had a bit of an argument, because I thought that he had gone too far. That's by the by now of course, but he mentioned you, and how you tried to save the priest from Dror."

"I reckoned Dror was overstepping his authority," I agreed. "I still do, it doesn't mean that I wasn't happy after the killing of the first squad, I had good friends there. I just wanted a fair trial, then a just punishment."

Rixon didn't answer that directly. "He told me that the troops in your shuttle were all dead, or so badly injured that killing them was a kindness. You and the two prisoners were the only ones strapped in so you survived. Dolmen thought you were dead and was going through your pockets when you started waking up. Anyway, he found your tags and your notebook. You shouldn't have been carrying it on a combat drop."

Of course; it explained a lot. "Dror put me in the shuttle at the last minute. I had no time to sanitise myself."

Rixon nodded. "Dror was a loose cannon, he got everyone so jumpy that protocol went out of the portholes. But as it happened, this time it was a good job. It was what saved you. Dolmen found out who you were. It turns out that he knew your father."

So that was the reason I had been left alive. All I could say was, "Oh." At least he hadn't been someone that my father had upset. There were quite a few of those.

Rixon carried on, "Yes, they had history, or so he said, something to do with the Holy Wars and his family. Apparently your father saved his father or something like it, anyhow that and your actions made him hesitate. He called me like I said and mentioned you. I could see your potential immediately, especially with the problems I had been having. So I asked him to drop you off on Basilan, after putting the frighteners on you."

"I won't give you Navy secrets," I stood. "I'm willing to work for you, because you gave me a chance, but I'm not betraying anyone or anything."

"Sit down," he ordered, and I heard steel in his voice. "I'm not going to do that, I just want you to know that I know your story, it might help you with the nightmares."

"That's fine then, but I've got some questions of my own." Rixon nodded. "Firstly, who was Dave Travise?"

"Well you are him now, but before that, he was the Nav here, now he's a wanted man, a Navy deserter, with a dodgy chip."

"What made him leave?" Rixon thought for a moment.

"We, well Griff actually, found out that he was being less than honest with us, so he had to go. Never mind why at the moment.

We got him drunk in a bar on Basilan, Rick fried his chip, and then we kept him here till you had been…" he grinned, "*legalised.* We had kept him drunk, so when you were on the way here we poured him in a taxi and sent it to the guards. The guards can be stupid but eventually they'll put the pieces together, a fried chip is an offence anyhow, but thanks to Rick and the way it's been set up he will never prove he was not Finn Douglas. At least not from the lock up."

"And the local guards on Basilan will deal with it?"

"Precisely, you're in the clear. Now drink your juice and sign these." It seemed like Rixon had thought of everything. He passed me the trans-papers, which were an apparently standard contract of employment, declaration of citizenship of the Federation and a couple of other things I didn't recognise.

Trans-papers were really plastic; the images on their surface hiding the layers of capacitors woven into them; to sign I merely had to tap the bar at the bottom, my ID chip would be interrogated. The information would be digitally encoded into the document, and the micro transmitter in it would store it on the ship's computer. It could then be passed to customs or anyone else as part of the crew list. The contract would be on my cabin viewer, so I could check that out later. Rixon was still talking.

"They're all required by various places we go to, keeps the customs happy, and the majority of the stuff we do is in the open, despite what the late Captain Dror thought."

I tapped them all, and passed the sheaf back to him.

"Thanks," he smiled, putting them into a drawer which he locked. "Now ask away, what else do you want to know?"

Suddenly, I couldn't think of anything much to ask. "Where do you turn on the Nav? And where do you get the food? It's the best packaged stuff I've ever tasted."

"But you don't recognise the boxes? Well Griff gets it, it's from the Independent Worlds, there's a place where we go on a semi-regular basis and we pick it up when we can. We don't get it all the time, so make the most of it. In between its frozen concentrates, I'm afraid. And the Nav control is on the port instrument panel, it's on all the time normally though, just say 'Hello, Nancy'."

"Okay, what about the stuff in my cabin?"

"It's your stuff, keep what you want and dump the rest, by the way, the laundry is down on–"

"Gamma deck port aft," I finished, and we laughed together.

I left Rixon and returned to my cabin. I attacked the pile of stuff, not really knowing what I would find. There was a large amount of clothing, most of which actually fitted me and was taken down to the laundry and washed. I also found some new clothes and toiletries in the drawers and washroom storage. There were a few things that I dumped in a pile for disposal, and some stuff that I really needed. I would have to get it when I could. Perhaps we would have time on Wishart.

Apart from the clothes, there was little to suggest what kind of a man Dave Travise had been, the personal effects were minimal, just a few action films and a viewer. There were various souvenirs from some of the more interesting places they had been and some encrypted letters. Then I found a flash drive, it was sewn into the leg of one of the overalls and I could feel it as I was putting them into the washer. Using my knife, I cut it out and stuffed it in my pocket. At the bottom of one of the drawers was a small locked box, which rattled when I shook it. It had a DNA key, and of course I had just put the best source of DNA in the washer.

Before I plugged the drive into the cabin viewer, I isolated it from the ship's network. I didn't want whatever was on it setting off any alarms.

Disappointingly, it was password protected. I didn't want to risk wiping it by guesswork so I would have to think of something else.

Someone knocked at my door. Quickly, I ejected the drive and stuffed it into my pocket. "Come in," I called and Griff entered, ducking under the doorway.

"How's it going, boy?" he asked. "You settling in, anything you need, clothes, luxuries? I can organise it for when we get to Wishart, I know a man there."

"Actually there is, Griff; can you get me some clothes and a few bits and pieces?"

"No problems, just message me a list and I'll pass it on," he eyed the much reduced pile of Dave Travise's things. "Need any help?"

"No thanks, I'm just about done, that lots all for the disposal."

"Find anything interesting?" it was said casually, but I didn't know him well enough to let on about the drive and the box. "Not really, just some letters and a few souvenirs."

"Okay, well don't forget you're on watch later, it might be an idea to get a snooze, see you." And he breezed out. It seemed like good advice. But first I put the box at the back of a drawer where I had found it, behind the spare blankets. I left the drive there as well. It wasn't the best hiding place but it would have to do. I retrieved my laundry and decided to take Griff's advice and have a snooze.

This time the dream was different, I missed the crash and it started when I came round.

Chapter 11, Then

I woke aching all over, I was in a dark cave and when I tried to move, my hands were tied together, as were my ankles. I was dressed in a Blessed robe and I wondered where my uniform was. Movement brought pain, and I remembered the crash and the destruction of the *Moth*. And the massacre; both of the marines and the settlers. My head throbbed and my neck felt stiff. How long had I been unconscious?

A figure loomed over me, light shining bright in my face. "Get up," a rough voice commanded. With difficulty I stood.

"Finn Douglas, Navigator Second Class, and that's all I'm saying," I tried to sound brave but it came out as a squeak. With my ankles tied I was finding it hard to balance.

"Don't be stupid, lad, you're alive, let's not spoil it." The voice softened. "There's been enough killing, I don't want secrets, I know as much about Dror, the Navy and the *Moth* as I need, especially now." The silence stretched out and I could hear water drip. I couldn't see where I was or who was asking because the light in my eyes was blinding.

"Alright then, who are you and what are you going to do with me?"

"I'm asking the questions," he said, "but fair's fair I guess. I'm Dolmen and I'm in charge here. The priest; he tells me you tried to argue with Dror about destroying the settlement, is that true?"

"Yes, it is," I replied carefully, aware of a possible trap. "I might not agree with your lifestyle, or your actions, but the law is the law and I felt Dror had gone too far when he shot the priest. But I don't see why you had to kill the first squad." The light moved away from my face.

His voice took on a harder tone. "They got too close to the truth and found some things that they weren't supposed to. Things got out of hand and the leader, stupid bitch, was the first to go, all her talk about justice." He spat. "She didn't know there were so many of us hidden here; she was surrounded and outgunned before she even started." My eyes were adjusting to the gloom, I could see large groups of people, there were a few dim lights and shadows flickered. That explained why there were so few men visible when we had arrived, they must all have been hiding here.

"Where are Tanner and the rest of the marines from my ship?" Even as I asked, I think I knew the answer.

He shook his head. "I'm sorry. They weren't strapped in when you crashed, messy business, there was blood everywhere and broken bones. The only reason you're still alive is that you stopped Dror killing the priest, and you spoke up for us. For that, and to show that we're not all bad, we are prepared to let you go, we've finished here anyhow."

He smiled. "You'll never see any of us again; we're off to the Independent Worlds to start over. And don't worry; you didn't kill all of us, just a few who wanted to be martyrs and the stupid ones who wouldn't keep their heads down."

He looked me over. "You know," he said, "you'd make a convincing acolyte, just the right amount of piety and honest eyes."

"Where's my uniform?" I asked, feeling self-conscious in the robe.

"Your uniform was covered in blood and worse, so it's gone now," he told me. "I'm sending you off to Basilan; the priest has got to go there for his knee, just remember to keep your mouth shut." This was pretty unnecessary advice; I was the one who would stand out there, not his men. I was starting to understand my situation, I was in deep trouble.

"But what am I going to do? I'm chipped and enlisted; I'll be scanned and stopped faster than you can say." I felt desperate, almost wishing that I had not survived. I certainly wouldn't last long once the authorities got hold of me, arriving with a bunch of criminals.

"Don't worry," Dolmen said, in a tone that suggested that I should worry a lot. "I've sorted it all out, you'll be taken to a man who will make it all go away." He paused. "And don't forget, we can always make it all come back again."

I didn't know what he intended but I wasn't in any position to argue, I was stuck with whatever he had in mind. Two men came over to us, my legs were untied and I was marched through the caves for an hour or so. We arrived in another clearing, there my ankles were retied and they bundled me into the hold of a Dragonfly scouter. The hatch slammed shut and we took off.

As soon as we had cleared atmosphere, my pilot, who said his name was Eric, took my bonds off, after nervously asking if I intended to kill him. As he was only about sixteen, the thought hadn't even occurred to me, and anyway, he had already told me that the ship was rigged to respond only to his voice.

It seemed to me that they had gone soft, after killing all the rest of my crew; why stop?

I asked Eric if he knew the reason why. "I don't really know," was his answer. "The priest was out of it, we had filled him with painkillers and he was delirious. At first Dolmen said that he couldn't kill you while you were unconscious, it wouldn't be right, then when he went through your pockets, he found something that made him think. Meanwhile your part in things had been explained by Maws, the other man you captured."

What had Dolmen found? I racked my brain; all that we carried into combat were our medic-tags. Then I realised, Dror had switched me to the shuttle and I had not been in combats, just my normal uniform. My notebook had been in the pocket. And my last letter, the thing we hoped would never be sent. Mine had been to my father. Of course my uniform was still on the surface, so I couldn't check, feeling in the pockets of the robes they were empty.

To be honest that had thrown me a bit, I had no connection to these people that I could think of, and although my mind was still in a state of shock about the deaths of all those people, I realised that I was out of the Navy now. There was no way I could explain my way out of this, maybe if I'd have stayed on Oonal, the only survivor, and somehow got rescued by whoever turned up looking for Dror, then I could have been alright. But accepting a lift from the 'enemy' put that course of action beyond me, the story was getting bigger and my chances of talking myself out of it were getting smaller.

"We've got the Black Box," continued Eric. "From the *Moth*, the last video and audio from the bridge, and the telemetry up to the missile strike; Dolmen says it might come in handy. Nothing was sent from when you arrived, we had a beacon in orbit jamming you, but you wouldn't have detected it."

I had never heard of a beacon that could do that. "Where did you get that sort of gear?" I asked him.

He looked pleased. "Independent Worlds," he said. "They have stuff you won't believe, it pretends to be the receiving station and soaks it all up, real clever."

Maybe the Black Box was handy for them, but if the Navy ever got it, all it would show would be my insubordination. And I was sure that if it came to it, the box would be discovered, and with carefully selected bits of the contents, it was another way of keeping me quiet. Nothing much I could do about that now. I changed the subject.

"Dolmen said you were taking me to Basilan," I said. I hadn't really thought about it up to now, I was just relieved to be alive. Eric grinned.

"That's right, you ever been before?"

"No, it's not got much of a Navy base on it, and it's relatively quiet, so it had never been on our patrol route, but I've heard of it." Basilan was an old world, not on the Rim, and a centre for craftsmen of all disciplines, if you needed specialists for big projects, then it was the place to go.

All the craft guilds had local offices, but the headquarters of most of them were on Basilan. Here, planet engineers rubbed shoulders with computer systems designers, and there were welders and builders who could live for months in a pressure suit, in poison atmosphere or under water, and build you a world while they were at it. It was the busiest planet in the Federation and the most polluted. But if you wanted to disappear, it was probably the best place to go. There was a ready market for skilled men, and I was a skilled man. The only problem was that I couldn't prove it. But I'd bet that I wasn't alone in that.

The trip to Basilan would take about a week, and because we were in such close proximity, Eric and I developed a friendship. Not the do or die best friend type, but a mutual respect and understanding. I came to see things from his point of view, particularly regarding the way of life that Dolmen and his group had made for themselves, and their resentment at the Federation's interference. The more he told me, the more I could see how the frustration had boiled over and we had ended up where we were.

His was the usual augment, if a law is unjust; it's almost your moral duty to break it. But I couldn't help thinking, if only Oonal had been in the Independent Worlds sphere of influence, none of this would have happened.

"Tell me about where we're headed on Basilan," I asked him, when we were still three days out. Eric had stopped locking me up overnight and whenever he went to the bathroom, which was progress.

"It's very industrial," he said. "Lots of factories and stuff, you'll miss the green open spaces because the whole of the landmass where we're going to is used, one way or another. And where there are no factories, there are mines and quarries. All the workers live in temporary shanties amongst the buildings, or in floating blocks on the coast."

It sounded awful, not the sort of way I would want to live. "How do they put up with it?"

"For the money," he said with a grin. "There's still one continent with no development, and people have their permanent homes there. They work hard and get good wages, there's plenty of work for everyone so most folk working on the planet do twelve hour shifts for a month and then have a month off. The ones working off-planet do whatever it takes. They might have to rough it for a time, but it's worth their while, in ten years they can retire. Then they go to Basilon. It's the biggest moon in the system; it's been terraformed and is just a big old folks home." He pulled a sour face. "It's all golf courses and spa resorts. It'd drive me crazy in a week or so."

I thought about it and could see the attraction of the freer lifestyle of Dolmen's approach.

Chapter 12, Now

The buzzer by my head sounded and Tan's voice entered my dream, waking me, "Hello, Dave, it's time to take the watch, come up to the bridge and I'll hand over."

I had a quick wash and dressed myself in some of my 'new' clothes. As I entered the wheelhouse Tan was sitting at the console, typing on a portable keypad. She looked up and grinned. "That was easy, I only had to call you once, your... namesake needed a small explosive charge to get him out of his bed. I've made you a coffee." She pointed to a cup sitting on the chart table.

"Thanks; Rixon said that he was trouble," I commented, and her face turned grim.

"When we found out," she didn't say what, "it had to be done, but I for one didn't enjoy it." She picked up some trans-papers and her keypad, folding them into a wallet, and stood. "Well, there you are then, everything is running smoothly; you can turn the alarms over to your cabin and go back to sleep, or if you have any work to do, take the remote." She pointed to a receiver clipped to the bulkhead. "I try to catch up on paperwork when it's quiet, but as long as one of us has the alarm, that's fine. I'll see you at breakfast, goodnight."

I didn't feel in the least tired, so after she had gone and I had drunk my coffee I took the remote and went to the empty mess room for a snack. It still seemed strange to be here in familiar surroundings with just a handful of people. I kept expecting to see Leonie or Dror or one of the others sitting in the mess or walking down an alleyway. Returning to the bridge my training took over and I spent about twenty minutes checking all the panels and displays for abnormalities. I wasn't used to this level of automation, and it made me feel happier to have seen for myself that all was running smoothly.

Feeling lost, I said, "Hello, Nancy," and she answered immediately.

"Hello, Dave, you're up late, what can I do for you?"

"Are we on course, Nancy?" I asked.

"Yes we are," she replied, sounding slightly annoyed, as if I was questioning her ability. "The engines are at seventy-five per cent, speed is five point two C squared and our ETA at Wishart is seventy-six hours and twelve minutes from now. There are no objects of any description in our vicinity. Will there be anything else?"

I took a chance. "Mode 101," I said nervously.

"I'm sorry, Dave, but mode 101 is not available to you."

It had been worth a try, I would have to be a bit cleverer. "Okay, Nancy, forget I said it." I hoped she would. "Can you show me the entry on Wishart, please?" The words and pictures flickered onto the chart screen and I sat down to read up on our destination.

Wishart had been the capital of the Blessed's time as rulers of the Federation. As well as being a huge agricultural planet it had a near monopoly on the manufacturing of farming machinery. It was the site of the last big battle in the Holy Wars, fought in orbit as the Blessed desperately tried to cling on to power on their home world. Debris still littered the orbital plane and symbolically, the Blessed's flagship had crashed from orbit at the climax of the fight. Everyone in the Federation knew the story and had seen the pictures and video of the event.

By one of those strange quirks of fate the ship fell to earth on the capital, Brethren's Host. The crash and subsequent explosion and fires wiped out more than half of the city's population and razed a lot of the skyscrapers to the ground. Earthquakes were triggered by the impact which completed the destruction. As you approached the old city across the plains it resembled a set of bad teeth jutting up in bent and broken disarray. Rather than try to rebuild it, or level it completely, the survivors left it as a monument and built a new city off to the other side of the space port. After all there was plenty of room.

The destruction of Brethren's Host was instrumental in stopping the war, which was past the point of winning by either side. Instead the conflict had degenerated into an exhausting and destructive stalemate, with low level terrorism on most worlds, and the odd space battle, though these were rare as the numbers of capital ships decreased. The massive loss of life on Wishart, particularly as it was not intended, forced the two groups to stop and talk to each other. Eventually they reached agreement on the only logical solution, the separation of the Federation into two parts, those who wanted rid of the Blessed and those who were happy to retain religious control. The surprise was that when all the votes were counted on all the worlds, Wishart wanted to remove the Blessed and stick with the new Federation. All of this was common knowledge, growing up it had been recent news. Dror and my father had probably been involved; obviously Dolmen had been there too.

The wheelhouse door hissed open and Myra came in; she seemed surprised to see me, and her face lit up. "Hello, Dave, I thought you had been avoiding me," she spoke in that soft purr that did things to my brain and scrambled my speech.

"No, of course not, sorry. I've been trying to sort myself out here; it's not easy being someone else." I gabbled, just like she had done on that first evening.

She came up close and I could smell sandalwood, one of my personal favourites. "I'm teasing you, silly," she said. "I've had a stack of things to do as well; I'm just here to check some of the gear before I turn in." She started opening panels on the console and checking the equipment inside. I peered over her shoulder as she looked inside, again I could see that the gear had been uprated from the Navy stuff I was used to.

"Who paid for all the improvements?" I asked.

She straightened up and flipped the panel shut. "I don't really know but I think that Griff got hold of the *Orca* from a contact. Whenever you ask him anything all he will say is 'someone owed me a favour'. We all joined up when it came out from the yard." She walked around in front of the space and knelt down; I heard the click of securing clips.

I was going to ask her all sorts of questions about Griff and the whole set up when Rixon came onto the bridge. "Hi, Dave," he greeted me. "Are you on duty tonight? You don't have to be here all night, you know. Didn't Tan tell you?"

"Yes she said," I replied. "Old habits, I'm just looking at all the differences from the Navy way. It's impressive, must have cost a fortune."

He was evasive. "Guess so," he muttered, searching in a drawer. "That's more Griff's department." There was a noise from the panel where Myra was working and instantly Rixon became alert. He walked quickly around to the console as Myra bobbed up.

"Hi, Boss," she said. "Just checking the repairs are holding up."

He looked at her and me and reached the wrong conclusion. Without a word he turned and left.

The embarrassed silence that followed his departure was broken by Myra. "Gotta go, good night, Dave," she said as she left, almost running.

So Rixon and Myra were an item then, which was a shame. I had finished my checks so I turned the alarms over to my cabin and went back there. There were enough questions buzzing round in my head that I knew I wouldn't sleep and I was right. At least it meant that I didn't have the dream again. Instead I just thought of Myra. For a time it had looked promising, now I was back to square one. The one positive thing was that I hadn't made a complete fool of myself.

The next three days passed relatively quickly as I got to grips with my new role. There were the usual Navigator duties, but other things were passed my way, things that on a Navy ship would have had a dedicated officer.

Here, for example, I was responsible for all the suits and safety gear and, together with Myra, for keeping all the surveys and equipment certificates up to date. That made a lot of things to keep your eye on, any of which were vital to our survival in deep space, and my cabin terminal downloaded a daily work sheet that had me crawling into corners and spaces that I hadn't visited since my training days. At least I didn't have to learn the ship's layout from scratch; it would have made life a lot harder. Myra was friendly and helpful but that was as far as it went.

Considering what I now knew about her relationship with Rixon I was probably a little more reserved with her than I might have been. Her comments had also started me wondering about Griff and how he had got his hands on the ship.

Speaking of Griff, he seemed to drift about and do very little, although he was a qualified watch-keeper and would stand a watch for you if you asked, he had no formal function. He was listed on the crew sheet as cargo officer, but as that was normally Tan's job it seemed to be a duplication.

I asked Tan how Griff was part of the crew.

"He knows so many people and what's going on that he's worth having on board," she replied. "He finds most of the work that we do, and you should see his traffic stats, he gets more messages than the rest of us put together. Like this job, he probably got it from a contact in the transport guild, normally it would go to one of their ships, but we do them favours and they remember."

The more I found out, the less I knew.

Chapter 13

Ten hours from Wishart and the gravitational field of its star became too great for the trans-light drive to overcome, so we dropped to sub-light speed. We were still going at about ninety per cent C, and we now started to organize ourselves for arrival.

Tan and the GFH, as Mitch, Stu and Ardullah were known, had been setting up the lashings for our cargo in the main hold, marking out the position of the various items with white chalk on the deck. This would ensure an even load distribution and avoid stressing the hull, always important, but more so during trans-light, which modified the laws of physics in a way thought impossible until it had been done.

As we approached orbit, we called the customs post and sent all the documents that Rixon had been compiling. Then we waited; sometimes you were boarded, he had told me, and sometimes they didn't bother, it all seemed to depend on their mood on the day. Being in the Navy, we had never had an issue with customs, we went where we wanted with no check, so it was all new to me. Anyway, we were empty on arrival so there was nothing to interest them and they left us alone. More proof of the effectiveness of my new identity.

After clearance was granted, we commenced our descent.

Wishart had no auto landing system, so I was free to take control, or at least programme Nancy with the instructions passed from the port. No doubt they were watching our passage and would intervene if they thought it was required, but they left it to me.

~~~~

We dropped through the clouds, which were extensive in what we learned was the Northern winter and started to be buffeted by strong winds; the tower had advised us of a little local turbulence. Nancy turned the dampers up to compensate, even so she struggled to keep us on the glide path, in the end I took manual control and managed to avoid the wrath of the tower with a fair amount of luck, and a little sweat.

Rixon was on the bridge drinking coffee and saying little as we descended, sure enough the land appeared as a featureless plain, dotted with houses and barns, linked by wide, straight roads. There were clusters of large sheds holding harvesters and other farm machinery. Lines of large yellow machines crossed the giant fields, it looked like they were ploughing or planting crops because they were followed by flocks of birds, fighting over worms and scraps.

There was a distortion to the line of the horizon ahead; it quickly grew into the ruins of Brethren's Host, a mass of twisted metal, now starting to show a green tinge from the ivy and other plants that were recolonizing its broken structure. It was a huge area, and the sight brought a sad feeling to me. I had heard of it, and seen the video in school, but it hadn't captured the magnitude of the event. It was easy to see how this one random act had changed the course of history.

As we passed over the city, in the distance past the port, we could see the new Brethren's Host rising from the plain, almost a copy of the first but this time the half-built buildings were covered in scaffold and surrounded by hovering cranes, showing the determination of the people to rise above the horrors and destruction of the Holy Wars.

We crossed the port threshold at reduced speed; a laser beam illuminated our assigned loading bay. All I had to do now was align with the beam and follow it to its source. As I flew down the beam I could see the bay we were headed to and realised that we were the wrong way round for loading; our stern ramp would not line up with the gap in the blast walls. That would slow down the load, as everything would have to be manoeuvred past the wings before it could be brought on board.

I considered going round again and approaching from the other direction, but that would take a few minutes. Hoping that I wasn't showing off too much, I slowed and put the *Orca* into a hover. Swivelling the ship around on the spot I lowered the gear and backed down to as soft a landing as I could make it in the breeze.

I called Myra and handed over control for shut-down. Rixon drained his coffee and put the cup down.

"Nice flying, Dave," he said. "Driving like that will be useful if we need any fancy stuff."

I basked in the praise. Dror had either grunted or managed to find some minor procedural fault in my manoeuvring. "Thanks, Boss. I just fly the way the Navy taught me, it's nothing special."

"Don't be so modest," he warned. "I've checked out your records remember, best cadet pilot, the Admiral Millman Award for precision flying and winner of the Cuthbert Cup three times running, the only time it's ever been retained."

These were all Navy honours for ship handling and navigation in a competition setting, and the depth of his background checks got me worried, what if he had spotted some of the other things on my service record?

Rixon said nothing more; he crossed to the ramp control panel and transferred control to the local position, by the door in the hold. "Tan," he called on the intercom, "you have the ramp; don't open it till you see one of the Chenkos on the monitor."

"Okay," the mate replied, her voice sounded hollow on the speaker as it bounced around the empty hold. Rixon turned to me, he looked tense, that was something I hadn't seen before.

"The Chenkos are Griff's contacts," he explained. "I haven't worked much with them. They have a reputation and I'm not a trusting soul so the ramp stays up till Griff says so." The way he said it showed there was some sort of history, clearly there was no honour amongst thieves as far as these Chenkos were concerned. I'd never heard of them.

"Well the name's not on the Navy list of POI," I told him. "But Wishart was right on the edge of our patrol area anyway."

"Typical Navy, all three letter abbreviations," Rixon muttered. "What's this one mean?"

"Sorry, old habit. It's Person of Interest, and you mean TLA." I tried to make a joke of it, but he was right, the service was obsessed with abbreviations, and it drove us all nuts trying to keep up with the new ones. The idea was to speed up communication, half the time it slowed it down as you worked out what people were talking about. "Anyhow," I continued, you call Mitch and Stu the GFH, so what's that if not a TLA?" Rixon grinned just as Griff called from the ramp.

"I've got Vlad Chenko on my cell, he's on the way and the gear is ready to load, the first crates will be here shortly."

Rixon relaxed. "At least it's Vlad," he said. Seeing my questioning look, he elaborated. "They're twin brothers, Vlad and Van Chenko. Vlad is the older, more sensible one, he keeps Van in check; most of the time."

"Okay," I replied, sensing that there was a story here.

"Like I said, I don't know them very well, except by what I've heard. Van is trouble. He's got some sort of mental problem, but he worships his big brother. There's more, but that's enough for now. I can deal with Vlad; like I said he's the sensible one, it's purely business with him."

We felt the rumble of the ramp opening, and through the outside camera we could see a line of lifters with wooden crates and pallets on them. The line stretched back to the blast walls. "Time to go and earn a crust," said Rixon, as he headed for the door. "Tell you what, come with me."

I followed him down towards the hold.

~ ~ ~ ~

By the time we had made our way down, loading was in full swing. Tan was identifying each crate and shepherding it into the correct position on the deck, where the GFH were lashing them down, using straps from the bins at the side of the hold. It was clearly an operation that they had performed many times, and the hold quickly filled.

I could see a group of men at the bottom of the ramp, Griff and some others. "Just wait here till I call you," he said as he walked down towards them, dodging the lifters and pallets.

I wondered why; maybe it was to do with not knowing them well.

As I watched, Rixon joined the group and Griff introduced him. My view was interrupted by the passage of crates but it seemed that the body language was strained, as if there was tension in the air, of emotions in check. Rixon called me down. "Dave, come and meet the customer."

I walked down the ramp, not really knowing what to expect. Why was I being presented like this? Rixon and Griff were talking to a tall blond man, dressed in expensive clothes, with a briefcase chained to his wrist. The gusting wind blew his hair across his face and he brushed it away, irritably. He was flanked by two large shaven headed men who I took to be bodyguards. They had dark glasses and ill-fitting suits, with the obligatory bulge under the armpit. What I could see of their necks was heavily tattooed; snakes in red and black writhed on their skin.

"Dave Travise," Rixon introduced me, "this is Vlad Chenko."

He looked at me and for an instant his expression flickered, as if a shadow had passed in front of his face; it seemed like he was disappointed about something.

Chapter 14

Out of the hull it was cloudy and chilly, a wind blew into our faces and it smelt of grain, a good earthy smell. I put out my hand, and the two guards twitched, Vlad inspected it and chose to ignore my gesture. Turning to Rixon he spoke, in a high pitched whisper, "No he's not, I know Dave Travise, and this is not him." Beside me I felt Griff tense, as if he had received a static charge, Rixon said nothing.

I retrieved my hand and tried not to look shocked. "Yes I am," I said, "and I should know, scan me if you want."

Chenko laughed, his bodyguards joined in. Vlad waved his hand and they stopped, instantly. "If you're with Rixon and Griff, then Rick has done his stuff, and I'm sure that's what the chip says. Look, whoever you are, don't take it personal but we both know the truth. I'm not out to expose you, but don't act the innocent." There was silence.

It started to rain, large cold drops of moisture bounced around us. I didn't know what to do so I just stood there. Even though no one was speaking I could tell that I was unwanted. Everyone ignored me, I felt like the embarrassing relative at a family party.

Vlad spoke to Griff, "Here are the papers." He unchained the briefcase and handed it over. "When you've taken off I'll send a message to give you the destination." He went to move away, but before he turned he gave me a knowing smile, a smile which said, 'I know all about you, and I've got the power because of it'. It part scared me and part made me very angry – angry with Vlad for knowing straight away; angry with Rixon for bringing me here and exposing me. And angry because Rixon and Myra were an item. I even began to wonder if I was really in the right place. While all this went round in my head, Vlad left with his two shadows in tow.

"I'm off to get the clearance then," said Griff. I thought that strange, he could do it over the radio, but maybe he had a bribe to pay or some other purpose. Rixon waved his arm in dismissal. Griff slapped me on the shoulder as he passed and whispered in my ear, "Don't sweat it, Vlad's a twisted bastard, he loves to stir it up, and getting us all fighting each other would suit him."

Rixon started to walk up the ramp, but I had had enough humiliation and wanted some answers, I grabbed him by the shoulder and spun him round. His face was a picture of shock and surprise; he shrank back as I lent in close. To make my point I grabbed a handful of his shirt, my fist under his chin lifted him onto his toes. A loaded lifter roared past.

"I don't know what your idea was there," I spoke slowly and with force, my head about an inch from his face. "But in case you think that was clever, try and show me up again, see what happens." I pushed him away and he sprawled onto the ramp. I walked away from him, and was about six feet past when I heard a click. I stopped.

"Got your attention then," he said, as I turned to see the pistol pointed at me. "I'm sorry, I wanted you to see him, because one day I might have to kill him and his psychotic brother and I might need your help to do it. There are things going on here that you don't know about. Let's just say that I need you to be angry with him, and not with me." He actually looked and sounded genuinely apologetic, a tone I had not heard from him before.

"Come on, Dave," he continued. "Would I give him a lever like that over me, think about it?"

He had a point. "Go on," I said.

"Look," he continued, "he just confirmed my suspicions. Surely a bit of humiliation was worth that."

"Not to me," I answered curtly, although I guess he was right, in a business like his, any advantage you might have or could get could be crucial. It was all 'I know that you know what I know' sort of stuff. I was just so out of my depth here, perhaps I was naive to think life away from the Navy would be all sweetness and light.

"Okay then," I told him, "if you might need me, put the pistol away and I'll forget it."

He returned it to its holster and stretched out his empty hand. "Give me a hand up; I think I've twisted my ankle."

As I leant over, he whipped his legs round, tripping me up. Before I knew it I was flat on my back and he was astride my chest, my arms pinned down by his lower legs. He drew the pistol again and put it close to my forehead.

His face cracked into a grin and rocking back, he rose to his feet. "I think I won that one," he said, still laughing. "Didn't expect you to fall for that. Come on then, let's get airborne."

I was seething as I walked back to my cabin, perhaps I was a fool but the thought that I had been used to make a point made me very concerned, even if Rixon felt justified. It was all very well to think that nothing about my identity could be proved, and I guess that the realisation that I was now on the fringe of the law hadn't really sunk in. At least they hadn't known my real name, just who I wasn't. And the look of disappointment that Vlad had tried to hide, was that something to do with my predecessor? And what was on the drive? Had I got involved in more than just a bit of trading?

I realised that I had to get to the bridge, there was departure and plotting the course to wherever we were going, although not a big job, it was what I was on board for, so with a sigh I headed topside. My hands shook as I opened and shut my cabin door. I took several deep breaths and headed for the wheelhouse.

As the door opened there was an argument going on in the forward part of the wheelhouse, out of my sight. Neither of the two involved had noticed my arrival, so intense was their shouting, and anyway, they were both out on the port side, facing the bow, so may not have heard the door. I moved closer.

Myra was screaming at Rixon, "Are you crazy, why expose Dave to Vlad like that, you know he's not stupid. I'll bet Vlad knows all about what happened on Basilan, maybe even on Oonal; what were you trying to prove?" She stopped for breath. "And what about poor Dave? His confidence in you must be shot to bits."

Rixon sounded embarrassed. "First of all, you don't talk to me like that; second, I couldn't warn him what I was going to do, but it proves that I was right about the other Dave, I saw it in Vlad's eyes. Your concern is touching, you falling for him?"

Her neck went red. "Keep your nose out," she said forcefully, "you might be my big brother and the captain here, but you're not my guardian; who I get involved with is my business."

That stopped me in my tracks, I hadn't realised that; I had thought that they were an item, not brother and sister. That changed things quite a bit.

They must have noticed me at that point. Rixon turned to me, "What did you hear of that?" he demanded.

"Nothing much, I was just coming up to get ready to lift off and as I came through the doorway I heard shouting, didn't get the drift of it all." Hopefully they would believe me.

Rixon looked relieved. "I need to talk to you; to explain," he paused and glanced at Myra, "I've been told my actions were… inappropriate. Myra, get down to the engine room and fire up the drive as soon as the ramp shuts. Give me a call when you're ready to hand over control." She left and he turned back to me, holding out his hand.

"Dave, I'm sorry, I couldn't warn you that was going to happen, you might have given the game away. I needed to know something. People like Vlad and Van, they have ears everywhere, and they're always looking for an advantage, same as we all are. Like I said, Vlad is the mastermind. Van likes to think he's clever but he's too slapdash. You know I had my suspicions about your namesake. Well, I thought that he was passing information about my business to them. Judging by the way things worked out I was right."

I couldn't argue with the logic of that, but even though I could understand, I still felt used. Rixon carried on talking, "What you have to remember is that underneath it all they're like us, only not quite such good people."

That was probably fair enough, I was getting a quick introduction to a whole new world.

"Forget it then." I changed the subject. "You said there were things I didn't know, is that why you want to kill him?"

"It's a long story, let's just say we have history, I'll tell you later."

The intercom buzzed. "I'm back on board, closing the ramp." It was Griff; he waved into the camera at the stern, he was carrying a large bundle, it must have been heavy but he handled it with ease. "Got a treat for tonight's meal, Skipper," he called. "Local delicacy."

There was a tremor as the ramp sealed; a light flashed on the console. The interlocks that stopped engine start-up until the hull was secure were released and the whine built as power was brought online. More lights changed colour until Myra's voice frostily announced, "You have control." I turned to the Nav controls on the panel and selected manual before Nancy could talk me out of it.

"Tower, this is *Orca*, we are ready to depart."

"Thank you, *Orca*, you are clear to proceed, follow the line to 50,000 and call again."

This time it was easier to handle the *Orca*, and my hands moved over the controls as we lifted, spun and rose, along the laser flightpath. Even heavily loaded the ship was responsive and there was power to spare. Calling again at 50,000 metres, I was released from tower control and was free to go where I wanted. "Nancy," I called, cancelling manual control, "Take us to orbit."

"Nice lift off, Dave," she replied. "It's good to work with an expert. Orbit in four minutes, I have control."

As we passed the edge of atmosphere, a message arrived, with coordinates. It was way out on the Rim, I'd never heard of the place but Nancy seemed happy and I left it to her to set up the voyage. My work was done; ignoring Rixon I went to my cabin. I needed to think about what had happened.

Griff buzzed the door about an hour later. "Food," he boomed. I went to the mess room, the 'local delicacy' was an enormous fish that had been wrapped in foil and steamed. It was delicious; flaky flesh that just fell off the bones, served with some small potatoes and a salad.

"How did you get that in the galley stove?" I asked. "And who's the genius chef?"

"I'm the chef," Griff answered, "and it didn't go in the stove."

"Heat exchanger on the generator," added Myra. "Don't worry, I gave it a wipe out first."

It hadn't affected the taste, but there was little conversation over the meal, everyone was waiting to see what the fallout between Rixon and me would be. I didn't know how to handle it; I was going to keep my head down for a while.

At full speed it was going to take us quite a few days to get to our destination, and I spent the time keeping out of Rixon's way and trying to get to know the rest of the crew a bit better. It was not an easy job; they all must have known what happened between me and Vlad and perhaps it made them uncomfortable around me. Or maybe they were annoyed that I had questioned Rixon, who they all seemed to regard as some sort of deity. I was the new boy, I felt like I was on trial.

Tan, I only saw at watch handover. She was very good at her job, friendly enough but I found that she was always ready to mock the Navy way I did things. The more I talked to her I realised that I just wasn't her type. Actually, men were not her type at all, as Mitch made clear to me when I accidentally caught the two of them together.

Stu and Ardullah were straightforward enough, very good at

what they did, but as long as they were fed and had heavy weights to lift or simple tasks to perform they were happy enough. They saw their time on the *Orca* as a means to enjoy themselves and seemed to have no ambitions after that. They both spent a lot of time in a spare cabin which had been converted to a gymnasium. There were racks of weights and top class exercise machines which they drove to destruction in intense circuits. I tried to join in for a while but found that I was unable to keep up, which slowed them down. On night watches I would go in at all hours and sweat out my frustrations, with the remote alarm box by my side, desperately trying to get to a level where I could compete with them.

Griff was an enigma, big and bluff, but I suspected it hid a myriad of things under all the booming. He was always really easy to talk to, and seemed to have been everywhere and knew all the important things and people. As I said before, he had no role on the ship but had enough knowledge to help out with anything that was going on. True to his word, a big box had been waiting in my cabin after Wishart; it had everything I had asked for, and a few other things that I hadn't. They were a nice touch and showed that he had done his homework. But I still had no answer about how he had got the ship. I asked him straight out and all he would say was, "Someone owed me a favour."

Rixon, after our difference of opinion, had become a bit distant. I suspected he had realised that I wasn't a pushover or maybe he thought that he had overplayed his hand. Whatever, I wanted to know more about the things he had said.

Particularly, I wanted to know what he had meant about Vlad Chenko, and why he had said what he did.

That left Myra, and the knowledge that she was available made the pursuit worth it. Leonie was a memory, and I had never really got anywhere with her before the shambles at Oonal, and before that I had had a few relationships, but never anything serious.

I thought that it would be best to play it cautious, but in the close proximity on board it was inevitable that we would be together a lot, especially as we had shared duties.

Every evening, she would come up to the bridge for her checks before leaving the machinery for the night and switching the alarms over. I usually tried to be there, in theory I was doing the same thing, checks before turning in, and I hoped it wasn't too obvious that I was always there. Before I knew it though, she made it clear that she could see what I was up to, and it turned out that she was doing the same, which made us both laugh.

I was still telling Myra the story of how I had ended up here and now I came almost up to date.

Chapter 15, Then

"There's one thing that bothers me," I was talking to Eric on the way to Basilan. "And that's how you're getting me to onto the planet. We will have to go through customs in orbit and they'll read my chip, I shouldn't be on a commercial transport. I shouldn't even be alive. I presume you have a cover story."

"That's alright," Eric was triumphant. "Where you'll be, they won't be able to read your chip, you're going to be a casualty." I understood what he meant immediately.

The Dragonfly class were long-range scouts and were often used as medevac ships; this one had a medic-bay containing two of the latest in automatic surgery pods. The priest, whose name I still didn't know, was in one pod, where his shattered knee had been receiving micro-surgery since we had left Oonal.

Eric informed me that I would be going in the other before we got to the customs post in orbit above Basilan.

"I'm afraid you'll be unconscious," he explained. "But if the customs see you in there they won't question it. Plus, you can't scan the pod. It has a shield so they won't be suspicious; the ship is a known medevac anyway. And we will be coming in on a transfer from a mining station that Dolmen uses as a front. We have a fake ID that I can show them. Don't worry, I've done this before."

We arrived in orbit and approached the customs post hovering above the arrival spiral, the queue of ships waiting to descend to the surface. I had never seen the Basilan spiral and wanted to get a closer look but Eric made me get into the pod while it was still a line of dots in the distance. The lid hissed shut, there was a smell like onions and I was asleep.

Basilan was the busiest planet in the Federation, and probably in the Galaxy. The arrival spiral was its answer to congestion. All arriving traffic was held in a circular stack, stretching from five kilometres right up into the orbital plane. The spiral was geo-stationary over the large ocean, and after customs clearance, you were allocated a number and position in the stack. In sequence you dropped from the stack into a spiral descent pattern, from the side it looked rather like a rotating DNA helix, position and rate of descent were controlled by the ground, your ship remote piloted.

At first, pilots had been allowed to drive themselves, but so many got dizzy and disorientated that central control by computer was introduced. Ships that had no auto landing system were boarded by specialist spiral pilots, who were used to the descent.

There were actually four interlocking queues of craft, so arranged to reach five kilometres altitude at ninety degree separation, and then proceed to their destination. It was the most efficient way of handling incoming traffic, one of the sights of the Federation, and I missed it.

I woke with a sore head and a raging thirst. As the lid lifted I could see that the other pod was empty; the priest must have already gone. I would have liked to have thanked him for his kindness. Eric came in with coffee. "I see you're awake, that's good. Get up and dressed, I'll take you to Wannatown, set you up." Wannatown was famous for all the wrong reasons and I didn't fancy being left in a bar on my own. Eric must have seen my look. "Don't worry," he said with a grin. "You're expected." Before we left he bandaged my arm. "This is a special bandage," he explained. "It generates static, enough to confuse a casual chip reader but appear innocent. Just in case."

Eric took me as far as the bar in a hover car that was stowed in the Dragonfly's hold; we passed belching chimneys and open furnaces, the whole planet was a hive of frantic activity and had none of the environmental controls that newer worlds have. No safety fences or machine guards. "It's not very safe here," Eric gestured at a line of injured men and women, queueing for a snack stand. "But there is so much money made that everyone takes the risk."

"What about the government? Don't they enforce protection?"

Eric laughed. "Government! They're the biggest crooks of the lot, they own all the factories that you can see; would cows vote for burgers?" A fair point I suppose. We pulled to a halt outside a run-down brick building in a narrow, deserted lane. Piles of rubbish flowed together like a frozen river. The building had red lights at the windows and a faded sign that read 'Paradise Bar'. It looked about as far away from paradise as you could get but it seemed to be my destination. Eric opened the door, the smell of hot metal and greasy food overwhelmed me as I clambered out of the seat and stood feeling conspicuous.

"You're on your own now," he shouted through the window as the door closed behind me. "Go in there and ask for Rick, if you tell him that Dolmen sent you, you'll be alright." I thanked him and he drove away.

This part of the planet was dingy, with close buildings and rubbish strewn streets, I had the feeling I was safe from a police scanner here; they probably never ventured this far into the slums. I couldn't blame them. And I had the bandage.

I pushed the door open and moved inside, it was gloomy and I could barely make out the few people huddled over drinks. They all appeared to be desperately avoiding eye contact with each other. Trying to appear both tough and inconspicuous, I strode nervously up to the bar, my feet alternately sticking and splashing in wet and dry sawdust. The bar was old and chipped with a large blotched mirror on the wall behind it, various half empty bottles arranged on a shelf and beer taps in front of me.

The bartender was a rough-looking man with three days' stubble that you could strike matches on. He gave me the once over. "Wad'all'it'be, boy?" was the nearest I could get to what he said; his accent was thick and hardly understandable, except for the sneering 'boy' which I found unsettling.

"Just give me a beer," I snapped. It came in a fairly clean glass and I sipped it slowly. The bartender was eyeing me, and I expect he was trying to figure out a way to part me from any money I might have.

"I'm looking for Rick," I said, after a bout of out-staring had gone my way. He raised an eyebrow, in a 'heard that one before' way. "Dolmen sent me," I tried again.

He jerked his head towards a corner, where silhouetted against a stained window I could make out what looked like a bear sitting behind a table. Seeing me look, the man waved me over. I picked up my glass and squelched towards him.

Close up, he was even bigger, with wild hair and eyes and a big bushy beard. I sat opposite him and put my glass on the table. Before I could speak, he stuck out his hand and boomed, "I hear you're looking for Rick, my name's Griff. I know just about everyone around here, I can take you to Rick, he owes me a favour. We'll do that later; for now just sit yourself down and tell me your story."

I shook his hand; his grip was like a trap. His face, behind all the hair, was kind and though I didn't really feel like spilling my life story to someone that I had never met before I gave him a rough re-edited version of events. He must have had some sort of telepathic connection with the bartender because bottles of beer kept appearing, brought by an old man who insisted on wiping the table every time, doing nothing but moving the beer stains about.

I hadn't intended to tell him about the *Moth*, but under the influence of the beer and his stare it all came out. I admitted that I was on the run from the Navy and that I had been delivered here with the promise of a new identity. I mentioned Dolmen and the fact that he had sent me here. All the time I was telling him, he nodded; as if he knew. I said that I had been told that it had been arranged for me to see Rick. I got the impression that I was merely confirming who I was; Rick's name must have convinced him he had the right man because he suddenly shouted across at the barman for a round of spirit chasers to go with our beers.

When the glasses appeared he sank his quickly and called for more. I couldn't keep up with him and as the night wore on, the full glasses stacked up and I realised I was getting more and more drunk. Having just awoken from an anaesthetic hadn't helped me cope with the alcohol and my stomach was empty. In between me trying to drink my way through the line of glasses and him telling me to catch up we swapped stories; he had been everywhere and met everyone, or maybe in my state it just seemed that way. He had a story about just about any place you could mention. In the end I must have just fallen asleep; the last thing I remembered was trying to stand to go to the men's room.

I woke up with the mother of all headaches; it felt like a gang of miners were opening a new section on the top of my head. Then I moved and it got worse. When the room stopped spinning quite so fast I raised my head again for a look around. I was fully clothed and lying on a bed in what looked like a cheap hotel room. The wallpaper was peeling and beneath me the bed-cover was stained and crackling. Worse, I had no memory of how I had got there, I remembered a man called Griff and hoped that he had put me here. Somehow I got vertical and staggered to the bathroom. The tap grudgingly ejected some warm, rusty water and I splashed it over my face. It made me feel a bit better. Looking around I spotted a coffee maker on the chest.

I was just working myself up to making a coffee when the door burst open and Griff reappeared. "Come on then, boy," he boomed, setting off another wave of pain in my skull. "It's way past lunchtime and I've got to take you to meet Rick the forger." He seemed no worse for wear himself and bounded away, calling, "Come on," over his shoulder every few steps.

I followed him downstairs, working on autopilot as he raced away from me. He led me through some backstreets, the sun was bright in my face and it made me wince. Finally, we stopped by a small door. As he hammered on it a slit opened at eye level and I could see we were being scrutinised. There was a rattle as several bolts and chains were removed, the door opened about an inch and a small dark face peered through the gap.

"Hello, Griff," he said. "Long time. What have you got here?"

"This is my mate Finn," said Griff. "He's looking for a new ID, he's a mate of Dolmen's. I figured that you could help me out?"

"For you, of course I can, come in and take a seat," the face replied, the door swung open and we entered the room. The curtains were drawn and the room was lit by the green glow of computer terminals. There must have been twenty or more screens hung on the wall, wires snaked everywhere and led to a row of printers. Paper and 3D models were strewn all over the floor. I found a chair and brushed a stack of coffee cups from it before sitting down. My head was clearing slowly, but I had a dry mouth and my stomach rumbled.

"Now to business," said the man I took to be Rick. "What's your full name?"

"Finn Donald Douglas," I replied. "Any chance of some coffee before we do much else?"

He waved his hands vaguely toward a doorway; Griff grunted and wandered off, returning with a couple of steaming cups. I gulped mine, the hot drink burnt my throat but the caffeine helped.

The man removed my bandage and chuckled. "I'll bet Eric gave you that," he said and Griff grinned as well. "Bet he told you it would confuse a reader."

"Eric is only a lad," said Griff. "Bless him; sometimes it's too easy to get him going."

"You mean it doesn't work then?" It looked like I was the butt of the joke.

"No, it's just a bandage, but it made you feel better so in a way I guess it did."

Griff just grinned some more and picked up a magazine from

the floor. Settling down in an armchair I thought he would start reading but as soon as he had got comfortable he closed his eyes.

Rick scanned my arm with a chip reader, close up he had particularly bad teeth and his clothes reeked of stale beer and tobacco. It didn't help my stomach. He crossed to one of the terminals where he tapped away for several minutes. "Ah, I've got you," he exclaimed, pointing to the screen.

Sure enough, there was my face and all my identity details from my Navy card. The realisation that my life was an open book to anyone with his knowledge was worrying to say the least. Looking at the screen, it had my movements listed, but not my arriving here, and in large letters it said that I was reported missing in action and if spotted should be detained for questioning. But there were no more details, so that was something. I still didn't see how he could alter my chip; they were supposed to be tamper-proof. You couldn't even remove them. Rick must have read my mind.

"Don't worry about the chip," he said. "That's my next job; now then, who would you like to be?" I hadn't really given it any thought; I had assumed that various bits of my past would just have been modified. I was about to say, 'I don't care, just make it an easy name for me to remember', when I found that Griff wasn't snoozing at all.

"He'll be Dave Travise," boomed Griff. "That's who he is from now on."

"Wait a minute," I said. "How do you know who I want to be?"

"That's as good a name as any," Griff replied, "and I think it suits you."

Rick tapped away again for a while. "I'm just transferring all your assets across to your new identity," he informed me. "I take it you don't want the loan that's listed here?"

"You can make it go away?" I asked. I'd been having trouble with the payments, it was a drain on my pay but at least I had a place of my own when I was on leave.

Rick just grinned. "Easy job. You'll have full ownership of the house and land and all your money; less a percentage for my trouble of course, unless you've got anything else to trade?"

"You'll do it for a very small fee," Griff growled. "You have his Navy details; they'll be worth a bit to you, won't they?"

Rick grinned. "Shouldn't you be asleep, Griff? Okay, I'll not fleece the boy, or should I say Dave Travise here, I don't want to end up on Rixon's wrong side."

This was the first time that Rixon had been mentioned and by the look that I saw Griff give, maybe I shouldn't have heard it at all just yet. Trouble was, I had heard of him, he was a person well known on the *Moth*, one who had made a fool of Captain Dror on several occasions, and while he had never actually been caught doing anything illegal, he was on the list for a friendly chat.

After a few moments, Rick stopped tapping and sat back with a smug grin. "Look at that now." He pointed, although it said Finn Donald Douglas the face on the screen was no longer mine.

"Say goodbye to Finn." He pushed a button and the screen dissolved, a new one appeared, with my face and the name Dave Travise.

"Check it out, Dave," he said, passing me a keyboard. I tapped away for a while, sure enough all the details of my life up to now had moved over, most of it was true, except for the loss of my Navy service and statement that I had arrived here three days ago on a ship called the *Orca*. The wanted notice had thankfully vanished; of course it was still attached to my other profile. I was no longer in the Navy, instead I was a 'trader and navigator', with a civilian qualification from some place I'd never been.

"How am I gonna remember all that?" I asked. "If I get stopped and don't know about my own life I'm going to look pretty stupid!"

"You'll have to do some reading then," replied Griff. "You could always say you lost your memory in a terrible accident."

"What, like having my ship shot out from under me by a bunch of psychopathic pirates?"

Griff said nothing but a grin flirted briefly with his lips.

"Right, children," said Rick, "that was the easy bit, now for the ID chip." He rummaged around in a corner, and came towards me holding something that looked lethal. "Don't worry," he said, grinning. "It's a lot of kit to do very little." He pointed it at my chip, embedded somewhere in my arm and it flashed.

I woke up with raging pain and Griff's face peering down at me from close range; I swear I could see small objects in his beard.

"Sorry, Dave," said Rick, "but if I had told you there was going to be a static discharge, you would tense your muscles, which makes it feel worse, and there's always the chance that the data transfer doesn't take." He waved a scanner at me.

"Hmmm…" he said, passing me the read-out. "Looks good."

The screen on his hand scanner said that I was Dave Travise, so his toy must have reprogrammed my bio-chip, which I had thought was impossible. No, I had been told was impossible.

"Bet you thought that was impossible," Rick said. "Well it used to be, and as far as the Feds are concerned it still is, so you're Dave Travise now, and you can prove it. Oh and I shorted out your Navy bio-transmitter while you were asleep."

That was the last link I had with the service and I had forgotten all about its presence, it could have incriminated me, now it was just junk in my arm.

Chapter 16, Now

I was still trying to work out how to get into the box, or unlock the password on the drive.

I needed a DNA sample for the box and had searched the cabin without success. It only needed to be a small thing, a piece of dead skin or a nail clipping. Even a hair would do it, I had peered into all the corners of the cabin and taken the washroom to bits to try and find hairs in the drains. But nothing I had found had worked. I knew that there were devices that could open DNA locks, Griff probably had one, but I didn't want the box to become general knowledge. The drive was different, after too many attempts it might wipe, with a bit of luck the password would be in the box or I might get a clue from somewhere else.

I reckoned that the two things were linked with the Chenkos somehow; probably they proved that Dave Mark One had been working for them. Since it wouldn't be a surprise to anyone, the question was how much more might I find out and did I really want to know?

All that would have to wait for a couple of days though, because I had a docking manoeuvre to plan. After having seen the details of the place we were headed I would need all my piloting skills to dock with our destination, which was a mining and research platform in orbit around a Gas Giant in an otherwise deserted system. We had already traded messages regarding the configuration of our stern ramp, and it was clear that whoever had converted the *Ona* had really thought about it. Our ramp and stern door seal were a standard size, unlike the Navy where nothing ever fitted anything else without a lot of adapters and fiddling. We could link our ramp with their flexible proboscis, which made everything easier. But first we had to secure. And of course there was a complication. The platform was spinning to create its own gravity.

Their docking bay had pylons that attached to us magnetically and held the hull secure, but on approach we would have to match its rotation and move sideways until the magnets could grab us.

The rotation was unusual; most orbiting facilities had field generators that created artificial gravity. When I went to the wheelhouse to do some planning, Griff was there doing something at the workbench. I asked him about it.

As usual he knew the answer. "They have some really delicate stuff on the station," he explained, "and the field generator would screw up their measurements. So they spin instead, and the centripetal force creates the gravity field. All the manned bits are on the outer Rim, where the spin is greatest."

"So in the middle there's weightlessness?"

"That's it, boy," he boomed, slapping me on the back again. "You're getting the idea, all the delicate stuff is in the middle." He bent back to the task he was attempting, fixing circuit boards together to make some unspecified item.

Funnily enough, his use of the 'boy' when he spoke to me didn't annoy me as much as when others said it. It was said without malice, just part of his persona.

"Nancy," I said, and once again she was a step ahead.

"Hi, Dave, I have the spin rate and docking details from the platform. I am computing a docking plan, unless of course you want to do it all manually."

I was getting used to her sense of humour and to be honest I liked it. The programme that created her was a source of fascination; the responses were so varied it was almost real. The more I interacted with her, the more her vocabulary and use of emotion changed; she was learning from me, becoming as sarcastic as I was, with a good line in riposte. It was like talking to a human assistant and sometimes I forgot that she was only a machine.

"You worry about the spin, Nancy, and I'll move us sideways," I answered.

"If you like," she said. "But I can manage to do both, you know." She sounded offended, crazy for a machine to have emotions like that but the more I talked to her the more she seemed human.

"I'd rather have something to do," I replied.

"Fine," she said. "It's nice working with you, Dave."

"Griff," I asked, "where did you get the Nav programme from?"

He glanced up and his eyes shone. "Someone owed me a favour," he said, predictably.

"Excuse me," said Nancy in a pained voice. "I'm still here, you know." Griff just rolled his eyes. "We could get that circuit changed," he answered. Nancy made a noise that sounded like 'Huh'.

"The cost of one of these is enormous," I stated the obvious, all the time trying not to laugh. I had read about the tech, developed on a place called New Devon. As with all new stuff, the price was crazy. In a few years it might be cheaper but now it was a rich man's toy. It was the sort of thing you would never see in the Navy. Especially if it answered back like that. Dror would have shot it.

"It was a big favour," he answered enigmatically. "Actually it was a matter of life and death, in more ways than one. I'll tell you about it, one day."

"I love a good story," added Nancy. "And some of yours, Griff, well…" I wondered then if she had recorded all the conversations on the bridge and if I could get her to play them back. That would be another late night mission, avoiding 'mode 101' this time.

Chapter 17

Two days later we dropped out of light-speed as we entered the system that was our destination. Before we could call and announce ourselves a patrol craft appeared in front of us. Small and bristling with missiles it blocked our path. However they had detected us, they were efficient.

"They worry about attacks," said Rixon. "Industrial espionage."

"Or people like Dolmen?" I suggested; my tone innocent. He caught on quickly.

"Precisely, but not like us, or at least not this time."

The craft interrogated us automatically via Nancy, which showed that there was money in whatever it was they did, and after the two computers had chatted for a while Nancy announced that we were cleared to follow them in. Their speed increased, and Nancy did the same, until we were moving at a speed close to light, even so they were faster and grew smaller as we tried to catch up.

They were headed towards the Gas Giant that already glowed as a purple crescent in the viewer, its large rings part lit by the system star. As we closed in we could see that there was a point of light visible on its dark side, in the shadow cast by the planet's bulk, and Nancy altered course until it was centred and just above our bow lights.

The patrol craft turned and left us, with a waggle of its stub wings, as we neared the station. Close up it was big and complex, consisting of lots of modules joined together around a central core. I could also glimpse the docking station as it spun past me; it was brightly lit and had a large, blank status board above it. It was only visible for an instant every time it flashed past. Its speed seemed to increase as we got closer and I briefly wondered if it wouldn't be easier to let Nancy do the whole thing. Then my pride and ego kicked back in.

"*Urssa* station, this is *Orca*, permission to dock, please," I called on the frequency given in our instructions.

A female voice, distorted but understandable, replied. "Roger, *Orca*, you have permission, and try not to do what the last clown did, we've only just finished repairs." Oh great!

I felt sweat break out on my brow as I took the controls, but I knew that I had a little help for the first bit, and the controller might not.

"Nancy, match us up with the rate of spin," I requested, trying to keep my voice neutral, but she spotted it.

"Relax, Dave," she said gently, and the engine note changed as we slowed to match the speed of the turning dock. Nancy juggled our engine thrust; reducing the power of the engine nearest the platform helped us to turn with it. As we started to circle it the planet flashed past the ports every few seconds. Our rate of turn would have been enough to make us all feel queasy, but the inertial dampers took care of the physical effects.

I focused my gaze on the docking arm, which was slowing relative to us, until it appeared stationary, just off our port beam. With delicate touches on the thruster, I inched us in closer, whilst Nancy took care of keeping us moving at the same relative speed. I tried not to look at anything but the pylon as it crept closer. Rixon tried to appear relaxed but he gripped the handrail as we closed in, I could see he was standing by the emergency control panel, probably ready to blast us away if it all went horribly wrong.

The status board above the dock flashed into life, counting down the distance, relative motion and angle of approach as we got closer. I juggled the controls, as we were slightly bows-in and the numbers changed. I was aiming for three zeros and achieved them as the range dropped to ten metres from our wingtip. The bulk of the station masked the background so it now looked like we were approaching a stationary platform.

Our wings slid under the structure and we hovered, the hull was now less than five metres off the arm. Close up I could see that the whole thing was mounted on huge buffers which would allow it to absorb the impact of a badly manoeuvred craft. The paintwork in the area was scratched and dented, with signs of many patched repairs. So far, I was doing alright, with Nancy's help. The controller called again, "Hold it there, we are starting the magnetic clamps." Our sideways motion resumed until, with a clang, we were held alongside. I immediately cut the power to the engines, before we could do any damage.

"*Orca*, this is *Urssa* control," crackled the voice. "Nice landing, we will deploy the walkway, standby."

I exhaled, releasing the tension I felt. Turning, I saw that all the crew were stood behind me and they broke into a round of applause. "Thank you," I bowed, "but now I need a lie down and my shirt needs wringing out."

"Thank you," echoed Nancy.

"Tan," said Rixon, "take the ramp control, open when ready and let's get started."

Tan nodded and taking the GFH with her, she left the bridge.

"Nice job," said Rixon. "You could have done that without Nancy, couldn't you?"

"Maybe," I answered. "I saw where you were standing though, and it helped me concentrate."

He grinned. "Captain always looks out for the safety of his ship, but I had confidence in you."

On the monitor, we watched as the unloader swung through its arc, eventually coming to rest on our stern. Its locking annular, on its flexible joint, fitted neatly into the recess around our stern door, guided into place by three suited figures. Once it was snug, the annular was inflated, filling the recess and creating a seal.

"*Orca*, we are pressurising now, you can open your doors when ready." Griff had gone to the stern and taken local control. He compared the pressure on both sides of the stern door and finding it equal started the motor and opened the ship. There was no need to slide the ramp out, one was attached to the shore walkway, and as soon as they could, the unloading crew bridged the gap.

Large hydraulic rams had come out from the station, and supported the *Orca*, holding it firmly in position for the discharge operation, which looked like it would commence as soon as the formalities were observed. Tan was waiting at the stern, where a self-propelled crane was poised to start unloading. Stu and Ardullah were removing lashings while Mitch dragged them out of the way.

Two white-suited men were checking the paperwork and inspecting the condition of the packaging. After a couple of minutes they waved the crane in and work began.

Chapter 18

I had nothing to do, I wasn't involved in cargo work, we had no onward destination and the surveys were all up to date. I fancied a look around; it seemed like an idea to get off the *Orca* for a while, so I walked down the discharge arm, avoiding the crane and the pallets. When I came to a fork in the corridor, I turned away from the cargo operation, and headed into the station.

The corridors were painted a very bright white and had airlocks every twenty or so metres. There were cameras and alarms everywhere, and lots of posters giving evacuation drills. Every section had its own lifepod, clearly marked. I guess that in the event of a problem each section would be isolated and it would be up to the people in each part to get to their own lifepod. The whole set-up was very professional looking but the most noticeable thing was the absence of many people. A few doors were open, surprisingly ordinary doors in the high tech environment but there was no clue as to what was behind them.

I hadn't gone far when a security guard came towards me. "Hold it there, sir," she said. "Can you tell me your business here, please?"

Of course I had not asked for permission to stroll around and had no ID badge. I must have been spotted by one of the cameras, or perhaps there were motion sensors in the floor. The guard scanned me with a handheld wand. "Are you from the ship on the pylon, Mr Travise?" she asked.

"That's right; I just wanted a change of scenery." She gave me a funny look; I could see her thinking, 'aren't all spaceships the same?' She was very polite, though. She turned away and I could hear her as she muttered something into her comms set. The words were indistinct, the reply made her turn her head back to me. She was smiling and nodding. She looked at me again, turned back and said a few more words.

"Well we can't have you wandering around without permission, sir. We spotted you on the cameras; of course we didn't know who you were. We can't scan the corridors, the field would interfere with the other things we do. The Duty Officer sent me to find out who was wandering around. Now she knows who you are she wants to see you; she was going to invite you over anyway."

"Is that the woman I heard on the radio?"

"That's right, sir; she wanted to ask you about your manoeuvre. Now you're here I can take you to the control room, we can get you a security badge."

"Okay," I said. "Sorry for the inconvenience; is she mad at me?"

"She was a bit upset, but I told her that you're cute. Once she's seen you she'll be okay."

I thought that was a funny thing to say.

She led the way through another airlock to a lift, which was the old continuous type, slow moving platforms without doors that you hopped on and off. We rode up for several decks. Down a corridor and through a door and we were in the control room, a large open space, crammed with tech and people. So this was where everyone was.

The guard took me over to the central desk, which was manned by a very attractive woman, her shaven head and make-up emphasising her features and blue eyes. Dressed in a skimpy vest and very small shorts, she was talking into a headset and typing with one hand on a virtual keyboard that was hovering in mid-air over the console. She had nice legs.

"Here he is," the security guard announced.

She looked me over and I realised that she was sizing me up. She had the sort of expression a cat has when it sees a mouse. The name badge hanging on one strap of her vest announced that she was 'Liesh', but whether that was her first or last name wasn't obvious.

"So you're the pain-in-the-ass guy setting off all the alarms?" she said. "Didn't you pick up a badge before you started wandering around? There should have been a box of them by the ramp."

"Sorry." It sounded inadequate. I hadn't seen them but then I hadn't really looked either. In the Navy we just went where we wanted and it hadn't occurred to me that I might need permission. She scanned me quickly and efficiently with a small handheld reader.

"So, Dave Travise, you're the pilot of the *Orca*?" I nodded. "I wanted to see you anyway, that was a pretty impressive docking," she said. "And quick. No messing about with you is there; straight in! You've done that before."

The way she said it and her wide eyed expression made me blush; there was too much innuendo here for my liking. "Beginner's luck," I said, trying to sound casual. I didn't mention Nancy; for some reason I wanted to impress her.

She licked her lips and I suddenly realised that it had gone quiet; everyone in earshot was hanging on her words. Call me slow but I got the impression that the cat thing was about right. She was still talking.

"Well the last one who tried to do it that quickly wrapped himself around our solar array when he bounced off for the second time, and HE said he was an expert. Didn't get anywhere with me after that. Where did you learn to fly?"

"Navy," I said and immediately wished that I hadn't.

"That explains the wandering around then," she said, with the familiar quote from the Blessed days, "Navy goes where they want! What ship?" she added.

And I was stuck, should I say *Moth* and risk more questions, or maybe they wouldn't know.

She solved my problem. "Have you heard the latest? One of the Rim fleet has gone missing, they think it's lost."

I tried to look shocked, but was conscious of the fact that I didn't know what my chip might say about my past. I hadn't read up much on Dave's history so I had to be careful. "Really? Any idea what happened?"

"The last report said they were sent from Michael's Hollow to investigate some dispute out in the sticks," she pulled a face. "It's sad for all the crew but there will be no love lost for the skipper. He was a nasty piece of work, you might have heard of him; Hermann Dror?"

"Oh everyone's heard of him," I said. "He's not the best recruiting tool, but very good at his job."

"You would defend him I suppose," was her slightly resigned response. "I guess you all stick together."

"That's a bit harsh," I said. "Anyway, I'm not Navy now. Tell you what, buy me a drink when you finish up here and I'll tell you my life story." I don't know why I said it, I thought that I would get knocked back, but instead, her eyes narrowed as she thought about it.

"I thought you'd never ask," she said. "Thought that I was going to have to suggest it. There are no interesting men left on here and it'll be a change from all the ugly, sweaty miners hitting on me. Come back here at twenty-two ship time." Her look changed. "And by the way, if I like your story you won't be leaving before tomorrow morning." She turned back to her task. I couldn't help noticing that I was attracting envious looks from everyone who had heard her.

Chapter 19

As I headed towards the lift, my escort gave me a visitor's security badge, which I hung round my neck. She rolled her eyes and smirked. "Liesh likes you," she said. "It's a sure thing. Lucky you, and lucky her! Go down to level eighteen and follow the signs for the Pylon." I realised what she was on about and felt myself blush as I walked to the lift.

Funnily enough, with everything going round in my head I missed my floor and got off at level seventeen. As I walked down the corridor I actually took notice of my surroundings and saw the signs on the passageway framing every few metres. Realising I was on the wrong level I was about to retrace my steps when I passed a lab with a lone worker bent over a keyboard. I had an idea, put my head round the door and said hello. "Hi," he replied, "can I help you?"

He was the archetypical techy, thick glasses, ill-fitting clothes and pathetically grateful to be involved in a conversation with a real person. He pushed his mop of greasy hair back over his forehead every few words, and even though I was metres away, I could tell he had bad breath.

I told him my problem. "I've got a DNA lock I need to open," and he gave me a patronising look.

"Is that all, I thought it would be something difficult. I can lend you a synthesiser, but I'll need it back."

"I'll be back to see Liesh later," I said. "I can drop it in then." At the mention of her, he looked deflated.

"Lucky you! She's friends with everyone but she never notices me," he said wistfully. Rummaging around on his bench he found a small grey pen. "Here you are," he handed it to me, "put the black end on the lock and press the contact."

"Thanks." I turned to go. "I'll bring it back to you later."

"I'll be here," he sighed. "I'm always here."

Now I knew about the signs, I was back on board in no time. The unloading was proceeding slowly, there was only room in the alleyway for one pallet to be unloaded at a time and because they were delicate they were being handled carefully.

I rushed to my cabin and got the box out, pressing the pen against it I mentally crossed my fingers and pressed the contact. There was a pause, a click and the box opened. Straight away I removed the pin from the locking bar, now I couldn't lock it again by accident.

After the anticipation, the contents were strange and a bit of a disappointment, a couple of ordinary looking pebbles and a screwed up piece of paper. I smoothed the paper out, it had a series of numbers written in blocks, they looked like coordinates, underneath were the letters V&VC. Now we might be getting somewhere. I would have to investigate them later.

My stomach was telling me it was time to eat; I had two hours before I needed to return to see Liesh so I stuffed everything back under the blankets in the drawer and went in search of food.

"Where have you been?" asked Rixon; we were in the mess room. "I wanted to ask you to sort out some routes. Never mind you can do them on watch tonight, we'll be finished and sailing in an hour."

I calculated, that would be 2100 station time, we kept our own time in space, based on the last place, or the next, and as we were only going to be here a short while we hadn't bothered adjusting. I was about to mention my meeting with Liesh but thought better of it. We would be long gone by 2200 and my sure thing would be receding into the distance.

"Where are we off to, Boss?" I said instead, trying not to sound disappointed.

"Come up to the bridge after you've eaten, I'll explain it all." He turned the conversation to other things, and as they were about things that had happened before my arrival I lost interest and went in search of food.

I was tucking into my meal when Tan, who had been watching the unloading, came into the room and took a cup of water from the cooler. Sitting down, she addressed Rixon. "We gotta problem, Boss," she said simply. My ears pricked up at this, but I kept quiet.

"Go on," said Rixon. "What has Vlad got us into this time?"

"I don't think it's him this time, it's the station Duty Officer," said Tan. "The stupid bitch has got some issues with the ship; she says we have to have an equipment inspection before they can let us go. The kicker is they can't do it till tomorrow sometime."

"That's crap," Rixon replied. "Dave, this is your department. You'd better tell me that everything's up to date."

"Of course it is," I answered. "And anyway it all checked out on arrival."

Rixon looked puzzled. "You're right, go and see her and sort it out." He pulled out a roll of notes. "Take some cash, or you could try and charm her." Beside him Myra looked disapproving. He shrugged, "I'd go myself but…"

"Will do, Boss." I knew what was going on but had to keep up the fiction.

Chapter 20

I had plenty of time but left anyway. I remembered to take a badge this time. On my way back to the control room, I took a detour and dropped the pen off; the tech was still in the same place.

"What are you up to?" I asked him, he gave me a pitying look as if I would never understand.

"Oh, just working out some gravity calculations, offsets for the results of our experiments. Did the pen work?"

"It did, and thanks, but it's only given me another puzzle." I figured, if no one ever talks to the guy, he would be safe with my secret, and he might even help me solve it.

He looked interested. "What you got?"

I told him about the blocks of numbers and the letters, his eyes glazed for a couple of seconds. "The numbers could be anything but the last bit sounds like it could be a case sensitive password," he said. "People forget the computer sees capital letters differently and put in lower case when they shouldn't, it happens all the time." He bent back to his task, I figured I was forgotten.

I was still early, so instead of going to the control room, I followed the signs to the lounge. I found that all the living spaces were nearer the centre of rotation and were extensive. There were gardens and walkways, large glazed panels and a feeling of space after the cramped, windowless alleyways. It looked like a good mess room as well, with the smell of real fresh food, maybe they grew it here.

The gravity was weaker and it almost felt like I would float away as I neared the centre of the station. There were a few people about and they looked at my badge, I guess everyone knew everyone.

I got back to the control room just before 2200; there was an argument in progress. Liesh was handing over the watch to a tall woman who was getting red around the face.

"Why is that bloody ship still on the pylon?" she shouted at Liesh. "They should have been gone by now."

"Safety gear inspection," she replied.

The woman's face changed to a knowing grin. "Well I hope he's worth it."

"Check him out," she said, pointing at me. "He's on time, must be keen." She got up from the seat and handed over the headset. "It's all yours then," she said. "Goodnight."

She walked over to me. "Hi, Dave," she greeted me, putting her arm around my waist. "Let's go." I could feel the gaze of most of the room, hot on my neck as we walked out.

"What was that all about?" I asked her as she led me into the centre of the station. Again I could feel my weight reducing as the gravity caused by our rotation decreased.

"Just jealousy; I saw you first," was her reply. It made me feel like a piece of meat, maybe that was how girls felt. It probably served me right.

We passed the open spaces that I had seen before and entered a different lift, tucked away in the corner. This one was card operated. It took us up to a row of cabins which must have been at the top of the station. We entered one of them and I almost stopped breathing.

One entire wall and all of the ceiling was made of plasto-glass, with a spider's web frame of metal. The cabin was above the rest of the station and seemed to be floating in space. The Gas Giant was in view, its rings tilted and sparkling, behind it was a carpet of stars. The motion was sedate and mind blowing.

"Nice view," I said, it sounded trite and broke the spell.

"Come and sit down," she called, and I turned. She was half-lying on a couch, in front of which was a low table with a bottle and two glasses. "Have a glass of wine, totally unofficial of course."

I took the glass and sat next to her, she wriggled in close, lifting her legs over mine. "So, Mr ex-Navy man Dave," she said. "What are you doing driving the *Orca*?"

"Long story," I answered, thinking of something to say that wouldn't drop me in it. "I'd had enough of the Navy and wanted a change. This came up."

The answer seemed to satisfy her. "A lot of interesting things on your chip." I wondered what they were; I just hoped she didn't want details. She put her hand on my arm and traced the line of my biceps, the touch electric.

"Anyway," I continued, "why keep us here for a safety inspection that you and I both know we don't need."

She grinned. "What's the point of having rank if you don't abuse it sometimes? I liked the look of you when I saw you, it's boring here; there's been no new male interest for ages."

"So my ship is being held up because you're bored?" Her hand moved to my chest, continuing the motion.

"Don't knock it, there's something in it for both of us."

The wine was starting to go to my head in the low gravity; Liesh leaned into me. "That's enough talk," she whispered into my ear. "Like it or not, and you will, you're here till the morning." She took my glass and put it on the table.

Chapter 21

I was back on board the *Orca* before breakfast, with clearance to depart, a sore body and had had little sleep. Cargo work was complete and the used lashings were stowed neatly. I walked into the mess room and Myra was the first person I saw. Before I had the chance to say anything she gave me a filthy look, turned and walked out. Feeling lousy, I got myself a coffee.

Rixon eyed me jealously and raised his eyebrows when I handed his money back. "You took your time," he said. "Looks like you managed to persuade her though. I suppose you want a day off now."

"I could do with a sleep," I told him. "But I've got clearance; we can go when we're ready."

"Well, get us on our way, set up the voyage and then you can disappear, I'll cover your watch. All the details are on the chart table."

I nodded. "Thanks, I think I've upset Myra though, I didn't want that."

"She'll be alright, she's an adult. Just leave her alone for a bit." Spoken like a big brother. Glumly, I took my coffee to the bridge.

"Good morning, Nancy," I said with as much enthusiasm as I could muster.

"Hello, Dave," she answered frostily. "Would you like me to speak quietly?" At least she was still talking to me.

I picked up the papers on the chart table and had a look at our destination, the name jumped out at me. It looked like I was going back to Michael's Hollow, a place I didn't really want to see again.

In all the vastness of the Federation, I had assumed that I had enough room to disappear, but I was being drawn back to the places where I could be remembered; next we would probably strike a deal with my father or my brothers.

I guessed that any objections I might have to that would be ignored. I was glad that I had grown some facial hair, maybe if I kept out of the way no one would spot me.

That was a problem for the future, first we had to pick up a load of food and some equipment from a trading station called Coopers Post.

"New route please, Nancy," I said. "Michael's Hollow via Coopers Post."

"Will do, Dave. Leave it to me, you sound like you need a rest." Even her voice sounded judgemental.

The departure was a lot simpler than the arrival. After we had shut the ramp and disconnected the proboscis the docking magnets had their polarity reversed and we were flung away from the arm, the inertial dampers stopped us from bouncing around too much and I piled the power on as soon as I could to compensate. I engaged the route to Coopers Post and went to my cabin for a sleep.

I felt like I was stuck, did I want Myra to think that we were leaving because of my overnight activities, or would it be better if I told her about Liesh and that we were delayed because of her desires. Either way, I would end up looking bad, and it made Myra and me less likely. And I realised that wasn't what I wanted.

I slept for about twelve hours straight and woke up hungry; my watch said it was the middle of the night. I went to the mess room for a bite.

Stu was eating when I got there, there were two empty plates in front of him and he was attacking a third, his free arm curled protectively around the meal.

He waved his fork in greeting as I looked through the boxes, there weren't so many left now. In the end I chose fish and rice and put it in the cooker.

"Hey, Dave," said Stu as I sat and opened the box. "You

recovered yet?"

I tried to make a joke out of it. "It's a job and someone had to do it."

He leered back at me between mouthfuls. "Lucky you, but I think it upset Myra."

He was spot on there, I knew that, and it wasn't what I had wanted. I shrugged. "That's life, we're not an item." I ate a few mouthfuls.

His perception surprised me. "Oh but you could be," he said. "I've seen the way she looks at you, and Mitch let slip that Myra thought you were... interesting I think the word was. You know," he warmed to his theme, "the last Nav, he fancied his chances with Myra, but Rixon did the same thing to him, made sure he embarrassed him in front of her, it was all downhill from then." He bent to his plate and attacked it.

"What do you mean, Stu?" I wanted to be sure that he meant what he was saying.

"Well, Dave, you seem like a nice guy, it's just that Rixon is very protective of his little sister, he feels responsible for keeping her safe." He chewed for a while. "Funny thing, after she knocked the other Dave back, it was from then that all our troubles started."

That was interesting news; it filled in a few gaps in my knowledge. Maybe Stu wasn't as unaware of things as I had thought.

"So what?" I asked around a mouthful of food. "Do you think that's why he started passing information to Vlad Chenko?"

"Dunno about that, but I know that he was always saying he had no money. Stone broke he used to say he was. He had a couple of stones and he used to fiddle with them, all the time rubbing them together, he kept saying 'stone broke' while he did it, like it was some sort of mantra. We used to reckon he was rubbing them for his luck to change."

I thought about what Stu had said, it could be enough to betray his crew, and in this world, as I was learning, there were no rules and apparently no honour either. Stu was stirring his food with a face like thunder; the memories had obviously got him wound up. He finally exploded.

"Those bloody Chenkos," he shouted, the sudden noise making me jump; clearly they were not on his list either, he jabbed his plastic fork into the defenceless plate with such force that it snapped.

Cursing, he picked another from the debris around him. "Suddenly they knew every move we made, and it couldn't have been blind luck. We all play the watching game and sometimes we get ahead of each other but this was every time. Rixon was going crazy and we were making no money. Wherever we went they were there in that old Bishop of theirs, undercutting us and taking the work."

My ears pricked up, on the *Moth* there had been reports of an old Bishop class frigate working as a freighter, but as it had not always been on the Rim it had not been high on our list of priorities.

So it was the Chenkos, I thought. Instead I said, "Where did they get a Bishop?"

"They found it," he answered, as if it was the most ordinary thing. "Abandoned and drifting. It was pretty shot up and deserted, no lifeboats, but they managed to tow it in and patch it up." His voice took on a contemptuous tone. "They don't look after it, and you wouldn't catch me on the thing. Now if you'll excuse me, my food's getting cold."

I'd finished my meal, so I went back to my cabin. There was a piece of paper wedged in the door: 'I've paid you. R'. Rixon must have been prowling around while I was talking to Stu. Perhaps he had heard our conversation, perhaps not.

I hadn't bothered checking my bank accounts since I had become Dave Travise and I suddenly realised that I didn't have a clue if I could still access them or even if they were still in the same place as Finn's had been. Panic set in; perhaps Rick had cleaned me out after all. I turned the paper over. To my relief Rixon had written the name of a bank and a series of numbers, which must be Dave Travise's account details. It was the same bank as I had always had; maybe the accounts were all together. Had he not given me that then I might not have been able to get at my money anyway. Perhaps I ought to take a look. But not now, I tossed it on the desk and went back to sleep.

I was busy for the next two days, checking all the safety gear in the shuttles and dropships. I had the craft to myself as I worked through my list of inspections so managed to avoid Myra apart from at mealtimes. And then she was always talking to someone else so it looked like she was doing the same. It kept us apart and stopped us shouting at each other, my attempts to explain would probably not have been believed anyway.

Finally I had the chance, I logged onto the hyperweb and found my way to the bank that Rixon said he had paid my wages into. The login as Dave Travise went without a hitch, using the numbers on the paper; I intended to transfer most of the wages into my old accounts, well out of anyone's way just as soon as I could. I knew I would have taken over the accounts that the other Dave would have had for his pay, and that there might be a bit left in it as well as what I had been paid, but I wasn't ready for what happened next.

When the screen opened I saw that Rick had renamed my two Finn Douglas accounts, they sat alongside the Dave Travise account that Rixon had used. Rick must have been in on the switch for longer than just the day he saw me, to get that much background. To my surprise there were now a total of five accounts listed under my name. I checked both of mine, it wasn't much but it was all there, so Rick hadn't taken anything out of either one. And the loan was marked as paid off as well.

Two of the other three were still password protected but the one that I had come to see had a significant amount, which must have been Dave's wages. He was paid more than my Navy pay, which wasn't really a surprise and over the last year he hadn't drawn much out. All the deposits were from Orca and Co. including the most recent. The account numbers on the other two looked familiar; referring to the note that I had found in Dave's box showed me that they matched up.

Maybe the geek on the station was right; the letters were the login code; taking a deep breath I entered them, remembering the case. The screen flashed up, 'enter your password'. Oh hell, what could that be?

What would Dave Travise use as a password? Stu's comment came into my head, 'he was always saying he had no money, stone broke he used to say he was'. I typed it in.

The screen went black and then opened again filled with numbers, I nearly fell off my chair.

Chapter 22

Altogether there was enough money in the two accounts combined to buy a ship like the *Orca*, or to use as collateral to equip a start-up colony. I could have my own planet and enough stuff to start up a farm or a factory. After my pitiful Navy pay, and the small savings I had managed to make, these three accounts had more money than I had ever seen in one place, somehow it was all mine.

Looking more closely through them, one account had been opened eight months ago and was filled with regular transfers from an unnamed account on Basilan, while the other one had no recent deposits, but only interest payments on the considerable capital.

I debated transferring the whole lot to my real accounts but in the end I decided against it; everything was in the same bank now so there would be little point. Instead I just changed the passwords for everything and logged out.

Maybe there was something in Stu's words, if the Chenkos had been paying Dave for information, that would explain the deposits, they had been doing it for a while but why hadn't they stopped, the last payment was only three days ago? Then I thought, now that the Chenkos knew Dave was gone, maybe they would want the money back. Hell, maybe Rixon would want it as compensation for all the work he had lost from Dave's spying.

I sat there numb; suddenly I could see that I was surrounded by people who had a reason to get me alone in a dark corner. Rixon to recover his losses, the Chenkos to get their investment back and Myra because of my dalliance at the station. And of them all, I was most worried about Myra.

As if I didn't have enough to worry about, I ticked them off on my fingers; the fear of being caught as a deserter, a change of identity and having to go back to a place where it could all fall apart. That was enough for anyone. Now here was another set of problems. To keep me sane I had tried to put some of them away in the back of my mind; the trouble was, it was getting crowded in there.

Next time I was on watch, alone in the wheelhouse I asked Nancy for information about Coopers Post. The computer system was turning into my source of information about my new life, I could ask her anything, even the stupid questions. I might get the odd sarcastic comment but at least I was getting an education in the real world.

Unsurprisingly in the vastness of the Rim, it was another place where I had never been, a genuine frontier world; there were no police, customs or traffic control, or even a proper spaceport, just a large field outside the settlement.

It was in quite a strategic position, in an area where the proximity of a number of stars squeezed the trans-light routes into a bottleneck. On the back of this, a ship repair yard had grown up. Of course, along with all the legitimate business, the chancers and criminals had moved in and the place had acquired a reputation for being somewhere where anything was available; for a price.

Nancy was very informative but a bit disparaging about Coopers Post and Nara, the planet on which it sat. She advised me to keep a close eye on my valuables and avoid the bars, especially one called Ma Esters. Apparently it had a reputation. She made it sound exciting and dangerous at the same time; the kind of place Dave Travise, Navy deserter and criminal double-dealer would like.

We arrived in the system during the local night time and settled into orbit.

"It'll be pointless landing before daylight," said Griff. "Everyone will be drunk or asleep and no use to us. Might as well relax safe up here and arrive after breakfast."

Next morning we dropped out of orbit, and at Rixon's insistence

Nancy took over, flying us through thick cloud with glimpses of the ground beneath. Turbulence buffeted the *Orca*; the dampers were working overtime to keep us level. Rain showers splattered the ports as the wipers struggled to give us a clear view; we were flying below one hundred metres and passed farms and homesteads dotted on the plains. Huge herds of cattle and flocks of sheep ignored us, intent only on the lush grass. We drank half-filled cups of coffee to avoid spilling most of it.

Rixon was lounging in his chair, drinking his coffee and chatting to Griff, while I stood feeling slightly redundant as Nancy homed in on the landing field.

"You been here before, Dave?" asked Griff, and when I answered in the negative he looked at Rixon and they smirked at some private joke.

"Well don't worry; your namesake never came here with us either. Nancy," said Rixon, "tell us at fifty kilometres out."

"Will do," she cheerfully replied, it sounded like she was in on the joke as well, whatever it was.

"We're crossing the high plains," Griff told me. "There's always a lot of cloud here, it bubbles up from the oceans and the lowlands and the wind blows it along. We keep low, there's nothing to hit and the turbulence is worse higher up." We were passing an enormous pen filled with pigs, some stopped their rooting around and looked up, we were that close to the ground.

"Fifty kilometres out," announced Nancy.

Looking ahead, I could see a line of clear air between the cloud and the ground; it shone silver and got bigger as we approached. "Hold on to your breakfast," said Griff as we broke into the clear air, the brightness temporarily blinding ahead. I looked down.

The land beneath us, which had been so close, suddenly fell away, not just a bit, but by around ten thousand metres, vertigo kicked in and I clutched at the console. Behind me I could hear Griff and Rixon laughing, I was too busy holding on to my dignity to comment. Nancy slowed the *Orca* and we turned to port, I realised that we had been dropping at the same time as we were turning when the cliffs reappeared above us. Waterfalls streamed over them and at the base; nestled in the shadows was Coopers Post.

"Exciting eh?" said Rixon between laughs at my discomfort. "It gets everyone like that the first time. It's a geological feature; we're not in a valley here. You can catch someone out next time." Griff gave me a slap on the back which didn't help.

The port was really only a large open space, off to one side of the town and dotted with craft. We dropped into a gap in the line.

I transferred engine control and Myra acknowledged me, I was glad to hear that her voice sounded a bit less frosty than it had in the few comments we had exchanged recently.

"Just so as you know, Dave," said Rixon. "No one ever rushes round here; it takes a bit of getting used to. Especially after your Navy way of doing things. I don't expect we'll start loading today. Let's get into Ma Esters for a beer, Griff; get on to Moraine's boys and tell him were here. Tan and the GFH can set the hold up; they can go for a beer when we come back."

We walked down to the hold where we found Myra; she had changed out of her overalls and looked very presentable in tight jeans and a blouse. Her hair was loose and looked freshly washed. There was make-up on her face and she swung a bag decorated with flowers. "Where you off to all dressed up?" asked Rixon, in big brother mode.

She gave him a stare. "It's none of your business but I need some spares. If I look like a helpless bimbo I'll distract them and I'll get a better price." Griff started up the ground car and the four of us headed into town. There was no paved roadway, just a set of ruts in the grass from heavy vehicles. When we got into town it was the same.

The dusty streets were lined with two-storey buildings; the wooden construction looked strange, festooned as they were with satellite receivers and power couplers. Small groups of people lounged around, watching the world go by. There were bodies asleep on verandas; at least I assumed they were asleep. We dropped Myra off by what looked like a scrapyard. "This is me," she said. "I'll meet you in Esters."

Chapter 23

Nancy had been right; Ma Esters was a dive, there was no other word for it, the chipped swing doors opened onto sawdust covered wooden floors with tables and chairs that showed wear and multiple repairs. It was the archetypical frontier bar, just like in a thousand bad movies. There were no windows; just holes in the wall with curtains and shutters. "It hardly ever rains here," Griff informed me, "that's all on the uplands, it's a desert down here. Anyway," he chuckled, "the glass wouldn't survive more than a couple of nights."

There were two very large men at the door checking out all the arrivals, they had the broken nosed look of bouncers, but their faces cracked into grins as they saw Griff. The three of them group-hugged, with lots of back-slapping and expressions of mutual admiration. Rixon shook his head. "Boys," he muttered. Eventually, they waved us in.

The place was packed and all conversation stopped as we entered, every face swung to inspect us. People were sat at tables, playing cards and drinking, while there were groups dressed as miners with girls hovering round them. The stairs were lined with more women, heavily made up and under-dressed. They all looked us over as we walked in, a few nodded at Griff and Rixon, who stopped and introduced me to so many people that I soon lost track. I noticed that he only ever called me Dave.

Eventually, we arrived at the bar, in front of a bony, rat-faced man sitting on a stool. He had his back to us; headphones in and was nodding. He must have suddenly seen us in the dirty mirror, or perhaps he had a sixth sense because in one fluid movement he drained his beer, stood and headed for the exit. He wore sweat-stained clothes that were too big for him and had patchy stubble on his pointed chin.

"Danno," rumbled Griff, "where are you off to then?" The man heard that over the noise in his ears. He pulled the 'phones out; stopped and swallowed, his throat twitching.

"Hello, Mr Griff," he whined, if he had been a dog his tail would have been wagging. "Fancy seeing you here," he licked his lips nervously. "Are you looking for someone in particular?" His head swivelled on his weedy neck. "Oh and Mr Rixon as well; who's this you've got with you then?"

"This, Danno, is Dave Travise," Rixon announced.

Danno's whole body shook, as if he had been shot. "Of course it is. Hello, Dave," he said, starting to edge sideways past us, towards the door.

Myra must have come in after us and was blocking his way. "Going somewhere, Danno?" she asked him; although she was dainty she was bigger than him, and more robust.

"And Myra too," he gulped. Sitting back down, he waved at the bartender. "Let's all have a drink."

"Thanks, Danno," she said, flirting with him, fluttering her eyes and altering her pose, pushing one hip out toward him. "Why are you acting so nervous?"

I noticed that she had undone more buttons on her blouse since we had dropped her off; was it for the shipyard or Danno's benefit? Either way it was worth it, at least as far as I was concerned. Rixon had noticed the display and looked annoyed, I wondered if there would be an argument.

"No reason," he answered.

Her voice dropped in tone, "Is it to do with Dave here?" she leant over and touched his arm and he twitched again.

"Of course not; I've never met him before." His Adam's apple was working overtime and sweat dripped from his face.

"That's funny," she continued in the husky whisper. She was

stroking his arm, her fingers tracing circles on the skin. "I'm sure you would have known him, I must have been mistaken."

Danno looked tortured as he bought the drinks; he kept looking at me as if trying to work something out. Clearly I had spooked him.

"Tell you what, Rixon," Danno said, swallowing half of his beer in one go. "It's funny you're here now. I've heard of a job, I was gonna call Griff about it, there's a miners' group that come in here most nights, they're setting up for a survey but their ship has fallen through. I figured you might want to cart them around."

"We've got a job, we're on the way to Michael's Hollow," said Rixon. "But thanks for the info."

"That's okay," said Danno. "They need another month before they're ready." He drained his beer. "I gotta go," he said and this time no one stopped him. With a longing glance at Myra he scuttled away.

"Who's he?" I asked after we had ordered more drinks, Griff was the first to answer.

"Danno is a low level trader, but based here, he buys and sells, mainly stuff that no one else will touch. He seems to be left alone by the local gangs so we think he has friends."

"My money's on the Chenkos," said Myra.

"Hang on a minute," I had déjà vu, I turned to Rixon. "Was this another little one of your ideas, using me to flush out answers without me knowing what the hell is going on?"

He looked embarrassed. "Not this time, I was as surprised as anyone to see him. I certainly hadn't planned it. I know it's his home planet, but the stuff we're loading wasn't arranged by him and meeting him here was random."

"He would know that we were coming in though," said Griff. "It's not his stuff but like everywhere, we all know who's doing what."

Fair enough, it wasn't planned but that didn't mean Rixon hadn't taken advantage. I remembered that he hadn't used the name

Travise in any of the other introductions. Perhaps I was getting paranoid.

The conversation turned to the cargo, and the possibility of taking Danno's job after we had finished on Michael's. After an hour or so Tan called to say they had finished setting up the hold. We drank up and went back to the *Orca* so they could go for a beer.

"Did you see his reaction when I introduced you? He knows," said Rixon when we were back on board. The hold was prepped and marked but there had been a call. Rixon had been right; we were not loading till the morning. Everyone accepted the news with resigned shrugs. Myra went off to sort out her purchases, which had been delivered and were on a pallet by the ramp. Food was supposed to be arriving and the fresh water we had ordered was dripping from a hose into our tanks, via a filter.

"He must have known about other Dave spying on us and he's probably talking to the Chenkos by now," agreed Griff. "He's a slimy little weasel but he keeps in everyone's good books by feeding them bits of information, making himself indispensable."

"A bit like you then," said Rixon, getting a punch on the shoulder for his trouble.

"But not so nice... or good looking," Griff added.

"But the Chenkos already know," I pointed out. "We saw Vlad on Wishart, remember."

"Yes, but Danno might not know that yet."

"And the miners, was that a real job?"

"Yeah probably, he's one of the men to see if you want to set up a job like that; at least if you want anything slightly dodgy, it probably won't be an official survey, more like claim jumping or removals."

This was all too familiar, on the *Moth* we had often had to try and sort out title disputes, where more than one person claimed mineral rights or settlement, they usually turned into a nightmare of 'He said. They said' going round in circles. Dror used to say, 'What's wrong with the planet next door', but a lot of the time it was down to people using force to steal what someone else had worked for. It was just proving it.

"Danno'll be on a percentage," explained Griff. "It's just business to him."

"Will you do it?"

"We'll see; if I think it's some poor settlers getting cheated then I'll pass." Rixon was proving to have standards; after all it was a job. He turned to Myra, who was walking past with a large box.

"You shouldn't lead Danno on like that," he said to her in an annoyed tone but Myra was in full feisty mood.

"Why not?" she said, glancing at me. "I've as much right as anyone to a bit of fun."

I got the message; she was teaching me a lesson. I tried to look contrite.

"Well I think it's stupid," Rixon replied. "Danno is not the sharpest tool in the box, if he thinks he's got a chance with you, he might just do something stupid."

"I can cope with Danno," she replied defiantly.

Chapter 24

I knew that the settlers on Michael's had had a rough time, I had been part of the relief operation after all, but as we flew over the rebuilt settlement we could see that they were getting back on their feet again. And it turned out that there was more to the job than just delivering the stuff they had ordered from Coopers Post, they had asked us to take a load of processed foods to market on a local planet, in convoy with one of their ships, which didn't have room for it all in their hold. It looked like they had started exporting again.

As we flew through the atmosphere we could see that nature was starting to cover the scars dug in the earth by the meteors. Although there were still plenty of gaps in the forests and burnt vegetation, there was grass covering the gouges in the ground.

The cut lumber had been put to good use, new buildings had grown up in the couple of months that I had been away, they had replaced the tents we had left behind and I was pleased to see that.

The beard that I had been growing since we had left Basilan had changed my features enough to make me less recognisable, last time here I had been in uniform, with a cap; that was all most folk saw. And if they were not using the Navy gear, there was less chance of them associating me with it.

We landed quite a distance from the settlement, by a large barn where they wanted the supplies we had brought.

Mind you, I still only intended to go off the *Orca* as little as possible. But when Myra asked me to help her with some maintenance I couldn't really refuse. Since she had flirted with Danno we were friendlier, as if she had paid me back and we could start again. On the trip over I had mentioned my fears about being on Michael's and she had been her usual practical self about it.

"You could have any number of good reasons for being here," she said. "It's only because you're feeling guilty. And it's not as if they knew your name last time, you were just one of the men from the Navy."

I met up with Myra and we carried our tools and kit down the ramp. We turned under the wing and I bumped straight into one of the settlers. We both stepped back and apologised.

Looking up I recognised the man; he was one of their council, Mal or something. How could I just walk straight into him? This was some sort of bad joke. I kept going but he called out. "Hey, don't I know you?" I tried to look blank.

"You were here on the relief, was it the *Moth* or one of the other ones? We can't thank you enough, you did a great job." I had to answer that, beside me Myra was quiet.

"Not the *Moth*," I answered, seeing a way out. "Dror wouldn't have had me on there, thank Gaia."

He laughed. "Lucky for you then, I heard that he was a surly bastard."

I've got away with it, I thought, and was starting to feel safer when he was joined by a woman.

"Hey, Greta," said Mal. "You'll never guess what, this fellow was here, on the relief." She was big and blonde and capable looking, a no-nonsense colonist if ever there was one. She looked me over and her eyes narrowed.

"Yes; I remember you, you were one of Dror's puppies."

"No, Greta, that's what I thought too," Mal replied before I had time to speak. "He says he was on one of the other ships." I kept silent.

"If you say so, Mal, but I'm sure he was from the *Moth*."

Typical, I thought, nosey and observant. "Anyway, you were Navy then; so what are you doing here with the traders?" She looked straight through me, as if she could read my mind and I almost panicked. I hoped I wasn't going red.

"My time was up," I said casually. "That was my last trip. I paid off when we left here, got this job straight after."

She thought about it for a moment. "Of course you're right," she said. "You can't have been from the *Moth* because it's gone."

I tried to look surprised and shocked. "What do you mean, gone?" Word had clearly got around, Liesh had known and now these people did.

"Well when they left here they just vanished, no wreckage, no boats; nothing."

I tried to remember what, if any, reason we had given for our departure, I seemed to recall that criminals were mentioned. Taking a deep breath I said, "They must have been jumped by the criminals."

I knew straight away that it was the wrong answer. She turned on me. "How would you know that and what do you mean, criminals?"

Oh how I hated her at that moment, her attitude was right for building a colony but I just wanted her to shut up and accept my story.

"Well that was the mess room talk." It was the only thing I could think of to say.

"And we were at a mining station recently," chipped in Myra. "They said they had heard the same, that they were after some criminals and got jumped."

She gave both of us a funny look, she was suspicious. "I need to see your captain," she said. "I've got another job for him, if he wants it." They both went up the ramp.

When they had gone I thanked Myra. "That's okay," she said. "Now you owe me one." Clearly relations were improving. I was pretty sure Rixon would deflect any enquiries if he had to.

We rigged a self-propelled hydraulic platform under the wing and were checking engine control lines and filters when Griff called from the ground. "Hey, Dave, can you get Myra down here for a minute?"

"Sure," I answered, I grabbed her ankle, about the only thing of hers outside the hull and gave it a tug. There was a bang and a curse, then she wriggled back out of the inspection hatch she was wedged in.

"What do you want?" she asked, rubbing her head.

"Griff wants a word." I helped her climb onto the platform and we descended.

"What is it, Griff?" she asked. "I was really busy there."

"Boss has been offered some salvage gear in payment for the job," he said. "He needs your opinion."

"I know what that is," I said. "It'll be the stuff we dropped off from the *Moth*." Griff grinned. "Well Dror won't be back for it will he? Perhaps you'd better come along as well then." I didn't fancy that; but what choice did I have?

"Give us half an hour," said Myra. "I have to finish what I'm doing up there."

He waited while Myra completed her work, we descended and he helped us stow all the gear away. As we walked over to the barn Griff said to Myra, "Rixon says pick the best bits, we need to make about twenty grand to cover the bill for transporting their produce so aim for half again. Lots of small things if you can, high value stuff; you know the drill."

Inside the barn was a large collection of the supplies that we had brought on the *Moth*, portable generators, pumps and a whole load of lifters and construction equipment. Altogether it was worth a sizeable amount to anyone wanting to start a settlement, and was in pretty good condition. But because we would be half loaded with produce there was no way we could carry it all. Greta was waiting for us and she watched in silence as Myra quickly checked it over.

"Well?" asked Greta, clearly she was keen to get on with things, and didn't appreciate being kept waiting while Myra examined every item. "You can see it's all new stuff, hardly used, just ask your bearded friend here."

Myra stopped her prodding and looked around. "I'm inspecting, not him, and I'll take my time."

Greta looked affronted that someone had dared to disagree with her. "He delivered most of it," she said, turning to me. "Didn't you?"

"Sorry, Ma'am," I answered. "She's in charge now, I'd just leave her to it."

"Spoken like one of Dror's puppies," she muttered. "I know you were on the *Moth*. The question is, where you got off if they went straight from here to their doom." She paused. "Unless you survived, that is."

The statement hung and I didn't answer, fortunately Myra had finished her inspection and came to my rescue.

"The stuff is in good condition," she said. "We can take some and sell it."

"Help yourself," she replied, still casting sideways glances at me. "Just pile it up and we'll see." Between Griff and Myra various items were selected, I just drove the lifter and made a separate stow. Greta saw what we had picked and grunted, removed a high-value compressor and a pump. "You can have that lot," she said. "We'll bring it over to you."

I drove us all back to the *Orca* on her lifter. She could have it back when she brought the pallets over.

Greta was as good as her word and the next morning the gear arrived. We stowed it clear of the produce and returned to checking the engines.

By mid-afternoon we were all done, the settlers transport was ready so we took off just after it, we would follow it to the market. It was only a short hop and less than a day later we were unloaded and free.

"So where will we take this kit?" I guessed that Griff, with his wide range of contacts, would have a buyer lined up.

"We'll just take them over to Passing Thru," he said. "Someone will buy them there." That was another place I hadn't heard of, Nancy would be due a round of questions on watch tonight.

Rixon was lounging in the mess room, coffee in hand. "Hi, Dave," he greeted me. "How's it going? Has Myra forgiven you yet?"

Certainly things were better between us, but I hadn't pushed. "Hard to say," I answered, and he laughed.

"She's not one to hold a grudge, and after all, it's life, but the fact that she was upset tells you how she thinks of you."

"No need for the big brother lecture," I told him. "And anyway, I'm not over Vlad yet."

Chapter 25

Our next destination was Passing Thru; I found out from Nancy that it was nothing more than a market place, a huge space station in the vastness of interstellar space.

My time post-Navy was turning into a very quick education on the realities of life, with places I had never heard of and things that I'd never imagined being involved in. On the way, when I had the wheelhouse to myself, I had asked Nancy; at least she wouldn't get fed up with me not knowing much about the Galaxy. In a patient tone she had explained a little about the place.

"Think of it as a market," she said. "The biggest market you could imagine, it's where all the traders go if they're looking for a job or a specific item. If you want anything from basic supplies to something a bit out of the ordinary you can send a request for re-broadcast. Griff gets the feed from the place all the time."

I had wondered how Griff seemed to know so much, it must have been one of his sources. We dropped from light-speed and approached, like I said it was a space station but like no other one I had ever seen. It seemed to have been built out of the leftovers from the Holy Wars, a load of patched up derelicts and old mining platforms all joined together. The surrounding space was thick with craft of all types. There were the latest model superyachts, beaten up freighters and everything else in between. All with the same thing in common; drifting around waiting for the big chance. *Moth* and Dror should have come here; they would have had a field day.

The station was inhabited by dealers of all kinds. Griff already posted details of the gear we had, and the station had re-broadcast the message. Of course you paid for the service, all payments went through the station and they deducted a percentage of the transaction. It was a lot easier than searching for buyers yourself though. And it worked. Within an hour of arrival, we had three potential customers and were on the way to the first; they were on a part of the station.

The station wasn't rotating so docking was a lot easier this time. They were there when we opened the ramp, two of them and a bodyguard, no names were asked and none were given. They boarded us, and Griff and I met them in the hold. The gear had been laid out for them to have a proper look. I hung around with Griff in case they wanted engines started or anything else. Stu and Mitch were on the walkway, armed and ready in case of any problems.

They poked about a bit and muttered to each other before coming back to us. The bodyguard stood watching Stu and Mitch, hand in his pocket.

"I'm not sure about the stuff," the thinner man of the two said. "It's all Navy gear and it looks new."

"We got it from Michael's Hollow," Griff explained. "Like it said on the bulletin; it's left over from the relief operations."

The fat one spoke this time, "Still, the Navy might decide that they want it back, have they sold it to you?"

"Not exactly," I chimed in. "We were delivering supplies to the settlers and they offered it in payment."

"That's your story but you can't prove it, can you?" He was right of course; but it made me angry. I didn't appreciate being called a liar.

Griff sensed the mood and spoke, "Look, we all know that it's Navy kit; we never said it wasn't and it was given to the settlers. It's not illegal to sell it on, it's second-hand."

"Well I'm not happy about taking it," said the thin one. "Especially if there's no paperwork with it. At least not at the price you're asking. Tell you what, think about how much you'll take for it and let us know. We can find our own way out." Still muttering to each other they left.

"They won't be back," said Rixon when we told him. "Unless I drop the price and that's not a good idea. Let's see what the next ones are like."

But they didn't want to know either. They said it wasn't the price. Perhaps we would be stuck with the stuff.

That only left one of the three and they were not on the station but on Bencon, a planet about a day away.

"Bencon is well down the food chain," Griff told me as we hopped across, saving me the bother of asking Nancy. "The place is one huge junkyard, a good front for all sorts of dubious transactions. We'll sell it all there alright, one way or another but we won't get much for it."

And it went without saying, the further down the list we went, the further we slipped away from legality.

When we dropped into atmosphere and broke through the cloud layer, I could see that Griff was right, Bencon could have been a planet made entirely of scrap metal and plastics. There was hardly any open ground visible and the atmosphere was choking, although the locals didn't seem to notice. We found our buyer and he passed a less than critical eye over the stuff. His yard was full of rusting junk, I wondered what he wanted such pristine gear for but taking my lead from Griff I kept quiet. He nodded at us. "I'll take the lot," he said. "I've got just the buyer for that."

He peeled notes off a roll that he took out of his pocket. "Cash okay?" he asked. "No questions asked, I'll give you twenty grand." That was far less than Rixon had hoped for, but we couldn't waste any more time trying to get a better deal.

After we had gone back to Passing and paid their commission we had enough to restock with food and a few spares. There was nothing left over for wages, let alone a bonus. We had another job to go anyway so we just had to accept it and move on.

Chapter 26

Our next job was a much better one. It involved a long flight to pick up some samples from a new mine out on the far Rim. They needed delivering to an analysis lab in the core; the job took us several weeks and was boring and uneventful as far as the work went. But we were extremely well paid. Apart from the relentless maintenance work, which we would have had to do anyway, we had plenty of free time.

The best thing that came out of it was that Myra and I resumed our evening talks in the wheelhouse. We had put our relationship back to where it was and dare I say it, Myra seemed to be starting to feel about me the way I felt about her. She admitted as much one evening.

"I flirted with Danno to pay you back," she announced in the middle of a conversation about something else. "I was annoyed that you did what you did on the station, I wanted you to notice me, see what you were missing."

Luckily I was paying attention. "I guess I deserved it," I answered. "But in my defence–"

"Stop," she said. "I don't want to hear it, I know the story, Griff told me but it's nothing I wouldn't have expected; you're only a male after all." And she laughed.

I joined in, all the time thinking that she didn't know all of Liesh's part in it.

We were well paid for the amount of time that the job took us and we got used to the life of leisure; I celebrated my first six months on board and I still hadn't broken any laws. My bank balance had improved and I had received another substantial payment from the unnamed source on Basilan. If it was the Chenkos then why were they still doing it? They knew by now who I wasn't.

All too soon we would be looking for work again, we had been out of circulation for a few weeks and had nothing lined up. Even Griff's contacts had nothing for us.

Rixon was tempted to hang around in the core systems after we had delivered the samples. He had spoken to the mine company, but they had no more jobs.

"The trouble is," said Griff, "we're out of place here, the established transports are well known and we're not. We'd be better off back where we belong."

"I know," agreed Rixon. "But it would be nice to get a load back out to the Rim, save us running all that way empty."

Ask as we might, there was nothing on offer so we set off on the long run back towards our own habitat.

"I have an idea," said Rixon one evening while we were eating, "let's get in touch with Danno and see if that mine job is still on. We can go back to Coopers; it's almost on the way. Griff, send him a message."

Late the next day Griff told us that he had heard from Danno, the miners were ready to go and would want to see the *Orca* before committing to hiring us.

"That's fair enough," Griff reckoned. "Probably Danno has tried to scam them and they're being careful." We altered course towards Nara.

Four days later, Rixon, Myra and I were sitting at a stained table in Ma Esters enjoying a cold beer. Griff and the others had stayed on board. Danno was supposed to be meeting us and he was late. The place was nearly empty.

Suddenly Danno was with us, he had appeared out of thin air and he looked even more seedy and furtive than he had last time.

Hello, Rixon, Myra, Dave," he said quickly. He kept looking around, as if expecting someone else to arrive. He bought us all beer and handed the glasses around.

"What's up, Danno?" asked Rixon.

He sat down. "Van Chenko's looking for you," he blurted out, "and he's not happy." What was he talking about? We had had no contact with the Chenkos since Wishart. We were here for the job he had told us about.

"What do you mean, Danno?" Rixon asked, looking both confused and worried. "And where are the miners?" Danno's weasel face twitched.

"They're not coming."

He looked at Myra, it was a look of longing; clearly he remembered last time. She was more conservatively dressed today and was ignoring him.

"I don't know all the details, Mr Rixon," he persisted, "but it's about some Navy gear that you sold on Passing. Vlad was getting searched by the police and they found it. That wasn't a problem in itself; they were after him for something else entirely."

"So," said Rixon, attentive now, "the Navy gear was legitimate."

"In conversation, they asked him how he'd got hold of the equipment; just out of interest like. They had a look and said it was from the *Moth*. Well Vlad saw his chance to try and do a deal. He said he knew of a survivor. Of course they didn't believe him but he said he could prove it. Anyhow, he's in jail now, along with half his gang. But the offer stands. It might just cut him some slack. Hence Van's looking for you." He looked at me while he said it.

"How did Vlad end up with the stuff?" I asked him. "We sold it to a guy out in the wilds."

"Yeah but you see, the man you sold it to on Bencon; he owed Vlad, and that was what he offered as payment. Of course he got leant on to find out where he got it from, but Vlad seemed to have an idea anyway."

Of course he would know, as soon as he heard where it was from, my name would pop up. And it would be too good a chance to miss to get at Rixon.

"Right," said Rixon, draining his beer. "Thanks, Danno, but we'd better get back to the ship, I feel kind of exposed without the boys about." We took his cue and drank up.

Before we could get to the door, it was opened by three large men, holding pry-bars. They looked heavy, but the men hefted them with ease. Smoothly Rixon turned and headed for the side exit. It too was blocked, and behind us we heard a scuffle and a moan. I turned to see the barman slump over the counter, whilst Danno was being held easily by another giant of a man. All the other customers had vanished.

The two men at the door parted and Vlad's twin entered. He had the same shiny suit and blond stubble. He was even thinner than Vlad; whip thin with sparkling blue eyes, but when he spoke I knew he wasn't Vlad. He had the same high pitched whisper, but this was more of a croak, it sounded like he had some throat trouble. "Well done, Danno," he said. "Come over here."

Danno was released and he raced over to him. "See, Mr Van, I got them here, just like I said." He grovelled, washing his hands with invisible soap.

"Thank you, Danno," said Van. "You can go now."

Danno stood his ground. "But, Mr Van," he whined, "we had a deal."

"Deal?" said Van dismissively. "I don't recall any sort of deal."

"But you said I could have the girl if I told you when they turned up, that's why I called you when I knew they were coming. She actually took notice of me after years of treating me like I was some sort of fool."

It seemed like Myra had set a train in motion. The colour drained from her face as the reality sank in. She gasped and gripped my hand.

Chapter 27

Van had crossed the room and was standing beside us, leaving Danno by the door. He turned to Myra, a sly grin on his face. "Well, were you, my dear," he inquired, "interested?"

Myra shuddered. "Not in a million years!" she exclaimed.

Van turned back to Danno who was squirming. "There you are then," he said.

Danno's shoulders slumped. "But she said... I thought..." he moved towards Myra and the henchmen tensed.

Van waved his hand dismissively and they relaxed. "Very well then," he said, "if you want her so badly come and get her."

Danno kept walking towards Myra, who moved behind me and Rixon; Van calmly took a pistol from his belt and shot him twice in the stomach, the noise echoed around the empty room. Danno took a step back with the force of the bullets, a mystified expression on his face. He coughed, the effort making him wince. He put his hand to his stomach and lifted it to his face. It was red with blood from the stain that was spreading across his shirt. The effort of raising his hand was suddenly too much for him and it fell back to his side. Blood dripped to the floor; in the shocked silence the splashes sounding as loud as the gunshot had been. Sighing, Danno dropped to his knees, pushing his hands in front of him to steady himself. As his strength faded, he slumped to the ground, the blood forming a pool around his body.

Van replaced the smoking pistol in his belt and turned back to us. We were all stunned by the casual way he had done it. Myra was sobbing.

"He would not have made you very happy, my dear," he said in that peculiar whisper of his, "whereas I will."

Van sat on a stool and looked at us. "My brother has got me looking for Mr Finn Douglas here. We've been all over the Rim, but Danno told us he had rather cleverly managed to get you to turn up. I believe it was something about a job for you." That stopped me dead, clearly there had been some research carried out. If Danno was really in the pay of the Chenkos, Myra arousing him to get at me might just have been the worst thing she could have done.

Rixon had his hands in his pockets; he stood in front of Myra.

"Mr Rixon, kindly stop fiddling with the transmitter in your pocket," lisped Van. "No one will be coming; my boys are at the *Orca*, keeping your crew occupied. I'm going to tell you a story. Danno may have told you some of it, I don't know, but," he waved his arm at the corpse, "he can hardly finish the story now." He settled himself and found a bottle behind the bar, pouring a glass he sipped.

"My brother has been found in possession of some Navy equipment, from a ship that mysteriously vanished. That in itself is not illegal. Vlad has explained that he bought the items in good faith from a man who claimed to be from the crew." He inclined his head at me. "Only of course that should not be possible, the ship being lost. Vlad has been told that if he can prove this, his case will be treated favourably by the authorities. So all that we need is for you," and he pointed at me, "to come with us and explain everything."

I felt drained, it looked like the game was up, my chip was one thing, but in custody a DNA test would be my undoing. And the Black Box might make an appearance. It wouldn't matter then about what Vlad had or hadn't done. And of course, Rixon and Griff would get drawn into it all.

"He's going nowhere," said Rixon.

"Yeah get lost," said Myra.

Van smiled. "Very noble, but this isn't your quarrel."

"Oh it is," said Rixon, "he's my navigator and one of my crew."

"Very well, you will all come with us, we will not harm Mr Douglas, but the rest of you are surplus to requirements. I hope I make myself clear."

We were bundled into the open back of a wheeled vehicle and chained to the floor. We set off towards the port. As we bounced along the road I said to Rixon, "Why come with me? It's madness."

He smiled. "You're my Nav, and I've got a reputation to uphold, I don't leave anyone behind, I never have and I'm not starting now. Besides, do you really think he'd let us go?"

Myra chimed in, "We stick together; if we hadn't stuck together he'd have killed us there. Anyway, who knows what chances we will get, Van is not as smart as Vlad; I don't expect he's thought it all out."

Her optimism was touching, but I couldn't help wondering at her fate on Van's ship. Probably the same one that Danno had planned for her; or worse.

We pulled into the field and there it was, an old Bishop Class frigate. Left over from the Blessed Navy, a relic of the Holy Wars, it was still a ship to reckon with. It dwarfed all the other ships around it. I had served on a Bishop in my training and in four months as the lowest form of life on board had got to know the layout pretty well. There were a group hanging round the stern, and we pulled up in front of them. I could see the *Ora* on the other side of the field; for all the good it was it might as well have been on Oonal.

One of the men, with a huge belly straining to escape his stained tee shirt and a hook nose, sneered at Rixon. "Look who it is."

He glanced at Van, as if seeking permission, who nodded. Suddenly he swung a fist into Rixon's stomach. His breath whooshed out and he doubled over. As his head dropped the man lifted his knee into his face. There was a sickening crunch and a spurt of blood as Rixon's nose broke. He collapsed onto the dusty ground and curled up. Myra tried to go to him but was held easily by two of the others. I couldn't move as I was held from behind although I tried. A voice in my ear advised me against it.

Rixon lay on the ground, blood was splashed around him in the dust and he was still for a moment, then he stirred and tried to stand. He failed the first time, but after another attempt got onto one knee. He shook his head and more blood splashed, and then he got unsteadily to his feet. His eyes were glazed and vacant as he swayed.

"That's for Barnyard's," the big man growled. He spat in Rixon's face and grabbed a handful of Rixon's hair with one enormous hand. The other swung in a lazy arc toward what was left of Rixon's nose.

"Enough," said Van, and Hook Nose lowered his fist. He let go of Rixon's hair and he fell again. Van was still talking, "We can settle up in space, Rixon and his little sister will get what's coming, but this one," and he indicated me, "this one is not to be harmed. Ricey, have you got it?"

A serious looking man in overalls carrying a holdall came forward. "Yes, Van," he said, he produced a bundle from his bag and Myra gasped.

"Exactly," grinned Van. "The flux tube from your Padget Inverter. Your Atlon won't be coming after you, even when the rest of them wake up and untie themselves."

"They won't all be waking up," Hook Nose announced. "One of them fancied his chances."

"Sad," said Van, in a voice devoid of any sadness. He reached out and took the tube from the man and casually tossed it up in the air.

Somehow, Myra broke free from the two men holding her and jumped towards the spinning tube, she got a hand on it, but it slipped through her fingers and shattered on the ground. Van laughed.

"Get them on board; it's time we were leaving." We were marched to the ramp. Close up, the hull was pock-marked and looked close to failure. The hold was dirty and chaotic, clearly the crew that Van had assembled cared little for maintenance as wires hung from holes in the panelling and the deck was covered with rubbish.

Myra looked around and whispered to me, "It's a mess, looks like it's all been patched up just to keep it flying." Her reward was a slap around the head from her captor, after that she was silent.

They threw us in a small cabin, and we sat dejected as we tried to come to terms with the way things had turned out. Rixon had ripped off the bottom of his shirt and was holding it to his nose, blood was still leaking but less now and he had moved more steadily as we had been marched to our prison. Myra sat in the corner, knees hugged to her chest. She looked frightened. I explored the cabin; it was all so familiar to me.

There were four beds in two sets of bunks, a desk and a terminal. I tried to set it up but it was dead. I wondered if it was broken or merely unplugged. I bent down under the desk, expecting to see a mass of ripped wiring, but instead I found Van's first mistake. And something else was playing around at the edge of my mind.

Chapter 28

Myra was distraught. "Who's dead?" she asked aloud. "And what's going to happen to us?"

Rixon had recovered a little; he removed the material from his nose. "Try not to worry about it," he said. "It looks like Dave has a plan."

"What are you doing, Dave?" she asked me.

"You were right about Van," I answered. "He's not realised that putting us in here is the worst thing he could have done." I plugged the terminal in and the screen sprang to life.

Rixon looked shocked. "You have got a plan!"

"You have to remember," I said, "I spent a lot of time on one of these Bishops as a cadet, and one of my tasks was to crawl around and learn the ship. After all, if you're gonna command it one day, it's good to know it inside out."

"And that helps us how?"

Well you learn a lot, and I know that this is a junior officer's cabin, there would have been four watch-keepers in here, and that makes it an important place." They were showing a lot more interest now, so I carried on. "You can log on to the ship's computer from here and take over control. It's a safety thing; if the bridge is compromised you can control the ship remotely from a terminal in a few selected places."

There was a noise outside and I pulled the plug, the screen went dark.

I got up quickly as the door opened. Hook Nose was outside. "Get topside, you lot." He waved a pistol in our direction and we complied. He backed away as we came out and waved us to walk in front of him.

I was in the lead and pretended that I didn't know the way to the bridge, taking pleasure in trying to go the wrong way at every opportunity; he was cursing us by the time we arrived.

Van was in discussion with someone who I guessed was the pilot. They stopped when we saw us.

"Ah," Van wheezed, "are you comfortable? Rixon, I must apologise for your treatment, but clearly you have issues with Lucas." We said nothing, I noticed that Rixon had had a relapse; perhaps he was trying to fool Van into thinking he was still out of it.

"Mr Douglas," he said, I had to remind myself that he was talking to me; I'd forgotten that was my real name. "You'll be pleased to hear that I have spoken to our man on Basilan. Vlad is on remand pending our arrival, but there is a lot of interest in his story. I got you up here because I thought you might like to watch as we lifted off, it will be your last view of freedom." He turned to Rixon. "And your last view of solid ground, until you leave the airlock."

Myra gasped and Van turned to her. "Don't be sad, my dear. I will make you very happy, for a while, how long it lasts will depend on you." She went pale and started trembling. I put my arm around her.

"Now, now," said Van. "Hands off, the lady is mine." Hook Nose dragged us apart and Myra started sobbing. "Oh dear," Van lisped, "I seem to have broken up the happy couple. Don't worry, my dear; you'll enjoy being with me more than you would have with him."

"I'll break it off," she snarled.

He smiled again. "No you won't, you'll behave because the better you behave the longer you'll live." He turned back to me.

"A final thought for you, Finn. We have been paying the real Dave Travis for information. That's money we would like returned; so perhaps you will give us the passwords to your accounts."

I might have guessed that was coming. I played dumb. "I don't know what you mean."

Van sighed, an exasperated sigh. He stepped forward quickly and slapped me around the head. He may have been scrawny but he was strong, I tried to move my head with the blow but I was held securely and it stung. "Please don't insult me; we know you accessed the accounts recently. You even changed the passwords. We watch these things. We have to deliver you to the police in exchange for Vlad; that will take us a few days. We can't kill you or hurt you too much, but of course you may be injured trying to escape. You will transfer all the money back to us, rest assured. After all, it's not yours."

He nodded to the pilot, who took control and lifted off, showing Navy training in his approach, but I got the feeling that he was not as loyal as Van thought. He looked like a man who was doing what he was told because he had to, not because he wanted to. It made me wonder about the loyalty of the crew. But we would probably have no chance to use disloyalty to help us. Once we were in orbit, I knew that the end would not be long coming. I expected that Van would want to drag it out though. So far he seemed the sadistic type.

"Well I'm going to eat now," he said, "and I suppose that I should let you have a last meal, Rixon. You can't go for a walk on an empty stomach." He paused. "Empty lungs maybe." There was laughter from Hook Nose and the pilot.

We were returned to the cabin and food packs were given to us, self-heating and filling, if not tasty. It was a last meal and we knew it. What we didn't know was how long we had.

"How much money is there?" Rixon asked. I told him and he whistled. "That would come in handy."

"I agree; all I have to do is survive but he's right of course it's not mine. And they've been paying me since Wishart."

"That'll be Van; he's slapdash, like I said."

"You can bet that he's been told off by Vlad," said Myra.

"Do you think that matters?" Rixon broke in. "You're still for the high jump. I'll bet the Chenkos have got hold of the video from the *Moth* from Dolmen. If they edit it up a bit you'll be seen arguing with Dror and if you get life you'll be lucky."

He was right of course, it was a good job that the ideas I had been working on were becoming clearer; the prospect of what was to come had got me motivated.

"Tell me about the ship," I said to Rixon, "how did the Chenkos get hold of it?"

"They found it drifting in space and just took it." He confirmed what Stu had told me.

"That's useful." There was a chance my plan could work.

"Why?" asked Myra, who was still trembling, after her comment she was back in the corner, avoiding eye contact.

"Well the Navy won't have decommissioned it; that gives me an idea. I expect the Chenkos just took off the secure transmitters and thought that was enough to keep the Navy from locating them."

"And isn't it?" Rixon had recovered most of his faculties. "It's what I'd do."

I shook my head. "It's not enough, it means they can't be tracked or remote controlled, but it also means that the ship's computer will think that the Navy is still in charge." The plan was coming together in my head, I felt excited; perhaps we could get out of this, if we had enough time.

"Where's this going, Dave," said Rixon. "In case you hadn't noticed we haven't much time for the big ideas. Any minute now I'm off for a walk. Get to the point."

Chapter 29

This was the crunch; I took a deep breath.

"I know Dror's passwords, and I can remember the Navy override codes for control systems. If the ship hasn't been decommissioned, then it should accept them as current."

"But don't they change?" asked Myra.

"Well yes," I replied, "and once Dror didn't respond then his would have been cancelled. But that's the point. They are changed remotely over the web and confirmed by secure message, if the Chenkos only disconnected the Navy uplink, then the download and the message won't have been received. The old codes should still work."

Realisation dawned on Rixon and he perked up. "So we're in with a chance then?"

I scanned the room. "We have to be quick; they might come for you at any moment. Let's see what else they missed, there should be a safety box under the lockers; it's painted red."

Myra had a look and dragged it out. She flipped the lid. Inside was all the safety gear that would see us right. Escape breathing sets, torches and a tool kit. And just to show that Van had no idea what he was dealing with when he took the ship over, a pistol and a wad of cash. "A junior officer's stash," I said. "Probably gambling winnings." Myra put it in her pocket, grinning. Rixon grabbed the pistol.

"Right, my plan is this; we hack into the systems, lockdown all the collision bulkheads and prepare a shuttle. Then we leave, after programming them to go trans-light."

Rixon nodded. "Can't we just start the self-destruct and blow them up?"

"The self-destruct is a myth," I told them. "There's too much chance of a mistake. There are other ways though." I plugged the terminal back in and turned the screen on.

The cursor blinked; Rixon and Myra crowded round. "What are you going to do?"

"I'm going to pretend to be Dror and sign in."

"Let's hope it works."

"I'm pretty sure it will." I typed and mentally crossed my fingers.

The screen cleared to a standard interface. "We're in," I said triumphantly. "Now I've gotta work fast."

"Isolate the communications set-up first," said Rixon. "We don't want them telling anyone what's going on."

I disabled their transmitter and then, fingers flying, I isolated and locked down the bridge and engine room and all the airtight doors, I was hoping that not too many people were in the alleyways. I got a shuttle online and initiated its pre-flight routines; the engines would be warming up while we got there, ready for a quick getaway. Now I had done that I could relax and finish off. We had time to sort ourselves out; there was nothing anyone outside this space could do to stop me.

Now the only thing to do was decide on the Bishop's fate; where could we send them out of the way? Already they must have noticed that they had lost control, not that they could do much about it. I had the manual override reset to a new code.

"We can open the doors manually as we go, the code is now 02215, as long as there are not too many people lurking. Now where can we send them?" I opened the Nav screen.

"How about somewhere in the deep patch?" This suggestion came from Myra; the deep patch was an area of the Rim with little in it, just clouds of gas and planetoids.

"Or we could just blow them up," said Rixon. "I don't feel inclined to let this carry on. Whatever happens, Vlad will be inside for a long while and most of his boys are here." He gently touched his face. "I owe them, for this and for lots more."

"I can turn off the cooling for the engine cores, which will do the job. Once I start it up, we only have about ten minutes to get in the shuttle and away. The speakers will count us down."

I opened the engine control screen. Van had excelled himself in his ignorance, it was all there. It felt like a big thing, but I could see that just letting them go would not help anyone.

"Your call," I said to Rixon, he barely hesitated.

"Do it!" he answered.

"Yes do it," echoed Myra.

I stopped the main cooling pumps; shut off the primary lighting and password-locked the sequence. Now a ship-wide voice started a countdown, if Van and his boys had been wondering what was going on, now they knew. I could imagine them, all locked in with their own thoughts as the numbers wound back. They had more notice than Dror had had.

"Now we've gotta move; follow me." I opened the door manually with my new code and a tool from the kit, a long metal spike that went into a small hole in the door. We moved quickly down the dark corridors, lit by blue strips. I knew exactly where I was going and manually opened each airtight door as we passed. They slid shut behind us with a clang.

We saw no one in the alleyways and after the last door was opened we sprinted across the hangar to the shuttle bay. The countdown continued in the background, relentless in that flat, mechanical voice, '*Six minutes to engine overload.*'

I opened the shuttle's ramp and Myra ran in. I was just about to follow her when I realised I was alone, where was Rixon? I turned at a noise.

'*Five minutes, thirty seconds to engine overload, restart cooling immediately,*' said the voice. I could hear a lifter start. "Rixon!" I shouted.

'*Five minutes, twenty seconds to overload.*'

"Over here, Dave," he called back. "I found us a profit, if I can just get it unlashed."

I sprinted towards him.

'Five minutes, ten seconds; you have one minute to restart cooling pumps.'

Behind me, Myra shouted, "What's going on?"

"Get ready for us, Myra," I called.

'Five minutes to overload.'

I reached him; he had a pallet on the lifter and was trying to release the lashing straps.

'Four minutes, fifty seconds to overload.'

"Help me, Dave," he shouted.

"There's no time," I answered.

'Four minutes, forty seconds to engine overload.'

"We can't leave this, it's worth a fortune."

"More than your life?"

'Four minutes, thirty seconds to engine overload, engine temperature critical, restart cooling pumps now.'

"Yes," he said.

"The shuttle's ready," called Myra, even in the dim lighting I knew where I would find what I wanted.

'Four minutes, twenty seconds to overload.'

I saw it in its stowage, good old Navy; I ran over and grabbed the fire axe.

'Four minutes, ten seconds; overload is now inevitable.'

Running back I swung the axe, hacking at the lashings; one by one they parted. Rixon lifted the pallet, there was one strap left, and it was bar-tight. It throbbed as I sliced through it.

'Three minutes, forty seconds...' Crackle-crackle *'... load.'*

The voice sounded distorted, systems must be failing.

We pushed the lifter and its cargo, a shapeless plastic covered machine of some sort, toward the shuttle's ramp.

Van's voice came over the intercom, interrupted by the countdown; he must have regained partial control of the transmitter. Hopefully he hadn't sent out any important signals.

"You bastard, Rixon."

'*Three minutes to overload.*'

"Vlad will get you."

'*Two minutes, fifty seconds to over–*' The countdown stopped.

We had the pallet on board and the ramp closed with a clunk. Myra was at the controls. "We need to go now," I said as we sat and strapped in. Her hands flew over the console. The bay depressurised as the doors opened, all the rubbish strewn over the deck and various other things flew out into space. Our acceleration pushed us back into the padded seats as we left the bay; the countdown voice had been replaced by a digital read-out on the overhead panel. Our speaker came to life as it entered the final minute.

"You'll never get far enough away from a Chenko." Van sounded faint, like an echo. "Keep looking over your shoulder."

Rixon leaned over Myra and turned the speaker off.

We swung in a lazy arc until the Bishop was a small dark shape in front of us, our eyes on the digital read-out. As it reached zero, it shuddered under internal explosions, the hull cracked and tongues of flame spurted out, consuming the last of the oxygen. The shock wave bounced us around a little and sent a rattle of debris over us, marking the end of the Bishop. I realised that I had been holding my breath and let it out with a gasp. I heard Rixon and Myra do the same.

I felt anger and relief, relief that Van was gone and we were safe, then anger that Rixon had almost spoilt it in the haste to make a profit. Wasn't his life enough profit out of the deal?

"Okay, Rixon," I shouted at him, "so what was so bloody important that we nearly didn't make it?"

His voice was calm; he had recovered from the beating and was buoyed by the adrenaline of our escape.

"It's a medical pod, fully automatic, top of the range."

I remembered them, I had hidden in one on my arrival in Basilan, and the priest had been in one having his knee fixed. They were a pretty expensive piece of kit and Rixon was right, it would more than cover his expenses and make up for the hassle. But I wouldn't give him the satisfaction, not yet.

He carried on talking, "It was them or us, I wouldn't have been able to protect Myra from Van and his boys, and now Vlad won't necessarily know we got away. You saw the state of the Bishop; it could have exploded at any time. We'll have to dump the shuttle, but first we go and get the *Orca* back."

"How about the Inverter?" I asked.

Myra smiled at me. "We have a spare, hidden on board, just in case; it's the one thing that will stop us so we keep one handy. We'll just have to lay our hands on another."

"I expect Griff knows where to get us one," I suggested and there was laughter. As long as Griff wasn't the one who had fancied his chances.

Chapter 30

We dropped into the port and landed the shuttle next to the *Orca*. The ramp was down and we hurried inside. Rixon had the pistol drawn but there were none of Van's men around.

Griff and the rest were awake and tied up in the mess room, Stu was missing. We released Griff, and he turned to help us untie the others.

"What happened to Stu?" Myra said.

Griff shook his head. "He's down at the back of the cargo hold."

We found him behind a container in a pool of blood, a pulse rifle in his hands. There was a hole in his chest from a large calibre pellet-gun; seeing his mangled torso made me feel sick, I had liked Stu; he was a bit eccentric but hadn't deserved to die like that. I was changing my mind; I had initially felt that we shouldn't have blown up the Bishop, seeing the broken body lying there was teaching me that Rixon was right. It had to end.

Myra vanished into the engine room whilst we cleared up, it didn't take her long to fit the spare Inverter and fire up the engines. We had decided that I would fly the shuttle into orbit and transfer to *Orca*, Stu would come with me.

Rixon shared his thinking. "I know you didn't want to destroy the ship but we had no option. Let me give you the background, Dave. We had to do that for Myra, she was terrified of Van. He's been watching her since she was little, and made it plain what he wanted her for. Vlad being around has kept her safe, when Van tried to grab her a couple of years ago, Vlad went crazy on him and that's when this all started."

He paused for breath. "Everything just fell into place for him there, he had us and Vlad wasn't around to stop him. He probably forgot to stop paying you after Wishart, I said he was sloppy. He hadn't reckoned on your knowledge of the Bishop, sloppy again." He paused. "I'd like you to take Myra and keep her out of trouble for a while, while I go to Basilan and try and sort this lot out. And I think I know the perfect place for you both. It's something that Griff mentioned to me."

I nodded my agreement; the background I had just heard made me more certain that we had done the right thing. And with the thawing of the tension between us, a bit of quality time with Myra could be just what the doctor ordered.

We put Stu into the shuttle and I flew it into orbit after we had scavenged what we could from it. I was joined by *Orca* and transferred across after setting the Nav to fly into the star. Rixon said a few words for Stu as we watched it fly away.

We had a conference in the mess room; everyone congratulated me on my escape plan, which I shrugged off. "Just a bit of luck, we happened to be in the right place for it all to work," was my response.

"Well you're definitely one of the crew now," said Rixon. "I owe you big, and I won't forget."

Our thoughts turned to the way we had been manipulated into capture.

"Danno must have called the Chenkos the first time he saw you," reckoned Griff. "He knew you weren't Dave and thought he might get some points for telling them."

"Only, they already knew," I said. "They must have cooked up the idea of getting back at Rixon through me; maybe they had spoken to Dolmen or one of his boys, perhaps they had the Black Box recording."

"Everyone knows everyone," agreed Griff. "And the stuff from the *Moth* was just the thing to set it all off."

"Danno's offer of a job was probably real enough to start with," suggested Rixon. "But Danno would have been told to get us back so we could get picked up."

We couldn't think of anything else to say about that; it had made Myra feel better, she had been sobbing and blaming herself for everything, talking it through like that made her realise that her play with Danno was not the reason for our plight.

"We're going to need another hand," said Rixon, changing the subject.

"I know where we can find someone," said Tan. "I keep in touch with the lads from my crew on the mine supply ships, any one of them would fit in nice."

"How about Max or Lyl?" suggested Mitch. "Their contracts must be nearly up."

"If they survived," said Tan dryly, I wondered what she meant.

"What's the plan now then, Rixon?" Griff asked. "Vlad will be slightly agitated when he finds out the Bishop's gone, with most of his boys and his baby brother. And he will."

Rixon nodded. "He's never going to believe that it was all an accident. I reckon I can square it all away with Vlad; after all he's the more sensible of the two. But it would be better if Dave and Myra were out of the way, just in case."

"I'm not going anywhere," was her reply.

"You'll do what you're told," said Rixon. She laughed at that; Rixon ignored her. "Dave, how would you feel about doing up a ship with Myra?"

"Doing what?" I had visions of hiding on some backwater world in a cheap hotel with Myra trying to run away from me.

"Well," he said, "Griff told me ages ago that there might be a ship for sale on Wishart. We could go and take a look. If it's okay you could buy it; you and Myra could do it up, then you can work for me."

To my surprise and relief Myra grabbed me. "Oh yes please."

Chapter 31, Then

Griff took me out of the forger's door; I was still a bit unsteady on my feet from the hangover and the static. Griff had his arm around my shoulders and he supported me easily.

"Come on then," he said. "I'm gonna take you to your new home, you can meet the boss." We walked down the rubbish strewn streets toward the port. The high buildings meant long shadows. Sunshine was fortunately absent; I don't think I could have dealt very well with bright lights. I tried to speak, and found that by really concentrating I could form thoughts and turn them into sounds.

"Do you mean Rixon?" My voice sounded slurred to me, like after a trip to the dentist, and Griff was obviously aware of my discomfort, because he told me to be quiet. To my dismay, he led me into a bar. Although it was well after lunchtime, the thought of more alcohol made me feel worse. Griff parked me at a table. "Stay there," he growled, as if I could run away; and wandered up to the bar. He returned with a glass of beer for himself and a small shot of a brown liquid for me.

"Drink it in one, boy," he advised and helped me to do so, holding my hand as I raised the shot glass. I took a sip, it was foul. His hand kept the glass to my lips and forced me to drink it all.

"Good," he said as I lowered the glass, his grip relaxed. "You'll thank me for that in about a minute." He took a long swig of his beer and watched me.

Suddenly, as if I had been plugged into a charger of some sort, I felt amazing. My headache and all the pain vanished and the day improved immeasurably. Griff smiled.

"What was in that?" I asked.

"You don't need to know, it flushes your system, when you go to the toilet over the next few days your stream will be a funny colour, that's fine, no need to worry."

"Thanks." I meant it; I was used to having a few beers but not that much that quickly. And then the chip thing had really disorientated me.

"Was meeting you a coincidence or part of the plan?" I asked him.

"Dolmen called us when he had his overreaction," he said flatly. "Stupid fool; all he had to do was to get rid of the *Moth* so he could complete the job whilst you were off to Mistiq. Even when the marines started finding things he should have hidden, he could probably have talked his way out of it. Did you know the place was a stronghold?"

Talking no longer felt like an effort, but I merely shook my head. Griff carried on, "Thought not, he could have said the pirates left all that stuff to ensure good behaviour, but no. Somehow shooting started, and of course once that road's been taken, it has to be walked to the end."

He looked genuinely sad and wistful. "There's been enough killing in the last couple of generations, most of us are sick of it. Dolmen called Rixon, he knew that we needed a new Nav. Apparently Dolmen told Rixon that here was something about you, that your turning up was a bit of synchronicity. I don't know all the details, but Dolmen believes in all that sort of thing. You know the rest."

"So I'm going to be working for Rixon?"

"Well, it's better than working for some of Dolmen's other… acquaintances or being in prison. Or back on Oonal with the rest of your shipmates. Now do you want some food? It's getting late, we have a party to go to and the stuff here is really good."

I hadn't eaten for ages and my stomach growled at the thought of solids, but Griff, who did nothing by halves ordered a huge array of local dishes.

"What do you mean," I asked him, as we waited, "a party to go to?"

"Didn't I say? I'm taking you there as soon as we've eaten; it's on the *Orca*, that's your new home. We're leaving tomorrow and we're having a farewell party tonight. It'll be fun. Come on; eat up."

The food had already started to arrive and plates soon filled the table. Although I didn't recognise half of them, I had a try and most of them were really tasty. More beer arrived; I stuck to the fruit juice. If I was meeting my new Captain I wanted to be sober when I did it. Griff never forced me to have a drop.

We left the bar just as it was starting to fill with workers coming off shift. Walking towards the port, we had reached the Gate and I was almost feeling human again. Griff and I were scanned at the barrier by a bored official. "Two crew for the *Orca*?" he said without looking up from his screen. "Griff no last name and Travise, Dave; Navigator." He called to his mate, "Let them through."

The barrier lifted and I walked towards my new home.

Chapter 32, Now

"There are a few things to sort out first," said Rixon. "We'll need a new engineer and a Nav as well as a replacement for Stu." We were sat in Rixon's cabin, just him, Myra, Griff, Tan and me.

"I reckon I can find the Nav and the Engineer easily enough," said Griff.

"But not from round here, Griff. I don't want anyone who has the slightest chance of knowing the Chenkos." Rixon was cautious "I don't want another Dave Travise situation, especially now."

"I know a shipping agent on New Devon," said Griff. "He can spread the word quietly."

Griff's tone was thoughtful. This was the first time I had heard New Devon mentioned on board; it had a reputation in the Navy as a good run ashore. Officially it was called Nova Five but nobody outside the government called it that. It was one of the first settled worlds and some said the first, despite the five in the name. It was a place dedicated to technology and well away from the Rim. I had never been there. Nancy had been invented and made on New Devon.

"Let me do some checking first," he continued.

Tan repeated her comments about the replacement for Stu. Rixon nodded. "Anyone who survives the mine supply ships will be tough enough for a job here," he said. "I'll leave that with you, Tan." She nodded.

Myra was excited, her eyes shone. Was she eager to do some engineering, or was it the thought of being with me? I knew which one I wanted it to be.

"What sort of ship are we talking about?" Myra asked. "Does

Dave have enough cash for that?"

"Like I said, Griff's heard that there's a Sprite for sale," Rixon announced. "It would be a perfect addition to our enterprise. And yes, if what Dave said on the Bishop was true, he has more than enough money to buy it and do it up." The fact that he thought of it as an enterprise meant that there was a future, a plan and that was good. "The two of you could run a Sprite; you could run it on your own, Dave, if you did a bit of work on it."

I thought that I'd rather run it with Myra but kept quiet.

"I'm grateful, Dave," he continued, "you saved my neck back there, you'll have to put the money up but I'll guarantee you plenty of work. There are a lot of jobs that we're too big and costly for, you can do them. We'll draw up a proper contract." It sounded more than reasonable to me, after all the money was just lying there in the bank; it might as well do some good. And I hadn't had to work for it, just stay alive.

"It's not just my money though, is it?" I said. "Morally some of it's yours and the crew's, the money you lost because of the other Dave's actions. And that's not all; the Chenkos were still paying it to me a week ago. Hell, with Van dead they might still be paying me now."

"That's worth looking into," Rixon said with interest. "I guess that must have been Van, with Vlad locked up. And we just found out how disorganised he can be. Buying the ship and running it will make money for us all, that's the right thing to do with it."

"I'll take a look at the accounts," I told him. "The payments were made every seven days, and the next one will be due the day after tomorrow." Perhaps the Chenkos would continue to finance my new life as a ship owner.

"Now let's get moving." Rixon stood. "Dave, plot your course, we're going back to Wishart.

Chapter 33

Myra and I stood side by side in the wheelhouse that evening; we were trans-light on the way to Wishart. The friction between us seemed to be a thing of the past, maybe it was reaction to the danger we had just faced, the realisation that we had nearly died or the loss of Stu. Either way it put our quarrel into perspective. She had applied the sandalwood again; I hadn't smelt it for a while.

"I feel terrible about Danno," Myra said. "I know it wasn't the reason for everything but I still feel like I shouldn't have led him on."

I put my arm around her and held her. "It's okay, I feel bad about what I did on the mining platform, I never meant to hurt you; maybe I could have just bribed her."

She put her head close into mine. "It's over; let's put it behind us, after all we weren't an item then."

I turned to face her, her eyes were misty and she had never looked more beautiful. I took a deep breath. "And could we be an item now?" I asked.

Her arms went round me; one hand pulling my face in close, as our lips met she whispered, "Yes."

The remote alarm unit buzzed, waking me. I reached over for it and beside me Myra stirred. "What is it?" she muttered.

I checked the read-out, suddenly awake as I read the alarm message, "High pressure alarm on the flux matrix, we're coming out of light-speed."

Quickly we both struggled into our overalls and as we headed for the door, there was a lurch as our speed dropped; the dampers must be off-line as well. The door opened and we tumbled into the alleyway. Picking ourselves up we saw Rixon emerge from his cabin, heading for the wheelhouse. He saw us together and frowned.

"What's happening, Nav?" he growled.

"High pressure on the flux matrix, Boss," I answered him, hoping that was what he was referring to. Myra had disappeared towards the engine room. He was obviously annoyed about something; he never called me 'Nav'.

Normally the alarm system gave you enough time to get organised before doing something radical, to have slowed down so suddenly meant that this must be more than a minor fault.

Rixon and I went around the wheelhouse cancelling alarms whilst we waited for Myra to report. The hull was intact and all systems except the main engine and the dampers were functioning so we were safe for the time being. Griff called from one of the shuttles, it was ready if we needed to abandon the *Orca*. Tan and the other two were loading supplies into it, in case we had a journey ahead.

We were between systems and there were only a few stars visible to us, out route was through a sparse area anyway, not a good place to get stuck.

"That spare Inverter that Griff got us might be duff," said Rixon. "We've had it a while."

I said nothing, I was wondering if Rixon would go into big brother mode after what he had seen. Maybe not, he had pushed us together with the promise of a ship of our own.

"You there, Dave?" the intercom buzzed. Rixon beat me to the pickup.

"I'm here," he announced. "What've you got?"

"Inverter's fried," she answered, her voice partly drowned by the crackle of sparking electricity and warbling alarms. "No plasma, no matrix, no light-speed. And instead of tripping the board like it should; it had enough residual charge to blow a few other things. Give me a minute to sort it out."

Rixon and I looked at each other; we were stranded in deep

space. Automatically I asked Nancy, "Nancy, where are we?"

Nancy took an age to answer; maybe some of her sensors were off-line. "Hi, Dave, sorry about the wait, we are halfway between Bellox and Raster, the nearest habitation is around thirteen days at maximum speed by shuttle."

"Stand by to raise them, Nance," said Rixon. "We may have to see if they have any spare parts we can buy."

"Will do," she replied. We stood in silence for a moment or two.

"Dave," said Rixon. Here it comes, I thought. In a flash I remembered what Stu had told me, how protective Rixon was. It was all very well me hiding Myra for him, we would be out of sight but he might not be too happy about the idea now he could see what was going on.

"Look after her for me," he said in a voice I had not heard before, a soft wistful voice unlike his normal sarcastic drawl. "I promised our mother I'd look after her and I nearly lost her just then, I would have without you. You can do a better job than me, she likes you a lot, keep her safe."

I didn't know what to say, this was a side of Rixon I had never seen, a fragile side away from the hard competence.

"Of course I will," I assured him. "I don't want to lose her either."

There was a cough; neither of us had heard the door. Myra was stood behind us. Covered in grease she still managed to look amazing. "That's enough sentiment from both of you or I might need to vomit. While you've been emotional with each other I've fixed things up."

She pulled a self-satisfied expression. "The Inverter wasn't totally broken, when it cooled down and I could have a proper look it was just one of the contacts that had worked loose. I've hard-welded it in; it'll hold till Wishart. I've restarted everything and handed control over; if you'd been paying attention you'd have heard."

Nancy piped up, "I spotted that, Myra; I have control, well done."

"Okay, Nancy, cancel the call; let's resume our journey," said

Rixon. "Then we can all go back to our own cabins to sleep." He emphasised the words *our own* and *sleep*.

"Nancy," I started but there was a whine and smooth acceleration.

"Already there, Dave," she said. The ports took on a red tinge as we passed the light barrier.

We all left the wheelhouse, Rixon last. I took the alarm box and Rixon watched carefully as Myra and I went into our own cabins.

For an hour at least. He should be asleep by then.

Chapter 34

We were on Wishart. Rixon and I were in a shuttle heading to meet the owner of the Sprite. Griff had taken the *Orca* to a shipyard near Brethren's Host where they could repair the Inverter and fix a few other things that needed looking at. A hull survey was due as well so that gave us a couple of days to do our business. Griff had called up and arranged a meeting.

Rixon filled me in on the farmer during the flight. We were headed for Sakkho; one of the islands in the Wishart Archipelago. It was about as far from Brethren's Host as you could get in either direction, isolated and remote. We followed the river from Brethren's Host to the sea, past small towns and wide open fields, filled with crops and animals. As we crossed the sea towards the islands it started to rain, it splashed against our hull and lightning flashed.

"His name's Evan Constable," said Rixon. "He grows corn and beans for sale, with a few fruit trees and his own hives for pollination. The farmers' co-op collects his produce twice a year but apart from that he's not disturbed."

The islands appeared; they were flat and featureless except for the huge barns that marked each settlement. Crops grew in ordered ranks and the occasional grove of trees flashed underneath us. The shuttle banked towards a set of barns with a small wooden house by the side, indistinguishable from the others we had passed. The rain had stopped as we landed and an old man came toward us.

I had imagined a lonely old timer; grumpy and distrustful of strangers, and I was about right. He was living in a rundown wooden shack, filled with old furniture and older memories.

Framed pictures showed him in various younger days, in uniform, around the farm and with a woman and a small girl. He was smiling in most of them. He wasn't smiling now, his body bent from years of hard physical labour; he spoke only the minimum needed to be civil. After introductions he called out, "Ria, come and meet the visitors." We were surprised when he said that Ria was his daughter and that she was still living with him. When she emerged from the other room she proved to be a strikingly attractive young woman.

She was tall and shapely; my immediate thought was 'wow', for some reason her long hair was bright green, matching her eyes and clothes. She said 'Hi' to us and languidly waved her hand. "I'll get tea," she said and departed the room. When she returned her hair was red, her eyes dark brown. I don't know how it was done, but no doubt Myra would ask her, assuming they got along.

We sat in saggy armchairs covered in patterned throws while Evan retreated to a rocking chair that creaked as he moved it. Ria fussed around her father; helping him with his tea and we realised that he only had one hand. Maybe that was why she had stayed.

"I don't know how you found out that I wanted to sell the *Seeker*," he said after tea had been poured and biscuits taken.

There was an anguished gasp from Ria. "Sell the *Seeker*? You said that I could have her. I was going to explore in her, I've been fixing her up myself."

Evan smiled. "I'm sorry, my dear, that was years ago when I still had my health and the farm was doing well. Now I can't afford to pay for the repairs she needs." Clearly shocked, Ria got up and marched out of the room, the door slammed.

"She longs for the bright lights she's seen on the video," said Evan. "I've seen them and I know that if she saw them, they would only disappoint her."

I thought, there's more to it than that, he has cheap labour here and has probably strung her along, keeping her with promises. It seemed unfair; after all it was her future not his. I said nothing as we finished our tea in an awkward silence. Evan seemed not to notice; maybe this conversation was a regular occurrence. We drank in silence, the only sound the rocking of his chair.

"Come on down then," said Evan eventually, "and I'll show you the ship."

There was no sign of Ria as Rixon and I walked across the damp fields with Evan towards the barns, scattering a small flock of bedraggled chickens that scratched in the mud. The barns dominated the flat landscape. It wasn't raining, but the grey skies were full of the promise of more. The lack of a background and the featureless plain made the barns look even more imposing, the nearest one was open and we could see farm machinery inside its cavernous interior, but the largest one was closed.

Evan kept talking, around the stem of his pipe, "Near the end of the war, she landed near here and then crew made a run for it. I guess that they were all conscripts, and when I got on board I found out that they had mutinied and killed the officers." It was a familiar tale, on the *Moth* and in the academy we had heard of the collapse of discipline on the government side in the closing days of the Holy Wars. The destruction of Brethren's Host had accelerated the process and eventually helped to bring about the peace.

Seeing my expression, Evan laughed. "Don't worry, I cleaned it all up. Until about a year or so ago I had been flying her every so often, just to keep the systems working, and the barn roof has solar panels charging the auxiliaries. Of course all the certification is out of date."

"That won't be a problem," said Rixon. "It sounds like you know what you're about."

He nodded. "I was an engineer, before…" He waved the stump. "And when my daughter was old enough, she helped me keep it space-worthy. As you heard, she always thought we were going to leave one day, but we never got round to it."

We reached the barn, and Evan jabbed at the door control with his stump. With a whine of hydraulics the main doors parted, and

I got a glimpse of my new home.

The Sprite class were a tried and trusted utility ship of about seventy-five metres, a flat ovoid hull with a tricycle undercarriage and stern ramp. Each side of the stern were rotating engine pods, it had no thruster but was still a very manoeuvrable ship. It had the raised bumps of an EM shield on the hull, and light cannon for defence.

Although it was a warship it was a scout and run-around; not designed to stand and fight. It carried a crew of up to ten, depending on its role. It had a moderate sized hold, and would be ideal for trading.

Evan showed us around the Sprite, which was in good condition throughout. There was no evidence of the previous occupants, all the cabins and public spaces were spotless and overall it looked like the ship has just come from the yard. The stores were well stocked with spares and the workshops had all the tools you could need.

Sure enough all the documentation was years out of date, but as long as we could get everything working that shouldn't be a problem. Evan had taken advantage of the amnesty for all combatant craft at the end of the Holy Wars, and had all the legal papers showing him as the owner. The papers noted that several items of Navy equipment had been removed, the cannon and the EM shield among them.

"It looks good to me," said Rixon after we had crawled around a few of the more inaccessible spaces. "Nothing that can't be sorted. What do you think, Dave?"

"The hull's sound and all the stuff seems to be there," I replied, cautious of expressing too much in Evan's earshot. It would be a poor negotiating ploy to tell him just how much I liked and wanted, no needed, this ship. A ship of my own. What would my father think of that? "Myra can take a look at the engines and services but on the face of it–" I said no more as Evan drew closer.

I had looked at a few sites on the web so had a rough idea of prices, I had plenty of cash courtesy of the Chenkos and the original Dave, still I didn't want to waste it from a weak position. Evan might not know what he had; anything around 200,000 would be a reasonable price.

"I reckon it'll take two of us about three months to get the *Seeker* working and certified for flight," I said and Evan nodded.

"We did what we could," he said. "So what do you think, Mr Rixon, do we have a deal?"

"I think so," replied Rixon, "although it's Dave's money, I'm just the chauffeur this time." Of course he was keen to see me buy the ship, he was thinking of Myra's safety, certainly no one would find us here, or even think of looking.

"I reckon she'll do," I nodded. "You've done a good job in the upkeep, I'll offer you 150,000 as she is."

Evan looked hurt. "How much?" he gasped. "I'd say nearer 250,000. There's all the tools and some spares as well." Obviously he knew what he had and was used to negotiating.

"But there are a few systems to fix," I protested, "and the certification to do, 175,000."

"No, no, no." Evan shook his head. "It won't cost that much and Ria will help you; 240,000."

"Ria's run off, she might not be back, and if the *Seeker* means that much to her she might not want to help."

"She'll do as she's told," Evan said defiantly.

Ria must have been lurking somewhere in earshot, although we hadn't noticed her. At Evan's words she came into view, her face was as red as her hair.

"No I will *not* do as I'm told, Father," she shouted. "I've done that for years, just one more crop, just one more planting season, and then we'll fly away. Well it ends now."

He didn't look particularly shocked; clearly this argument had been festering for a while. She turned away again and went back to wherever it was she had come from.

"Ria," he called, "come back, let's talk." There was no reply. I saw his shoulders drop.

"Very well, 175,000 then," he said with a resigned sigh. "Just promise me that you'll get it off my land as quickly as you can, leave me in peace." We shook on the deal but it left a sour taste in my mouth.

"We'll be back to start work in a few days," I told him. "Just two of us; me and Myra the engineer, we'll bring our own stuff and live on board; out of your way. If Ria wants to help that will be appreciated but she doesn't have to." Evan said nothing more.

We flew back to the *Orca* in a subdued mood. "Rather you than me," said Rixon and I agreed with him. "Living on board means you'll be out of the way I guess; at least you won't be watching happy families."

"I got a bargain," I said, "but it felt wrong."

"I know what you mean," Rixon agreed. "But as it wasn't your money at the start I reckon it was a good deal."

What would Ria do? I wondered; would she even be there when we returned?

Chapter 35

Myra listened in silence as I told her what had happened. "Poor girl," she said. "How awful to think you're going away then finding it was all a lie." We were sorting out the stuff we would need to get started, just a few specialised tools and diagnostic programmes to start with. And some food stores as well. Then there was Myra's wardrobe.

In the end it was quite a pile of stuff. We fixed it all on a pallet. Rixon was dropping us off and heading for New Devon. Griff's agent buddy had a few prospective people lined up.

I landed the *Orca* by the big barn, Evan had seen us coming in and had brought a lifter to help carry our gear, there was no sign of Ria. I made the most of it, it would be the last time I manoeuvred the *Orca* for a while and I was getting to like the job. It was far better than doing it with Dror standing over me, ready to criticise. The money had all been transferred to Evan so apart from the formalities, the *Seeker* was mine. And I fancied changing the name, as soon as I could.

I felt awkward after our last meeting, because of the tension between Evan and Ria. "Day all," Evan said, quite a speech for him. He shook my hand, nodded to Rixon, and I introduced him to Myra.

"Hello, Myra," he said, and there was a pause. He was obviously deciding what to say so we let him think for a minute. Finally he cleared his throat, "I guess I should say, Ria and I, well after you left and we both calmed down a little; well we've had a good old chat, it's cleared the air between us."

That was a relief to me; I hated the idea of being in the middle of an argument between the two of them, and having to involve Myra in it. Ria would probably have tried to use her to advance her position and Myra would be stuck, forced to take sides.

"I'm pleased to hear it," I said. "The last thing I wanted was to cause trouble."

"I understand that," he continued, "and I've realised that I should have done things differently. Anyway, we've agreed, I'm using some of the money from selling the *Seeker* to hire a man from a place up near Brethren's Host. He wants a change of scene and he's agreed to help me on the farm. When he's learnt the routine Ria will be off to the city, but she wants to help you first if that's okay."

"Of course it is," said Myra. "I'd be grateful for any help, she must know just about everything about the ship."

"She does at that," said Evan and there was pride in his voice. And a little regret.

Evan drove the lifter into *Orca*'s hold and picked up the loaded pallet. He reversed it down the ramp and headed for the barn.

Rixon and Myra embraced. "Keep in touch," he said. "Griff will bring your stuff over as and when he can; try to order full loads though."

"You look after my engines," she said. "Don't hire anyone who'll cut corners."

He nodded and turned to me, one eyebrow raised. "Good luck, Dave, remember what I told you," he said. We shook hands and he went back up the ramp without another glance. Griff hadn't put in an appearance; he was probably doing my job.

We followed Evan into the barn; he had driven the lifter up to the *Seeker*'s ramp. We heard *Orca* take off, we were alone. Ria's voice came from inside the hold, "Who's there, is that you, Father?"

"Yes it's me," he replied, "with the *Seeker*'s new owners."

"Are they here to start work?"

"Yes, Ria," said Evan, gently, "and they'd be grateful if you'll help out."

We walked up the ramp, to the port side was a small workshop;

Ria was inside, she stood as we approached. Her hair was a dull brown with russet streaks today; it complemented the colour of her overalls. She looked sad as she saw us.

"I've been trying to fix it for Father," she said, pointing to a prosthetic hand on the bench. Its plasto-skin cover was peeled back, exposing circuit boards and wiring. "But I need smaller drivers for the hydraulic valves."

"I have a set in my gear," said Myra. "I can get them in a bit."

And with that gesture the ice was broken. "You must be Myra," she said, smiling broadly. "I'll be glad to show you around tomorrow. Come over to the house later," she added, "there'll be steak and some beer."

"Yes, come over," agreed Evan, who had joined us. "There's more than enough and it's all home grown."

They left deep in conversation, perhaps our arrival had done some good; at least they weren't at each other's throats.

Chapter 36

We moved in, unloading the pallet of equipment and stowing the packs of food in the mess room. It was getting late in the day to start work, but Myra got her drivers out and after a few minutes' work had fixed Evan's hand.

"Ria had most of it done," she told me, "just the articulated joints to torque up." I didn't know what she meant but I made appreciative noises. After a shower, we wandered over to Evan's porch, following the smell of a barbeque.

Evan and Ria were sat gazing out into the night; the sky was thick with stars in the moonless sky. With no background lights and the flat land it seemed like the whole of the Galaxy was on display.

Myra passed Evan's hand over to Ria. "Here you are, it's done," she said. Evan's face lit up.

"You've done it!" Ria said. "Thank you so much, I didn't have the tools and it's been broken for so long."

She took it and held it in front of Evan's arm. He pushed the stump into the prosthetic and the fingers came to life. He beamed and we saw him how he must have been.

Evan passed us glasses of cold beer and we drank, sitting in companionable silence while the huge steaks grilled. There were bowls of salads, fresh bread and fruit, enough for about ten people.

"Everything here is from this farm," said Evan proudly, "even the beer; I have an automatic micro-brewery."

"It makes decent wine as well," said Ria, holding up a glass of something red.

While we ate, Evan talked of his time in the service, the beer had loosened his tongue a little, or maybe it was the more relaxed atmosphere between him and Ria.

He told us about the Holy Wars, and his part in them. He had been a young conscript, newly married when called up and had seen active service. Although it was obvious that parts of the story he told us were missing, I got the impression that the Sprite's arrival here had not been a completely random act. Anyhow, his wife had produced Ria, and then died when she was young.

"I've never been off the planet," said Ria wistfully, "and I've only been to the city a handful of times." She had changed out of her overalls into a sarong in bright colours, and her hair was now silver and gold, shimmering as her conversation became more animated. "I always thought that I would use the Sprite to get off-planet and see the Federation, now it's yours and I'm still stuck here. But we've come to an understanding," she looked at Evan who nodded, "I'll help you and then I'm off to the city, I'll get a job as an engineer."

Evan broke in, "She used to sit in the pilot chair and dream of going to all the places she saw on the televisor; I was going to take her, but there was always another harvest, always another bill and somehow the years went." There was regret in his voice. "After my May passed, it never seemed to be the right time. I'm sorry, Ria, but I let you down." He stopped, almost sobbing and she put her arm around him.

"I know, Father, and I understand." And in a strained silence we finished our steaks.

Chapter 37

Next day, we started in earnest, Myra disappeared into the machinery spaces and I went to the bridge. I was looking at everything and I had the advantage that Evan didn't; I had money to spend.

I had Evan's registration trans-papers and his password and for a fee was now able to log onto the type-specific pages of the hyperweb for this vessel. I used its official number to read its history.

It was one of a batch of twenty built at the Navy yards on Prem in the last days of the Blessed. Fearing civil war they had massively increased the size of the fleet, of course that all backfired on them when the officers revolted.

The *Seeker* had had an uneventful life until the day the crew had mutinied, just patrols and some scouting behind the lines. It had seen a little action, using its superior speed it was in and out before anyone could react. No mention was made of a mutiny on board; merely that it had been 'superseded'. Evan had kept the records up at first but the entries had been become fewer as time passed; probably as his money and enthusiasm waned.

I created a new owner's account, now I could pay to use the web to download checklists and diagnostic software. The first thing I did was set up an automatic update on all the ship's software; the result of this would tell me of any major problems in the ship's computers.

Next I downloaded the 'Checklist for Operational Preparation', which I could use to make sure we missed nothing. It had a separate section for Myra which I copied to the engine room workstation. It took an age to download and when it opened it had over 3000 pages. I sighed and pressed the 'start analysis' button.

After a few seconds of thinking about it the screen lit up in red. 'DO NOT START MAIN ENGINE' it said in bold letters. 'SOFTWARE UPDATE IN PROGRESS, 37 FLIGHT UNSERVICABLE SYSTEMS DETECTED'. As I watched, the number changed to 44.

I called the engine room. "I'm getting the same," said Myra. "Don't worry, we'll work through it." While the update proceeded I had nothing to do so I wandered around the accommodation.

There were cabins for ten and all the associated stores and public rooms. Even though I had never served on a Sprite, I had been on one for a look when I was a cadet and could remember a few things. All the features that I looked for were here, including a large selection of spare parts and tools in the main workshop. These would all need to be tested.

We met up at lunchtime; the analysis was still going on, sixty-seven per cent completed according to the screen. Ria had appeared with a basket of food and we sat outside on the grass behind the barn. The sun was bright and warming under a cloudless sky of deep turquoise and flocks of birds drifted overhead as we ate.

Ria apologised for leaving us to it, she had been busy showing the man her father had employed the workings of the farm. He was getting the hang of things and she would be able to help us soon. There was little we could do anyway until the update had finished; Myra said that it would generate a priority list for both of us, with details of the work and the parts needed. It would show what we needed to get and in what order to do the jobs. The computer had locked the main engines down until the checklist was done and all the systems were fixed. I told her about the amount of spares I had seen in the stores and her face lit up. "That's good, we can get on and check them out, and it might save us some waiting around."

Lunch over, we went back to work. The update had finished and sure enough a list was displayed, it ran to seventy pages. "Meet you in the stores," called Myra on the intercom and I set off.

It was really cramped in the stores and we had to squeeze in close together, one thing led to another and it was just getting interesting when there was a cough. Red-faced, we disentangled to see Ria standing at the doorway. "Excuse me," she said, trying not to laugh, "I've come over to help, but if you're… busy, I'll come back later."

Now we were embarrassed. "We needed to check out the spares," Myra said.

"It's cramped in here," I added. Our activities had not fazed her, with all the animals on the farm she had probably seen worse.

"Perhaps you should put a sign up, or lock the ramp," she suggested, she had given up trying not to laugh and we joined in.

"Let's get up to the mess and have coffee," Myra suggested.

"I can help you with the spares situation," Ria said as we drank our coffee. "I've written a spares catalogue on the mainframe, you can cross reference it to the priority list and it will tell you what we need."

"Show me," asked Myra and using the workstation in the mess room, Ria set up the relevant pages, her hands flying over the keys; it was obvious that she knew as much about the workings of the ship as Myra. Between them, Evan and Ria had kept the ship in as good a condition as you would have expected, given their lack of specialised facilities and money.

"There you are," she said triumphantly after a couple of minutes had passed. She copied the list to Myra's diagnostic tablet, it was much shorter now. "Wow," said Myra, "good work, we have a lot of the stuff we need right here, as long as it all works."

"Look," Ria pointed to the screen, "all the spares were checked on these dates."

I felt left out as the two women chatted away, I was superfluous to requirements as they nodded and laughed together, basking in their mutual knowledge and a growing friendship.

Ria gave us her views on the work and we debated when to send for parts, there were still going to be a lot of things we needed. Some of the spares we could use to get the ship running but we would need to replace them before we could be certified. Myra thought we should wait till we had enough for a full load of one of the *Orca*'s shuttles, I reckoned that we should set up a regular delivery of stuff as we needed it, otherwise there would be so much that waiting for it would cause a delay. In the end we compromised, Griff could get the big stuff and the local yard at Brethren's could supply the run of the mill gear. Ria said their prices were reasonable.

As we chatted, it became clear that Ria was very well versed in the mechanics of the Sprite, and considering her admitted isolation, pretty up to speed on current affairs. Perhaps I was being particularly slow but until Myra mentioned it I never realised what she was up to.

"I don't think Ria is going to stay in the city," she said. "I know she's told Evan that but once she gets away from the farm she'll keep going." I had to agree with her on that. There was something different about her, the aura of a bird about to fly.

"Who's this Griff you keep on about," she asked after we had been discussing a particularly expensive piece of kit. She was dubious that he could get things for us at a lower price.

"You'd like him," said Myra. "He's a big man, with a big personality, he can get just about anything you care to think of, he knows everyone and they all seem to owe him a favour."

"Sounds interesting," Ria replied with a polite smile.

Chapter 38

Myra and I had words. I wanted to rename the ship, she didn't. "It's bad luck," she said, pouting. It made her look even more beautiful.

"And the old name didn't bring the last crew much luck did it?" was my reply. "I don't like *Seeker*; it's boring and might bring back memories somewhere."

She had no answer to that so she went off to sulk in the engine room. It was a silly row, ships got renamed whenever it was useful or the owners changed or for any number of reasons.

"What's the matter with Myra?" asked Ria. She had come over to help out and must have heard the shouting. She looked upset, her hair turned blue as I watched.

"How does that work?" I asked. "Your hair, it's always a different colour."

She laughed and produced a small box from her pocket. "This," she waved it in front of me, "it's a field generator, it polarizes the molecules of a special shampoo that I use. I can set it to change on a timer, or by sensing my pheromones."

"Where did you get something like that?"

"It's from New Devon, we had a man come round trying to sell us machinery and he gave me it. I think he reckoned I would make Evan spend his money."

"And did he?" She laughed again and the happy thoughts must have been detected by the box. The blue hair vanished, replaced by a flame red.

"No, we just took all his samples and told him to clear off."

"I want to change the name," I told her. "I hope you don't mind."

"And that's why? That's silly, change it. If it makes any difference,

I want you to change it as well; it'll keep reminding me if you leave it." At least she understood.

"That was my point." Ria nodded.

"Leave it to me, Dave. I'll tell her."

We had sent Griff a list of the parts that we needed and the order we needed them in. I told him to get the best quality spares that he could. Even with the money I had there were still some things that I couldn't afford. I really wanted a Nav system like Nancy but that was beyond me after I had got the necessities, including a spare Inverter tube.

I hadn't really thought about how he would send them to us, I figured that he would probably use a commercial transport so I was surprised to see one of the *Orca*'s shuttles sinking down toward us one morning as we walked across to the barn. We were living on the Sprite but eating at Evan's table, a sort of peace offering.

The shuttle landed near the barn and the ramp dropped. Behind us I heard Ria come out of the big house, alerted by the noise.

Griff bounded down the ramp and ran towards us. He scooped Myra up and hugged her till she shouted that she couldn't breathe. Dropping her he approached me; I was just contemplating a defensive strategy when he stopped, as if he had hit a wall. His gaze was fixed way past me. I turned.

Ria was running towards us; her hair was orange today I noticed. It flowed and bounced as she moved. She had a long floaty dress on; the abstract pattern was dancing as she came towards us on long legs. She suddenly realised that Griff was watching her and she faltered like a startled fawn. There was a confused look on her face. Then the feminine took over and she smoothed her hair and her clothes. She walked demurely up to us.

"Ria, this is Griff," Myra introduced them. "Griff; Ria."

"Hello," they both said at once, and then they both burst out laughing. I looked at Myra and she looked at me, realising what we were seeing. It was the same moment as ours, on the *Orca*.

"Who the hell are you," Evan shouted out, breaking the moment. He had come out as well and approached unnoticed, there was a large gun in his hands.

"Good morning, sir," said Griff, ever so formally. "I'm Griff, and I've just brought some spare parts for Dave and Myra here. And…" he paused, "a few other things for you both."

"I'll get the lifter," said Ria and raced away, decorum forgotten.

Evan grunted, "You can get on with your chores after you've done that," he shouted at her retreating back. "Harly will be along presently." He must be the new man, Ria's ticket away from here.

"So how are you both?" Griff asked. "I got all your stuff here, managed to squeeze it all into one load. I knew someone who was selling a load of spares and we did a deal. And I'm sticking around for a few days to help you get it all set up."

We started unloading the shuttle, Griff had everything we had asked for and a few more things besides. Thoughtful things that would come in handy. He also had a pallet of stuff for Evan, some farm equipment and a spare prosthetic hand with a charger and repair kit. Myra must have sent him the details. It would be useful for when Evan was alone.

Over the next few days Griff busied himself helping us out. The work went quickly at first; then his help became more sporadic and the reason wasn't hard to spot, he and Ria were obviously becoming more than friendly, they would disappear together for hours. They were an item, no doubt about it. The funny thing was they were so indiscrete it was laughable, in the end I had to try and subtly tell them that Evan wasn't really pleased. He had cornered me and asked how old Griff was. When I told him he shook his head and muttered. After that he tried to keep his eye on them. But Ria was not to be dissuaded. Her hair was never blue in those days, always red or orange.

"I'll have to go," Griff said one morning, out of Ria's hearing. "Rixon will be wondering where I've got to and he's got places to be. And Evan will probably take a shot at me soon."

"Okay, Griff," I laughed. "What will we do once we are all certified?"

"Call us up and we'll arrange a meeting. Then we can set about organising things."

"That'll be great," Myra was excited, "seeing my big brother again and getting the rest of my gear."

Abruptly he was gone. Ria came over looking for him and stopped short when she saw the shuttle had gone. She just stood there sobbing; Myra went to comfort her. The hair was dark blue, almost black, beautiful but sombre.

"He's gone without saying goodbye," she said into Myra's shoulder while I stood there feeling like a spare part. "I can't be without him." She sniffed and tried to stop her shoulders shaking.

"Griff's like that," said Myra, "he hates saying goodbye; it's nothing personal with him."

"I'll call him," she said and she did, every day. He didn't always answer but she got used to that, she reckoned she could train him, given time.

Chapter 39

Now that Griff had gone we reviewed what we had to do. To our surprise Griff had actually got a lot of the work done. As ever, things just seemed to have happened even with all the time he had spent with Ria. Now he was gone we set about finishing up and with Ria's help we soon got the work done.

I reckoned we were ready to be certified so we called the testing station at Brethren's and booked in. We were given permission for a one way flight.

"What's this then?" asked Myra, she had been sorting out the cabin and held a drive in her hand. It was the one from the real Dave, I had forgotten all about it since I had accessed the accounts, leaving it in my gear. It had been carried across to the Sprite with my spare clothes.

"It was Dave's but it's password protected," I explained to her. "I found it ages ago but once I got into his bank accounts I forgot all about it."

"Ah! I reckon I can get into it." She plugged it into the console and tapped.

The screen opened. "What did you do?" I asked her.

"I used his password." She said it as if it was the most natural thing to do.

"How did you know his password? I only found it out after talking to Stu."

"It was obvious," she said. "He was always saying it."

"That's exactly what Stu said, he was always saying it. Sort of hiding it in plain sight."

"Or so he wouldn't forget it," she laughed. "I'm stone broke," she said, "not stony broke; just stone broke." Like Stu had said, and it had worked for his bank accounts. It seemed like everyone had known it. But had anyone else used it?

There was a list of files stored on the drive and Myra opened one at random.

"This proves it," she said. "Look! Dave had all Rixon's contacts and itineraries stored on here, he must have been copying them from Rixon's personal directory and passing them on."

She scrolled through the files and directories on the drive; it looked like there had been a copy of just about everything that the *Orca* had got up to.

"Look at this," she said, pointing to a list of messages. "These messages were sent to someone else on the *Orca* and here are the replies." The addresses were encrypted, a jumble of letters and numbers.

"You know what this means," said Myra, with a worried voice.

"Dave wasn't the only traitor on the *Orca*; someone else was working with him."

"Looks like it, but who?"

"We'll find out, I don't want to tell Rixon yet in case someone else gets hold of the message, I'll tell him when I see him."

Afterwards, I thought about things and it wasn't a comfortable thought. There was a second traitor and both Stu and Myra had known the password for the drive. Stu was dead, could it be Myra? Surely she would never have revealed her knowledge like that? Or had she just got carried away and forgotten? Could she have turned against her brother?

I remembered what Stu had told me, how Rixon would sabotage her relationships. Would that be enough to make her plan to destroy him? It went round and round in my head. Van had lusted after her but I didn't know how she felt about Vlad.

Chapter 40

I had a sleepless night; was I cuddled up next to someone who would destroy me? I decided against asking her straight out, it could kill our relationship. I would just keep my eyes and ears open, hoping I was wrong but ready in case I wasn't. The trick would be to pretend everything was normal.

It wasn't like I had nothing else to think about. It was time for the first flight. We had been granted permission to fly in atmosphere to the testing and certification station. Ria wanted to come with us but Evan forbade it. Myra said it was safe though and despite anything else, I trusted her as an engineer.

It was a cold day when the Sprite was towed out of the barn with Evan's tractor. Rain blew around the barn and the cloud was low and scudding as the Sprite was dragged into the open air for the first time in goodness knew how many years. I didn't want to use the engines in case the thrust got out of hand and demolished Evan's barn. We were dragged well clear and rotated so we faced into the wind and the exhaust pointed harmlessly across the fields.

Ria jumped from the tractor's cab, her yellow waterproof jacket was slick with rain and her hair wet and matted around her face. It was plain brown, maybe the box wasn't in use. Or maybe it just wasn't waterproof. She disconnected the tow-line and Evan backed off. Ria looked up at me and waved before moving away, her feet splashing in the damp ground as she followed the disappearing tractor.

I was on the bridge and Myra was in the engine space. I called down on the intercom to let her know we were clear.

"I'm starting the main engines," she said and there was a low rumble as they spun up. Lights changed on the panel as more systems came online. When Myra was happy she handed over control. I gently lifted the Sprite into a hover, about two metres off the ground. We drifted sideways in the wind and I rotated the thrust-baffles to keep us in position. The controls worked smoothly and I revelled in doing what I loved. I glanced down at the panels, all the lights were green. "Myra," I called, "we're airborne. How's it looking down there?"

Her voice sounded slightly agitated. "Just hold it there for a minute." I could hear alarms in the background, it felt like déjà vu from that night on the *Orca*.

I felt powerless to help and had to juggle the controls to hold station in the light crosswind. I hadn't retracted the wheels so could drop quickly if there was a major problem; at least I still had main power. Whatever was going on couldn't be that serious.

After what felt like an age, Myra called back, "All sorted, Dave, just a couple of low pressure leaks on the auxiliary systems," while behind her voice it was silent. I lifted up to 200 metres, the vast barns shrinking below. The clouds engulfed us but the scanner showed clear air all around us. As I turned the Sprite onto the heading required for our destination I called traffic control to let them know we were airborne. They confirmed that they had us tracked and cleared me to proceed, giving me course and altitude.

"Are you ready?" I asked. This was it; everything was going well so far, now for the big test.

"All green down here," said Myra and I put on the power. The Sprite might have been old but it still had the acceleration the class had been famous for. We broke through the clouds into bright sunlight as we reached our flight level, outrunning the storm. In no time we were back over the ruins of Brethren's Host and approaching the shipyard.

We landed and introduced ourselves. The mechanic came out to have a look and whistled, "Wow," he said appreciatively, "haven't seen one of these for a while, I used to work on them, this'll be fun."

He plugged the Sprite into their analyser and fired it up. "The checks will take about three hours," said the mechanic. "If you want to go into the town you can get a meal while you wait. I'll call you if there's going to be a delay."

We found a monorail just outside the yard; it whisked us into the centre of the new city. The car was full and we stood, straphanging for the short ride. When we climbed down to street level we found a huge map of the city on a stand by the exit. In 3D it showed the state of the reconstruction and at the press of a button illuminated all the restaurants in green.

The whole place was in chaos, buildings were built and half built all around us, and everyone ignored the work and carried on with their lives as if it was perfectly ordinary. The rebuilding had been going on for years and was still only half completed so I guess it was.

"What do you fancy for lunch?" I asked Myra as we approached a street full of restaurants.

"Something to celebrate with," was her answer. The food we eventually had was good, but it wasn't any better than Evan's. And we couldn't drink wine anyway.

The atmosphere was strained, probably because of the knowledge that we shared about the second Chenko spy on the *Orca*. Obviously I was having disturbing thoughts about Myra's involvement, if she was guilty she hid it well, she was itching to get back to see Rixon and tell him what we had found out.

Not only that but I knew that the whole renaming thing was about to come up again and I wasn't keen on another argument. So in the end we ate in silence, walked back to the station in silence, and returned to the yard in silence.

When we got back to the yard, certification had been completed and we were ready to go. All we had to do was sign the register, pay the fee and we would be official.

"She's in really good condition," said the mechanic, "you've done a wonderful job."

"How about the trans-light systems?" asked Myra, this was important; we hadn't been able to test it out, for obvious reasons; and we were relying on the analyser to reassure us.

"The trans-light checks were all good, you shouldn't be vaporised when you flick the switch," he said with grim humour. "If you are, you can come back for a refund." Very comforting, the humour was pure Navy. It took me back.

"One more thing, what's the name of the vessel?" the mechanic asked. "Do you want to keep *Seeker* or have you got another."

And that's when we argued about it for the second time. "We'll keep *Seeker*," Myra said, at the same time as I said, "*Freefall*."

"I thought Ria had talked to you," I said.

"She did but I'm not convinced," she replied, "and it's a bit low, getting her to argue for you."

"She has her reasons as well you know. Anyway, I'm paying." I played my trump card.

She glared at me. "No you're not," she said with perfect logic. "Vlad Chenko is paying. It'll be bad luck," she repeated her prediction. I shrugged it all off.

"Change the name to *Freefall*," I told the man. He nodded and sent his apprentice to carve it on the main beam.

"Why *Freefall*?" asked Myra as we flew back to Evans.

"It's a reminder of my slide down the social scale," I told her, "from naval officer to smuggler with a false name."

"Ah," she replied, "but now you've stopped falling," she said. "You've got me and you're a ship owner and trader. Things are looking up."

Chapter 41

Now that we had got the *Freefall* certified we were ready to meet up with Rixon and start earning. I still had a little bit of the Chenkos' money left, and all of my own but the lack of movement was starting to get me down. At least my relationship with Myra had survived the renaming episode and things between us were good, although the presence of Ria was becoming a bit of a nuisance, she was always hanging around asking about Griff, it was love and hate depending on whether they had spoken or not. She gave us a load of message disks for him and made us promise to persuade him to call her more, or even better, come and see her.

On the way back to Evan's we had sent a message to Rixon, telling him we were ready to start work. We heard nothing for several days, eventually he answered, just a brief message giving us a rendezvous. I worked out a route and let him know our ETA. We had time for a last meal with Evan and Ria.

We went over but it was an uncomfortable evening, it was obvious that Ria didn't want us to go; we were the last link she had with Griff. She drank a lot of wine and started getting maudlin, she sobbed that she would never see Griff again. Evan got angry; he disapproved of Griff anyway and thought that he was a waste of her time. It looked like we were going to have a repeat of my first meeting with them when Evan wound up the evening and we said our goodbyes.

Early next morning we took our leave, lifting off into the clear skies of Wishart, the barns dwindling below us. I reached orbit and set up our route to meet Rixon. I was still missing the ease of working with Nancy but the new system that Griff had installed was better than the Navy way, and I couldn't afford my own Nancy at the moment.

There was a brief moment of worry as we worked up to light-speed. I was alone in the wheelhouse; Myra was at the controls in the engine room. Apart from the tests, the trans-light drive had not worked for many years, and I delayed engaging the drive long past when we could have fired it up.

In the end, Myra forced the issue. "Are you going to have the balls to do it or should I?" she asked. "We'll never get anywhere like this."

She was right of course; I opened the cover on the panel and pushed the button. On the intercom I heard the whine as the Inverter fired up, creating the flux field. The view from the port flickered as we overtook the light from the stars, the ports tinged red and to my relief the instruments showed no problems.

"It's all good down here," said Myra over the intercom. "I'm coming back up for lunch." If she said it was alright then it was, I relaxed and went to the mess to meet her.

"We need to talk to Rixon about the other traitor, show him the files." Myra was desperate to see her brother; the thought of him in danger had unsettled her. If she had have been involved she was a very good actress.

"What if it was Griff?" I wondered out loud; although it was painful to consider and didn't bear thinking about it had to be said, and it moved suspicion from her.

"That makes no sense," Myra dismissed my idea. "He's been around forever, he doesn't need Vlad's money, he has a bigger network of friends than the Chenkos and as much clout."

We were just tucking in to some of the food that Ria had left on board for us when there was a nervous cough from the alleyway.

"Who's there?" Myra called out and Ria sheepishly put her head round the door.

"I couldn't stay there and now I feel bad for leaving him," she said. "But I want to see Griff again. I need to see him again. Evan didn't want me to but I don't care about that any more either."

"I think you had better call Evan and explain," said Myra. "He'll worry and be cross."

Ria hedged, "He says that Griff is too old for me. I'll do it later."

We had quite a way to go to the rendezvous and I called the *Orca* a couple of times to say we were on the way. They never answered but I was sure that they would be there. I assumed that Ria called Evan; she was very quiet for the rest of our trip, keeping out of the way except for mealtimes. Myra was busy in the engine room all day, which left me with a lot of time that I used to set up a maintenance schedule and perform a full inventory of the ship's gear. I could have done with her help but I didn't like to ask.

Almost before we knew it, we had arrived. We dropped out of light-speed and approached the system that was our destination. *Freefall* had performed faultlessly on the journey; just a couple of minor faults that Myra had sorted easily. We were even early on my ETA.

Our long-range scanner showed that there was no one in orbit around the Gas Giant that was our destination, but they could be in its shadow. As we got closer no one appeared.

"They're not here yet," I said, and again tried to call. There was no answer, so I put the *Freefall* into orbit around the nearest moon, set up a listening watch and we settled down to wait.

On one of our orbits, in the middle of the night, we passed through a debris field, objects bumped against the hull, waking us up.

"Must be asteroids," said Myra.

"Let's take a look, some of them are filled with valuable stuff," I suggested. Plenty of people had got serious amounts of money from scooping asteroids, the tec market was screaming for a lot of the rare materials that seemed to congregate in asteroids.

"It's two in the morning," Myra grumbled. "We'll have a look later."

"They might not be there next time around," I persisted.

"I'm awake now," she sighed. "I might as well."

We went to the wheelhouse; Ria joined us. "What's going on?" she yawned.

"Dave thinks he's made us all very rich," Myra laughed as she manipulated the scanner, suddenly the smile faded and she turned very pale, her shoulders shook.

"What is it?" I asked.

"It's the *Orca*," she sobbed as Ria and I went to comfort her. "It's the wreckage of the *Orca*. There's metal from their hull; whatever happened to them must have been catastrophic."

"What about the shuttles and troopships?"

"I can't tell," she sobbed. I switched our receiver to the emergency frequency and we listened for beacons as the moon and the Gas Giant turned below us. We were all stunned and forgot sleep, drinking hot coffee as we listened.

Six hours later we picked up a faint beacon and headed down. I piloted the *Freefall* towards the rock and lava strewn surface, homing in on the signal, which got stronger as we approached. We found the source under a high cliff, it was definitely one of the *Orca*'s troopships, and it looked the worse for wear.

Chapter 42

We touched down as near as we could to the wreck; it had had a rough landing. We left Ria on board; she had no suit experience so Myra and I went over to investigate. We found that the hull was intact and the airlock had not been damaged, the outer door could still be opened. Perhaps everyone would be on board, unable to communicate.

Inside we found Griff. He was alone and unconscious. He had lost a lot of blood, judging from the state of the cabin. His face was a mass of cuts where flying equipment had hit him. His left arm had suffered the worst damage, but at least he had managed to bind it up before passing out. The first aid had probably saved him from bleeding to death; his breathing was faint and his pulse hardly noticeable.

"What's going on?" Ria called from the *Freefall*, she was following our progress from the wheelhouse.

"We've found Griff," Myra said. "He's badly injured." There was a gasp over the radio. We had a modest medical set-up on the *Freefall*, nothing as grand as the pod we had salvaged from the Bishop, but good enough for basic field surgery. It would have to do for the time though.

Myra and I managed to get Griff into a marine combat suit and carried him as gently as possible back to the *Freefall*. Before we left, Myra went to the data recorder on the control panel and shoved the chip in her pocket. As *Freefall*'s hold pressurised and the access opened Ria was there with the diagnostic trolley and we rushed him into the bay.

I cut the sleeve of his suit off and exposed his arm, below the elbow it was a mess, the skin was peeled back and bones and tendons showed. Blood welled as I took off the tourniquet and put the scanner sleeve over his arm. Myra meanwhile hooked him up to the monitor, following the instructions the machine put up on the screen. Lights flashed and the scanner whirred, I could hear the sound of the parts moving over his arm as his injuries were analysed and surgery attempted. The screen showed his vitals and although they were low, it seemed happy enough with them.

After a few hours it was obvious that his arm couldn't be saved. If we had the pod from the Bishop we might have done but the *Freefall*'s gear was just too basic. Automatically it amputated the shattered forearm and the elbow joint. Ria was in tears and I dreaded to think what Griff's reaction would be. He was going to have to make some serious adjustments to his lifestyle.

Ria sat in the bay by Griff's side refusing food and only leaving to use the bathroom. Myra and I kept her supplied with coffee; free from her presence we discussed our next move.

We agreed that there wasn't much we could do until Griff woke up and we could find out what he remembered. *Orca* was gone; it looked like our planned working arrangement was out of the window. The data recorder chip Myra had recovered was inconclusive, all it showed was the craft separating then being hit by a shock wave and tumbling out of control to the planet. Just before it had hit the ground it had fired engines to cushion its landing, although whether that had been automatic or manual was impossible to discover. And there was no way we could find out any more about the *Orca* from it, the chip was only written to when the troopship was detached.

Myra suited and went back over to the wreck; she looked around for quite a while, with the comms link off. I didn't think that there would be much to see, the hull was badly damaged by the impact and it was unlikely that there would be traces of anything untoward, like explosive residues in the internal atmosphere or other signs of sabotage. I think she was just looking to keep herself busy, and to have a bit of time to reflect on Rixon, he was her brother after all. At night she cried in my arms and I tried to comfort her, but I was pretty grief-stricken as well. Time blurred as we sat on the moon, the only one of us who got any rest was Griff.

It couldn't have been anything to do with her, my suspicions were just that and I mentally apologised to her. 'Look after her,' Rixon had said; I would have to do that now.

On the third day, Ria ran into the mess. "He's awake," she shouted, turning straight back to the bay. We followed her. Griff was trying to get the sleeve off, weakly grabbing at it as alarms buzzed.

"Calm down," Myra and Ria called. "It's alright now," and at the sound he flopped back.

"Take it easy, Griff," I said and he turned his head. "That you, boy?" he weakly muttered. Ria held his right hand, he squeezed it.

"I'm here, Griff, what happened?"

He shook his head; "I don't know much, my head is throbbing and I can't remember. I know I was doing a job in the troopship, fixing some alarms and checking the stores when we launched and started bouncing about. I strapped myself in but my tools and other stuff were flying all around the cabin. Something must have clobbered me because the next thing I know, I'm awake on the planet, the ship is wrecked, there's blood everywhere and the radio's bust." He took a deep breath. "Rixon must have jettisoned me."

"Have you any idea why?" Myra asked.

He shook his head. "No, it was all quiet. We were early to meet you. Why is my arm so cold?" We had to tell him. "Oh," he said. "At least it wasn't my drinking arm, or the one with my chip in. I would have had to go see Rick again." His attempt at humour was lost on Ria, who sat there numb. The read-outs said that I could remove the sleeve, I did and the extent of the surgery was revealed. A line of neat sutures encircled the stump of his arm, just above the elbow. The flesh was coated in a plastic film to keep it clean.

Griff just looked at it, then at Ria as she helped him sit up.

"I'm not much good to you now," he said, waving the stump. It sounded brutal but it was probably better for him to get it out, now we would see what she was made of.

"It's okay, Griff," she said, strength in her voice, "you've still got me, we'll be alright." It was said with such emotion that I knew that she meant it. She was going nowhere, she had her man. Griff smiled and put his other arm around her shoulders.

"Okay," he said, "it is what it is. I'm alive and that's a start. It's nothing to do with me, you're in command here, Dave; but for what it's worth here's what I'd do, I'd scoop up the debris and see what's in there."

He was right of course, I was in command and he was reminding me of my obligations without usurping me, just like a good chief mate would. I felt the weight of responsibility, it was no longer a game played by Myra and me, things were getting serious.

We secured the *Freefall* and lifted off. Once we were in orbit we found the debris field again. Myra scanned for the largest objects; she found a lot of bits and pieces which I scooped up. But there was nothing there to help us.

Griff improved over the next few days, he was soon up and about and started to fill his skin again. Ria was a constant presence, but he didn't let her do too much. "Let me try and do it," we heard him say gently, time and again. The boom in his voice gradually returned, he was adjusting to the loss of his arm remarkably well, like he did everything.

"I need to get online," he announced. "Time's wasting. Rixon and I had an arrangement, if anything happened to either of us; there were things we had to do."

"Help yourself," I said and he sat at a terminal for several hours, typing one handed and muttering as he had to keep correcting his spelling.

"Right, that's all done," he announced. "I've secured all the money and set up a message to say that we're busy for any callers.

And I've downloaded the latest traffic, on and off, the Black Box data, and Rixon's log from our cloud. It'll take a bit of going through but it might give us some answers. I'll make a start; it'll give me something to do."

"I can help, maybe set up a search in the computer for keywords," suggested Ria. Griff took her hand and squeezed it. "We're going to make a good team," he said, his love obvious.

"How long were you in the troopship before it was jettisoned?" asked Myra.

"About four hours," he replied, I was just about to come out for lunch when… Wait a minute!" He frowned, trying to remember the details. "There's something, I can't recall it," he muttered and shook his head, as if trying to physically align his neurons.

"What?" we all asked at once.

"I remember bits and pieces," he answered. "The job wasn't due but Rixon insisted I do it that morning."

"Does that mean that he knew something was wrong, maybe he was trying to protect you?"

"Maybe, things were different since you and Myra had gone, the whole atmosphere had changed on board."

"How do you mean?"

"The new crew, the ones we got from New Devon, they were not ideal, there was a lot of tension."

It sounded like the happy world we had left had gone downhill.

"Rixon, me and Tan were in one group," Griff explained. "The new engineer and Nav kept to themselves, they were okay and onside with Rixon. They were a couple and highly recommended. The fly in the ointment was the man we got to replace Stu. He was Marik, he said he used to be a security guard at one of Pennington's mines; he was hanging round the port looking for work. Well we hadn't got anyone from the agency and we were ready to leave so we took him, we thought we could check him out on the way to Farista."

That was just about as wrong a place to get crew as you could find. All the dubious types hung around the ports, safe from the customs and discovery.

"Why did you take him?"

"I don't really know why," he said with a perplexed expression. "Maybe I can't remember because of the bump on my head? He was signed on by Rixon. He got off on the wrong foot with Mitch and Ardullah, instead of keeping his head down and getting established, he made it plain from the off that he didn't like the way they did things, said they were sloppy."

It sounded like a disaster, in a small crew, the last thing you needed was a troublemaker.

"In the Navy," I said, "we'd have got rid of him straightaway, presumably he was on a trial?"

"Oh yes, that was the plan, we could see he was wrong for us but before we got to Farista and could; well it all got messy. Marik made a play for Mitch, she knocked him back, obviously he hadn't been paying attention. Tan got upset at that and wanted to get involved. Mitch stopped her, words were said and the whole thing fell apart. Marik had a rethink, he sat back. Then, when we got to Farista, Mitch and Ardullah walked off the ship."

This was terrible news. "Then what happened?"

"Tan went crazy, she had to be restrained, we locked her in her cabin. Rixon said it was the first time he had ever had to do that. Marik realised that he had overstepped the mark. He apologised to everyone and said it would be best if he went. He did but of course it was too late."

What a mess. "So when you came to get us, you were three men light?"

Griff nodded. "That's why we weren't answering your calls; we had all that going on. Tan was not best pleased without Mitch… well let's just say that things were strained and work took longer than it might have. And with the jobs we had, we all had to do extra to make up. I was doing lashings, at my age!"

There was a lot of food for thought, maybe a reason in there for the destruction of the *Orca*. I had a sudden thought, "Could the Chenkos have hacked Nancy and set up something while they had the *Orca*, back on Nara? Maybe there was a bit of code hidden in a message to trigger a virus or subroutine."

"I don't think so," said Myra. "I went over all the systems after we got free, I couldn't find anything."

"I know!" Griff shouted out. "That's it!"

"What?"

"The reason I found Marik logged in. He must have been a Chenko plant, I caught him fiddling in the database, he said he was trying to find a movie to watch."

"You think he was doing something he shouldn't?"

"I went over his history but couldn't spot anything, I told Rixon, the night before. It's possible he was hacking the system. Trouble is, unless we find him and ask him, we'll never know, best to get over it and move on."

We absorbed this and it certainly made us think. We had all been changed by the events of the last few days. And in a way he was right.

But then there was the drive, and the proof that there was a second man. It hadn't been Marik, we were no closer. It all seemed immaterial now though.

We scooped a few more times in the debris but found nothing, any evidence had gone. There seemed little point in staying here any longer.

"What was Rixon's plan after we had met up here, Griff," I asked.

"It was my plan really," he said. "You know the man on New Devon; he was a shipping agent and cargo broker. We used him to get an introduction to the crewing company and he told me that he wanted to sell up and retire. I think I could do a deal with him. His agency was going to get work for both ships, no reason I couldn't buy him out and do it for you though."

"How would you feel being stuck on the planet?" In answer he waved his stump. "Wouldn't be much use out here anyhow would I?

And you'll need someone with contacts while you get organised."

Ria spoke up, "I'll keep him happy, he won't want to stray from me."

"What? You be a businessman, Griff?"

"Don't laugh, boy. I'm not getting any younger and New Devon is a good place to be, as good as any and I've seen a few."

Chapter 43

New Devon was a revelation, probably the most beautiful place I had ever been. The scenery was breathtakingly glorious, unspoilt by man's colonisation. If it hadn't been for the fact that it seemed to rain all the time, it would have been perfect. The people were friendly and the food was good. Griff explained that the port had a gang of young women, the locals called them Gyrls, who guarded the ships from theft or damage in exchange for food and a few coins. In itself that was no surprise, a lot of ports had them in one form or another, but all female gangs were unusual.

One wandered over as we opened the ramp, a scruffily dressed teenager, all in black with dark hair and eyes. She walked with shoulders forward and a fixed, determined stare. Griff said, "Leave this to me, I've been here before." He talked to her for a while and when he came back he introduced us. "This is Hannah," he said. "She'll be watching the ship for us."

She waved her hand. "'right all," she nodded. "Like the Sprite! Griff 'ere says you're seeing Ivan. Tell Benj I got it so far."

I was confused by that, but Griff seemed pleased.

As we rode into town he explained. "The port wouldn't run without the Gyrls," he said. "Unofficially of course, you keep them onside or else. They're all tec wizards; they can get in to your ship anyway so it's easier to work with them. They can do small jobs or supervise cargo work for you, once you get their trust or get vouched for."

'Interplanetary Freight', the agency that had provided Griff with my replacement was a run-down concern; with one old man and his wife in charge. Ivan and Eva were lovely people and the six of us got on really well. The agency had clearly seen better days though, they were losing interest, and wanted to retire and explore all the places they had been sending ships to while they still could. That was dependant on the price being right. After some haggling they agreed to sell Griff the business and all the goodwill they had built up over the years. They made a point of introducing him to as many of their customers that they could find, growers of fruit and vegetables and manufacturers of electronic goods.

And they stuck around for a while to help us pick up the way of working, which on New Devon was very laid back and relaxed. "Never put off till tomorrow what you can put off till the day after," Ivan told me. "That's the New Devon way." As I said, the Federation would rather the place was called Nova Five but the locals just weren't that keen.

The Gyrl called Benj was their contact in the port, she organised the watchers in return for food and a bed in the back of the office. They had been training her up in the legal and financial aspects of agency work and pleaded with Griff to keep her on. "She will be a big help with your first harvest," Ivan said. "She knows the ropes and you'll be glad of her help."

We signed the deal and they departed on a grand tour of the sector. We saw them off and they seemed to have got ten years younger just by selling us their lives' work.

Griff used the money from the *Orca*'s accounts to buy the agency, it covered most of the costs of setting us up, even though it was a small outfit it had good contacts and Griff was right, there was money to be made. The small loan that we had taken out was soon paid off. Once Griff and Ria had looked through the books they discovered several ways to save money and make the company more efficient. There were a few freighters on contract to the agency; I joined them and found to my relief that the other skippers were a friendly bunch.

I was worried that they might see me as a threat to their livelihoods but with Griff and Ria taking a different approach to running the business there was more than enough work for all of us. With Benj helping, Griff and Ria soon got the hang of the job. Myra meanwhile kept busy working with me on the *Freefall*.

We settled into a routine, the work was varied with plenty of return cargoes; the trips weren't too long and pretty soon the events of the past retreated in my mind until they were just memories, faded at the edges and full of uncertainties and contradictions.

Myra wanted a place to call home, I still had the apartment that I'd bought as Finn Douglas, but I was never there so it seemed logical to sell it. Rick, all that time ago on Basilan had changed the title deeds to show that Dave Travise owned it. In the end, I actually made a good profit on the deal, now Myra and I could get a place of our own.

Property prices on Nova were high, but between us we managed to get an old house on the coast. It looked out over the ocean and was in desperate need of renovation, it was the only reason we had been able to afford it. Myra immediately took it over as her project, Griff found cheap materials and a few workmen for the heavy lifting. In his usual way, he had quickly added to his network of 'contacts' and I made a few trips on my own while they were doing the place up. I'd never really had a proper home on land, I'd only spent the odd week in the apartment and it felt like a novelty shutting the world out behind our own door.

Between them they did a fantastic job, Ria helped out with the decorating and soon we were ready to move in.

"I can see myself getting old here," she said one evening as we sat outside watching the sunset over the ocean, the blue turned to crimson by the last rays of daylight. A gentle breeze riffled her hair, she had never looked lovelier. "And I can't think of a better place to have ended up." At that moment, I couldn't have been happier, everything was sorted and the future was ahead.

After six months I asked Griff if he had ever tried to find out any more about what had happened to Rixon. He said that he hadn't; after all, the wreckage was conclusive enough to show that survival was very unlikely. "It could have been an asteroid strike or some rapid depressurisation," he said. "I was just lucky that I was in the troopship."

"But there was another troopship plus the two shuttles," I pointed out. "Someone else might have got off. You said that Rixon made you go in there that morning; he must have had some inkling that something was happening." It occurred to me that if he had been the second traitor on board then that was all a lie. I couldn't bring myself to think it could be him though.

Myra had been fidgeting around for several weeks now and I sensed that something was not right. I left her to her grumpy moods and mumbling for a while, she was too proud to ask for help, I had found that out the hard way already, when she was ready she would let me know what was on her mind.

In the end, we were sitting having breakfast, overlooking the sea. There were whales close in under our piece of cliff, blowing and sounding in the clear, unpolluted waters, saved from the persecution they had endured on Old Earth by carriage to this new world. They had thrived in the rich waters on Nova, now the native fishes were under threat, nature would find the balance; as long as we kept out of it.

"I have to go away," Myra announced, tears in her eyes. I moved to hold her and she snuggled into me. "It's Mother," she said.

This was the first I had heard of her mother but then I had never mentioned mine.

"What about her," I replied, expecting to hear of some illness or desire to visit her daughter's new home.

"She doesn't know," Myra said. "And every day I don't tell her it's worse, now I can't put it off any longer."

"She doesn't know about Rixon?" I was surprised. Even if Myra and she weren't close I would have thought that she would have been told, so she could mourn her son.

"I didn't tell her at first because I didn't want to believe it. And as time went on I knew I should tell her but it seemed so final, as if I was admitting that he was gone." She stopped and sobbed again as I held her, her body shaking. "I don't want to believe it. You and Griff talking, well it made me realise that I had to do it, so I'm going."

"I'll take time off, come with you." She shook her head.

"No, I'll go alone." It was said with force and invited no argument. "But I'll keep in touch," she said in a softer tone, mollifying me.

"Okay." I had no choice. "When will you leave?"

"Tomorrow," she said. And in the morning, when I awoke she had already gone. She left a note, 'Dave', it said, 'I'll be gone a while, I have to catch up with Mother, she works as a surveyor and I need to find her. And I need to get my head around all the things that have happened. Don't worry I'll be okay and I'll be back as soon as I can, Myra'.

I asked Griff if he knew, he was surprised. "Messinya and Myra weren't close," he explained. "Rixon was always her little boy and I think it annoyed Myra that she never really treated him like a man. She was always a tomboy anyway but it always felt to her like Messinya thought she was the son that Rixon hadn't been."

Ria seemed to have known for a while longer than I had about her going, she thought that it was brave of her to go and tell her that her son was in atoms orbiting a moon somewhere in the Rim. "I couldn't do that," she said, awe in her voice. "Myra is so strong, so sure of herself and what to do."

Rixon always seemed like a man to me, but then, I wasn't his mother.

"Did she tell you when she would be coming back?" I asked.

"She thought maybe six months."

"Six months?" I couldn't be without her for six months, the thought of a week or so had been bad enough.

I lost interest in the empty house after that, it didn't feel the same, I started living on *Freefall*, and Myra called me a lot at first, then as the weeks turned into months it gradually got longer and longer between calls. I knew then that she wasn't coming back and the thought depressed me. I threw myself into work, taking any and all the jobs I could, just to keep busy and stay away from Nova. When I was in the office I was miserable and distracted.

Ria noticed that my mood was deteriorating, to be fair it wasn't hard, and one day after Myra had been away about five months, she grabbed me and dragged me into the inner office. "Sit down," she ordered, shutting the door. "We're having a little chat."

It was then that I broke down and told her that I felt I had lost her. She reassured me, "Silly," she said in the practical way she approached everything, "you men have such fragile egos. She's fine, it's just been a stressful few months for her, getting involved with you, getting the *Freefall* and then losing her brother. And seeing Griff lose an arm as well. She just needs time on her own, she talks about you all the time."

"You hear from her?" I asked, annoyed. "She never contacts me, well only once a fortnight or so."

She backpedalled, "Well we send messages, look, Dave, don't worry, she'll be back."

About three weeks later, I was sitting in the office, sorting out the details of the next few trips when there was the sound of a car stopping outside. The door swung open and Myra appeared. She saw me and ran to hug me as I stood. We embraced for ages and I felt my spirits soar. Eventually, we broke apart and I looked at her. She looked pale and tired and different somehow, her eyes had changed, lost a bit of their sparkle.

"Are you alright?" I asked. "I've been so worried."

"He thought you'd gone," Ria helpfully added.

"You silly man," she said. "I'm tired and I've been halfway around the Rim but I'm glad I did it. Messinya and I are getting on so much better now and I've finally got it all clear in my head. Rixon's gone and I'm at peace with it. I know what I want."

"What do you want?" I said, thinking, whatever it is, it'll be worth it.

"You," she said and grabbed me again.

I tried to talk to her about where she had been, but she would not say much except that she had found Messinya, told her and comforted her through the grief. Then Messinya had asked her to stay with her for a while, she was all the family that was left. Myra couldn't tear herself away until the thought of me had made her leave; then the peace between them had threatened to fracture again.

"It was hard, emotionally hard," she said. "I don't want to bring it all up again; let's just say we talked a lot and I realised that she just wanted to keep me with her, I was all she had left."

"And yet till you said you were leaving I never knew she existed," I had to say it, that was the one thing that had bothered me, Messinya had been so peripheral; then she was suddenly the most important person in the sector.

There was silence from Myra, as though I had discovered a guilty secret and I realised that I had said the wrong thing. "How do you get on with your parents?" she asked. "Wouldn't you want to see them in similar circumstances?"

"You're right, I guess," I answered, my relationship with my parents wasn't exactly conventional, perhaps it wasn't up to me to judge. Myra glared until I gave in. "Sorry," I said.

She smiled, "Okay, after I sorted Messinya out I had to take some time to get my head straight. I went into a meditation retreat, that's why I didn't call so often. That made me focus on what was really important, and then one day, I just felt ready to come back." In other words, don't ask.

And then things got so busy that we forgot all about it. We were facing the harvest, the busiest time of the year for the produce producers, the fruit and vegetables from New Devon were famed all over and it was a race to get them to the markets. I needed Myra with me, despite Benj and her contacts there were simply not enough people to do all the work. We were doing the jobs the stevedores normally did, such was the pressure on the port. We left the house, we could finish it later.

The pressure to ship the harvest coupled with the continual and never ceasing movement of the technology that New Devon produced made it even more manic. Time on the ground was non-existent; we were often discharging and loading at the same time. At least once we were full and away, we could only go as fast as we could go. And there was usually some extra produce left on board for the crew, which made a change from the usual boring food. If there were no immediate return cargoes we came back empty for the next load. Griff and Ria were glad of Benj; she had worked harvest before and kept everything on track.

At last the season tailed off, work got easier and we actually had a few days off with no job planned. We went back to the house and spent time there, just the two of us.

After a few days relaxing, Griff called us, a long trip had come up, it would mean nearly a month away and I was relieved when Myra said that she would come with me. I had to deliver a load of technology, weather conditioners and generators, to a planet called Deccan, it was a one way load; that was okay from our point of view because the fee more than covered the return empty but I didn't want to spend that much time on my own; away from Myra.

We filled up with lots of good food and drink for the trip; hopefully we would be able to do a bit of sightseeing on the way home. We planned to make it into a holiday.

When we got to Deccan, we found that it was a new world they were setting up and had little to trade anyway, which meant that we were clear to make a lazy return to New Devon. We unloaded and sorted out the usual things, fresh water, garbage and a couple of small inspections outside the hull, all part of the never-ending job of keeping *Freefall* in good condition.

The planet itself was quite different, mostly rocky with small seas and large ice-caps; it was cool and dry. It was ideal for the needs of the settlement, they were researching quantum engineering. In conversation the leader explained that the atmospheric conditions, low humidity and lack of a strong magnetic field were perfect for their experiments.

We had decided where we would go on the way back; there were several of the wonders of the sector that we could explore. We were just about ready to leave when we were approached by a systems engineer called Morrie Klein. He had been working on different planets for nearly a year and was desperate to get home. He said that he missed his family on New Devon and had heard that we were on the way back. Could he come with us? That put paid to our holiday. I talked to Myra.

"It's okay," she said. "He's been away from his home for so long; we've got to take him."

I still tried to put him off; I wanted her to myself, to have this time while we could. I offered him passage at a ridiculous price and his face fell.

"I've not got that sort of money," he said. "But I tell you what; I've got something else you might want." He held up a glossy brochure. "Look!"

That was it, my selfishness was forgotten. "Let's talk." I was hooked, I knew I was helpless to resist.

Chapter 44

I only had to consider it for a few seconds. The trip back at maximum speed would take us just over a week and it would be long enough for him to get the work done. Myra agreed to provide the missing piece that he needed to pay for his passage. Her input took all of a minute. He said that he needed twenty-four hours with *Freefall* totally shut down, so he could set up the hardware and install the main part of the software. The rest of the job he could do on passage. Myra wasn't happy about letting him have the run of 'her' engine room but he promised to take good care of it.

"All the hardware has standard plugs," he said and she nodded.

"I know all that, it's just my engine room…"

"Don't worry," he reassured her. "I'm used to engineers; you won't know I've been there."

We used the time to explore Deccan in a ground car, taking a tent we camped in a secluded valley, cooked on an open fire and slept under the stars. It wasn't the long holiday we had hoped for but would have to do.

When we returned, Morrie looked pleased. "I've got the unit working," he said. "And all the main systems are cross-connected; I can tune it up on the way home."

"I'll go and have a look," said Myra. She was gone an hour and I sweated, she was a perfectionist and I could imagine her trying to find fault. Morrie looked relaxed.

"It's an occupational hazard," he said as we drank tea. "Probably the worst bit of the job, invading someone else's space."

He needn't have worried, she returned with a smile. "Sorry," she said, giving him a hug. "You've done a very neat job, the wiring is all hidden and there's only one extra unit that I could find, on the racks with the auxiliaries."

Now it was his turn to smile. "Thanks," he said, "but there are four extra units, I'll leave it to you to find the other three."

We were ready to leave so I went to the wheelhouse with Morrie; Myra was in the engine room. I called her after the ramp was closed and she started the engines and transferred power. Now was my chance to see if Morrie had made good on his part of the deal. I cleared my throat.

"Good morning," I said.

"Hello, Dave," replied Myra's voice from the speaker. "What can I do for you?"

Morrie's grin said it all. "I reckon that pays for your flight," I told him, as the computer lifted *Freefall* off and set a course for home.

Over dinner, Morrie told us a bit about the projects he had been working on. I would have thought that a systems engineer would have had a quiet life but not Morrie. There was enough excitement in his tales for a lifetime; he seemed to have been involved in all sorts of adventures. There was a lot more to it than just installing hardware and getting it working.

Every day he worked on fine tuning and testing the new Nav system and in the evenings he told us more of his story.

Now, two days out of Nova, we came almost up to date. He told us that he had come to Deccan from Hulm. Hulm is the Federation's prison planet and he had been upgrading the management software.

Myra's eyes lit up at that. "Oh, tell us some stories about Hulm," she pleaded. "The Federation keeps it all secret; we only get rumours and gossip."

"I'm not supposed to talk about it," he said seriously. "But you've been good to me so I'll tell you a bit, but not tonight, it's late and there's a lot to tell. It'll keep till tomorrow."

I went to the wheelhouse for my nightly checks, Myra departed to the engine room for the same. Feeling a sense of déjà vu, I asked the computer for information on Hulm.

"Sure, Dave," 'Myra' said. "There's not a lot, most of it is classified." It felt strange hearing Myra when I knew she was in the engine room. But on my solo trips it would be invaluable. Morrie had got me to fill out a personality survey and put the results into the system. Now the computer was starting to understand me and my sense of humour a lot better.

It was a lot more sophisticated than the system the *Orca* had been fitted with, although that one had attuned itself to me pretty sharpish, this one was more subtle. I thought that Myra might have had some input in the programming as well, a lot of her personality was there in the voice, not just the sound. I wondered for the first time who Nancy had been based on. I would have to ask Myra or Griff.

"Okay," she said, "Hulm is the place where all the bad guys are kept. The whole planet has been turned into a fortress. There are widely spaced islands and the prisoners are segregated on them. The lower grade criminals live in supervised communities; they fend for themselves, grow crops and survive as best they can. There's a gang culture, the guards keep out of it and leave the inmates to it. And they do actually get released at the end of their sentence, if they make it. As the severity of the crime increases the population are housed in more and more secure facilities. The worst are in solitary confinement in tunnels underground. They get allowed into sunlight once a month, always alone."

Pretty grim stuff, even the small time criminals had to fight to survive.

Myra continued, "The planet is surrounded by armed defence satellites and patrolled constantly. It's run by the Federation armed forces, they used it for training." She paused for a moment. "That's about it, but unofficially the word is they use the worst of the prisoners in live firing exercises."

It sounded awful; I couldn't help thinking that I would have ended up there if I had been caught before Basilan. No wonder the death penalty had been abolished; it wasn't needed. Just the threat was enough to keep the Federation quiet.

After dinner the next day, we settled into our seats and Morrie carried on with the story.

It was all a bit disappointing; Morrie repeated a lot of what the Nav had told me.

"What about the juicy stuff?" asked Myra.

"What, you mean the tales of heroic hardened criminals fighting brutal guards, of brave resistance to hardship and injustice; all that sort of stuff?"

She nodded. "Yes please."

"Okay," he said and told us stories that the guards had told him, the grisly ends of famous murderers and robbers, rebellions squashed and escape attempts. And I recognised a few names from my days on the *Moth*, we had put them there. If I had been captured and sent there as a Navy deserter I would have been in more trouble than I had been with Rixon.

"Of course, a lot of what went on there is still secret," he said. "I was kept in the control rooms and didn't see much. But there was one other great story, a recent one too."

"Go on then," said Myra, eyes shining. "Don't keep me in suspense any longer."

"You know that they say no one has ever escaped from Hulm?" he said. We both nodded; it was common knowledge and part of the mystique, after all how could you get off a heavily defended planet? There were no commercial facilities; the whole place was locked down.

"Well it's not true, there has been one, and I was there when it happened. A maximum security prisoner called Vlad Chenko. He's the first person ever to escape from Hulm."

Myra went pale. "Do you know him?" asked Morrie, noticing the change in atmosphere in the room.

"Heard of him," I replied for her. "How did he get out?"

"Long story," said Morrie. "He was in a fight in the prison and was thrown over a balcony. He landed on a table, it broke his back. He was patched up but the spinal fusion didn't work, his spine was too badly damaged and couldn't be repaired. He would need a wheelchair. The authorities weren't going to bother, after all he was never going to be released but his lawyers argued for it and in the end he got permission."

That figured, the Chenkos had a lot of clout and people on the payroll.

"On one of the fittings," Morrie continued, "he was broken out by his gang; they were pretending to be the wheelchair makers. They had been several times before and were all supposed to have been checked out. They swapped him for a lookalike they had hidden on their ship. It was so brazen that no one noticed. When they left they just took him off-planet, easy as that. No one has seen him since."

Chapter 45

"That's amazing," said Myra. "Vlad Chenko was well known where we used to work; we heard that he'd been caught for something."

Morrie nodded. "He'd been running a huge racket with his brother; apparently the brother disappeared around the same time as Vlad was arrested, he must have got wind of the way things were and scarpered."

We knew the true story about that, but didn't say. "How long ago did he get out?" I asked. Morrie screwed up his face and thought for a moment.

"About two months ago I guess; I'd been on Deccan six weeks so yeah, about two months."

We speculated about it for a time, just for something to talk about, we couldn't concentrate and really wanted to get Morrie out of the way to decide our next move. Eventually he turned in and we could talk.

"We need to get onto Griff," said Myra. "He can put out some feelers. He has a great network of contacts; they can let him know if Vlad is sniffing around."

"At least we will be arriving tomorrow. Two months is a long time, you could find anyone in that time."

"Even legally," said Myra. "And we've not been hiding; we've left a trail a blind man could follow, never mind one in a wheelchair with a grudge."

"I wouldn't have thought that the Chenkos would have had enough people still loyal after what we did to organise that sort of operation," I said. "With no leaders left I'm surprised that they didn't just melt away, join up with some other gang."

"The thing is," Myra told me, "you never knew them that well. They were so far under the radar that they were considered above suspicion on some worlds. They had political connections; probably a lot of people owed them favours. They could have planned the rescue, found someone to make a wheelchair like that and got someone to hide him, like you were hidden by Dolmen."

"Perhaps Vlad will just give up and settle down, after all his argument was with Rixon and when he finds out that he's gone he might assume that we've gone too." I tried to sound hopeful.

"I doubt that," said Myra. "They lost a lot of money with you and Rixon, and don't forget that Vlad lost a brother. That sort of thing makes for long memories. We'll have to keep our ears open and be a bit more discreet in our dealings for a while."

The next day we landed on Nova, Morrie said goodbye and left. He had kept out of the way after his revelation, I think he realised that we knew more about the Chenkos than we were letting on. Still, he had done a great job with the computer and I was grateful.

Chapter 46

Griff was very concerned about our news. "Vlad won't rest till he gets us all," he warned us. "I know you think you know all about it, Dave, but it goes back a lot longer than your involvement. Well before the other Dave was involved he wanted Rixon out of the way, he was a competitor. He'll find out easily enough that you're still alive, and the last he knew from Van was that you were captive. So he'll want you for destroying his ship and killing his brother. Even if he can't prove that it was you. He wants Myra for... well you know why and he wants me because I've managed to shaft him more than once." Said like that our chances were not good.

"Who's this Vlad Chenko?" asked Benj, she was in the office doing something that looked technical. She was like a mini-Griff; she just drifted around and got a remarkable amount of things done with no obvious effort. She was quiet and inconspicuous as well, and so efficient that we hardly noticed her unless she wasn't there.

"He's a name from our past," said Griff. "Perhaps we'd better get you away to somewhere safe, it's not your argument but he won't see it that way if he turns up."

Benj stuck out her chin. "I'm with you," she said. She leant down and pulled a wicked looking knife from her boot. The blade was about eight inches long and serrated. "He'll have me to mess with as well." Her loyalty was touching but I remembered Danno. The Chenkos wouldn't let a Gyrl stand in their way; she would be swatted like a fly. Even if he was in a wheelchair.

"Let's hope it doesn't come to that," said Myra.

Griff put his network of contacts onto the job of discreetly finding out what Vlad was up to. All the pilots on our books were given the story of Rixon's demise to pass around, hoping it would spread and get noticed. We had an anxious wait for information; I didn't want to go anywhere until we had an idea what he was up to. Myra stayed close; Ria wondered what all the fuss was about till we told her the full story, then she stayed close as well.

We all ended up living on *Freefall*, jumping at shadows. We kept the ship fully stocked with food and ready for a quick getaway. Our wonderful house was neglected. Benj stayed in the office, fielding calls and keeping the knife handy. In fact, she took over the day to day running of the agency. We had to fill her in on more of the Chenko story, her eyes widened and despite the threat, she was obviously excited, it must have sounded like a story out of some video adventure.

Griff soon started to hear things; Vlad was spotted on several planets, in his wheelchair, together with a couple of his old henchmen. The word was that he had fitted guns into the arms of the chair. He was heard asking if anyone knew of Rixon's whereabouts. Then he must have got to hear of the *Orca's* disappearance because he suddenly went quiet and seemed to have lost interest. Then we heard from one of our pilots that he had gone to the Independent Worlds.

We decided that it was safe to relax a bit, we moved into Griff's apartment over the agency and I started doing short trips, local hops that got me back every three or four days. This went on for a month or so. Then it happened.

Chapter 47

I was just about to land when Myra called from the office, there was a problem. "I don't want to discuss it on the radio," she said. "Just get in here as quick as you can." She sounded very agitated. I didn't even shut down the engines; I just left *Freefall* with Hannah.

"Can't stop," I shouted. "Watch the shop for me."

"No problem, Dave," she shouted as I ran towards the station and headed to the office. As I moved through the port, I saw a line of pallets with *Freefall* stencilled on them, my next cargo had turned up, and the stores. Hannah would sort all that out for me.

When I arrived, everyone was sitting in the office, Myra was dispensing tea, she rushed to me and held me.

Ria was in a terrible state. "I called Evan as usual last night," she said, "and it was obvious that something was wrong, he had been frightened and was agitated. 'I had visitors looking for you and your friends', he told me. 'They wanted to know where you were, Harly tried to get rid of them but they beat him up'." I remembered Harly; he was the man that Evan had hired to help him, a good man, loyal and dependable. "I asked him who it was," said Ria, but I think we all knew.

She continued, "Don't know, he said that he didn't introduce himself, just started breaking things. He was blond, very thin, in a wheelchair. He had two men with him; there might have been more on the ship. They had snakes tattooed on their necks and down their arms. He said he wanted to speak to Dave but you might know him as Finn."

It was definitely Vlad; he must have traced us, not that we had been hiding. The Rixon story hadn't stopped him. He could have found me from the ship's register or my house that I'd sold or they might have found Griff through the agency and worked backwards. There was so much evidence that Myra, Griff and I were still alive after *Orca* had vanished.

Ria carried on with her father's message, "The man said that you had put him in the chair, he reckoned he needed to find you. His wheelchair, it had guns fitted into the arms, he used them on our hogs. He said he'd give him a few days to think about it. He laughed while he shot the hogs. If father doesn't tell him where you are when he comes back, he'll use the guns on him." Ria was distraught. "He's trying to get me to get you all to Wishart," she said. "He obviously knows a lot about you."

"We haven't been keeping ourselves a secret," said Myra, we had all thought that we were safe with Vlad in prison and Van gone. Until we had heard from Morrie, at least that had given us a warning, we had forgotten about Ria and her father's part in this.

Griff said what we were all thinking. "We'll have to get to Wishart sharpish, get Evan to safety before Vlad goes back."

Freefall had only been on the ground a few hours, I had clearance to leave again and we were all going this time. Ria was desperate with worry; I think Griff was looking forward to the chance of finishing things off once and for all.

We got ready to leave the office; there was no need for us to go anywhere else before the port.

The door opened and two Federation guards came in, wearing full uniform and body armour. They superseded the local police, you only saw them if something big was going on, something interplanetary, like an escaped criminal maybe? We relaxed.

"How can I help you?" asked Ria. We all stopped and waited.

"We're looking for Griffon Alyoushan," said the larger one, waving his ID card around.

"That's me," said Griff and the second scanned his arm and nodded. "Looks like you've had some action," he said, gesturing at Griff's missing appendage.

"Long story," Griff agreed.

"And who are these four?"

We were all scanned, my heart stopped but I tried to appear relaxed about it. Then when the guard reached across to scan Myra, his sleeve rode up his arm and I saw it, the tail of a snake tattooed on his arm.

Now I felt really scared. We were in deep trouble.

"Just a routine check, Mr Alyoushan," the first guard said. "We're searching for an escaped criminal and your name came up."

"This one's Dave Travise, the Gyrl's Benj Solan," said the second guard. "The other two are Myra Rixon and Ria Constable."

"Who are you looking for?" Griff asked.

The two looked at each other. "Nothing to worry you, sir, that's classified information. We had a report he might be here, do you mind if we take a quick look around?" The pair moved through the reception area into the office. There was a cellar leading off it, hopefully they would be a while. I put my finger to my lips, grabbed Griff and dragged him into the street. Myra and Ria followed, looking puzzled.

"What are you up to?" Griff asked.

"They're not guards," I explained. "They're Vlad's men."

Griff was instantly alert. "How do you know?"

"I saw the snake tattoo on one," I answered and he looked shocked.

Benj came out into the street, she looked pleased with herself. "Are they the guys you were worried about, Mr Griff?" she asked. "I heard Ria saying what had happened to her father."

"Yes that's right," Griff said. "Make yourself scarce for the rest of the day, Benj. Come back here tomorrow and if you don't see us again for a while, just keep the place going."

She looked shocked. "But you'll be back, won't you? And I've just locked them in the cellar for you. I followed them in, quiet like, they never noticed me. I saw them both go into the cellar so I shut it and locked it. Was that the right thing to do?"

"You're a genius, Benj," said Myra. "That was exactly the right thing to do. Of course we'll be back, now scram." Benj ran off down the road.

"Let's go then," Griff said. "They'll be out any second, there's not much of a lock on that door."

We went to the guards' patrol car; the doors were unlocked. "Jump in," said Griff. "If we take their car, they can't follow us, at least not as quickly."

"Can you start it without the key-card?"

He gave me a look. "Watch me; if I can't then I deserve to get caught."

Chapter 48

He pulled something out of his pocket and waved it in front of the sensor, the engine burst into life. Griff floored the pedal and we shot away, just as the two fake guards came out of the office. There were shouts and shots, followed by thumps as bullets struck the rear of the car. Then there was a crash and the rear window and the windscreen exploded. I felt the bullet pass by my ear, like a burning hot wasp.

"Get down," shouted Griff and the girls hit the floor, we slid around a corner; tyres screeching.

"Everyone alright?" I called out and both girls answered.

"Head for the port," Myra shouted and Griff shook his head.

"And what if they have the *Freefall* staked out?"

"There were two of them, that's how many Evan said there were with Vlad." Myra was practical, assessing the odds. "Vlad can't have many of his old crew left. We got most of them on the Bishop and the rest would have melted away when he went down, those that weren't caught with him. And scores would have been settled with him inside. No, two is probably all there are."

It made sense; I just hoped she was right.

"We'll have to chance it anyway, there's nowhere else to go," said Ria. "And I want to get to Evan if I can."

"Were they real guards or just Vlad's men pretending?" I wondered aloud.

"Does it matter?" replied Griff.

"Well it might if the real police spot us," I said. "You're driving like a maniac."

"Good point." Griff slowed down and we drove sedately to the port, we attracted little attention and got there quickly. The pen with *Freefall* in was deserted, where was Hannah? I had left her sitting in a chair by the entrance; the chair was still there but it was empty. We found out when we went into the pen, she was huddled in the corner, an ugly bruise on the side of her head. Her breathing was shallow; at least she was alive. "We'll have to leave her here," Griff said. "I'll call the medics when we're away."

We ran on board, cargo had been loaded and lashed in my absence; I hadn't had time to think about my next trip, Hannah's organisation had got ahead of our plans.

There was a shout behind me, and a shot; it hit the frame of the ramp and pinged away with a shrill whine. I jabbed at the controls and the ramp started to close.

As it lifted I saw a man run towards the *Freefall*, a gun in his hand. It was one of the guards from the office, he must have had another vehicle ready somewhere, and clearly there were more than two of them. At least he wasn't going to make it aboard. That should improve the odds a little; hopefully we only had one man in a wheelchair and one less guard to deal with.

Myra had carried on and was halfway up the ladder to the accommodation deck, following Griff and Ria. "I've shut one outside," I shouted, dodging into the workshop. I used the remote Nav pickup to prime the engines and ready us for a quick getaway. Remembering what had happened on the Bishop I put the computer on silent, and rigged it to obey me only; I didn't want anyone else in charge. At least I hadn't shut it down; if I had it would have taken us a while to get ready to take off. And it couldn't have been done quietly. Who knows where we would go though, if Vlad had found us here then we were in serious trouble. He must have come on a ship, they could follow us, we weren't armed, it would be easy for them to attack us. We'd just have to face that if it happened. I grabbed the pistol I kept hidden in the tool-rack and headed topside. If one man was outside, that still made the odds better. I had only been a couple of minutes sorting things out, once I caught up with the others and lifted off we might be okay.

I ran towards the bridge, my heart pounding, feeling comfort from the pistol in my hand. My feet clanged on the deck, and I slowed. What if there was someone already there? I walked silently, so as not to advertise my arrival. In my head I could see possible outcomes, and silently prayed that I wasn't too late.

The wheelhouse door was open and Myra was facing the doorway, I could see that she was tied to the handrail along the bridge front. She saw me approach. She tried to hide her smile and inclined her head to the left, to indicate that someone was there.

"Is that you, Finn? Come in," called Vlad. "But put the pistol down first, we are all reasonable people here." His tone was so calm that I almost did. Myra looked at the deck and I understood. I dived into the space and rolled, hoping my momentum would take me behind the console, and out of Vlad's sight. As I moved through the air a shot rang out, hitting the bulkhead roughly where my chest should have been, denting the panel. The bullet ricocheted around the space. Then I saw the second of Vlad's men; as I rolled upright in what I thought was cover. He was on the other side of the console, creeping up on me with a smirk on his face. Vlad's bullet bounced around and hit him just above the left eye. I watched the back of his head blow open in a burst of red. There was blood everywhere. One of the girls screamed. He toppled without a sound still with the same expression.

As I peered cautiously round the corner I could see Vlad's reflection in the ports. He was in his chair, a pistol in his hand. There were two shapes built into the armrests of the chair, they must have been the guns that Evan had mentioned. The barrels looked like two cannons. Surely he wouldn't use them in here? They would ruin the hull and control gear.

I could see that Griff and Ria were next to Myra, all three of them tied to the handrail. An idea was forming in my head, and I wondered about the strength of the rail.

Vlad was moving, I could hear the tyres squeaking on his chair as it crossed the metal deck, coming my way.

He was talking as I scrambled around the console, keeping away from him. "Mr Douglas, I just want my money back. Now I have found out that you spent it on this ship and some other things. I'm afraid to tell you that it's mine now, of course after what you did to my brother it would only be fair that I should take something of value to you as well."

It was time for me to find out just how strong the rail was.

"Nav, immediate lift off, up angle sixty degrees, dampers off, execute," I shouted out the orders. "Okay, Dave," replied Myra and Vlad looked around to see where the noise was coming from. Below me there was a rumble as the thrusters rotated and the engines, already primed, fired.

Chapter 49

Instantly the deck tilted as we rose, I was already tight to the console and pressed back against it as we accelerated, without the dampers the G force was immense. There was a howl from Vlad and the whine of his chair motor as the wheels spun for purchase. In the end they gave up and by craning my head I could see his reflection in the port as the chair slid backwards into the bulkhead. I lost sight of him but heard the crash as they met. There was a rattle from the alleyway as the henchman's body bounced aft, and from the cabins and everywhere else as unsecured items fell to the rear. I pulled myself up and risked a look, Vlad's chair was wedged against the bulkhead and he was unconscious, head lolling in time to the vibration as the engines roared. Clouds scudded past the ports as we rose into the sky. The radio squawked, "*Freefall*, what are you doing, you haven't called departure control."

I ignored it. "Level flight, dampers on," I called and our motion changed. It was suddenly quiet as everything fell to the deck, except for a fine haze of dust that hung in the air. Standing, I crossed to the rail and untied Myra, we hugged each other in relief.

Griff coughed. "Let me go then," he said.

Myra turned to Ria and undid her wrists, while I did the same for Griff. It was their turn to embrace.

"Let's get Vlad secure," I said. "There are all sorts of questions I want to ask him."

"You're not the only one," Myra had a catch in her voice. "Before he dies I want to know if he killed my brother."

I turned back to Vlad, but he was gone. There was a crash from the alleyway.

"Come on," shouted Griff. "He's gone aft." We all ran for the exit.

"He can't be far." His wheel tracks were visible in the bloodstains left by the henchman's body as it had bounced down the alleyway, but at the top of the hold access they stopped.

I opened the stowage and pulled out the pistols that I kept there. Griff took one from me but Myra refused with a shake of her head. Ria had no reservations and cradled the weapon in a grip that showed she had used a gun before. I already had one so I left the rest in the stowage and we split up. I sent Myra and Ria back to the wheelhouse. "You'll be safe there," I said.

"Go!" echoed Griff. I flipped the main hold lighting on and we peered into the space.

The first thing we saw was the chair, it had fallen down the ladder but there was no sign of Vlad. Even if he had not been thrown clear of the chair he must have been hurt by all the acrobatics, but somehow he had managed to crawl out of sight.

The hold was half full of crates, they had been well lashed so they hadn't shifted, but it meant that there were dark shadows and corners, any one of which could hide Vlad. Griff put his finger to his lips in a gesture for silence. I passed him a torch and took one myself.

Cautiously, we went down the ladder, I felt very exposed to a bullet and I was sweating; I lost my grip and slid down a couple of steps, making a racket. Nothing happened.

Reaching the deck, we split up and searched the hold. I saw the henchman's body, at the end of a long red smear, but no sign of Vlad. We met up again at the bottom of the ladder. "Anything?" I asked Griff, he shook his head. Where was he?

Suddenly there was a scream from the wheelhouse and we both made a lunge for the steps. We jammed each other on the ladder and in the time it took to sort ourselves out we heard two shots. Lungs bursting, we jumped up the steps and raced to the bridge, me in front. Vlad's corpse was blocking the doorway, he must have sent the chair down the alley as a decoy and hidden in the heads, his withered legs were tangled and bloodstained and it was obvious that he was dead. Shoving his body out of the way I went to Myra and Ria, who were both on the floor.

Ria had a gun in her hand, the barrel smoking. "I shot him," she whispered in a shocked tone. "I shot him." Why wasn't Myra speaking? Turning my head I could see where the second shot had ended up.

She was sitting against the bulkhead, looking relaxed; there was a neat red dot over her heart. The light had gone out in her eyes and my tears welled up as I looked at her face, the calm expression spoiled by their blank stare. I had told her to go to the wheelhouse, told her she would be safe there. I would have to face the guilt I felt. And I wouldn't have been alive if it hadn't been for her warning; I looked at the dent in the panel, she had saved me, but I didn't save her. I felt guilty for surviving.

Ria saw my face. "It's not your fault, Dave," instinctively she had read my mind. "I should have been quicker."

Griff sat beside her and held her. "It was logical, Dave," he said. "We all thought he had gone aft."

Ria looked straight at me. "I'm sorry, Dave," she said. "I wasn't quick enough." She was in shock, repeating herself.

She sobbed. I felt numb, as if I wasn't here and that none of this was happening.

"*Freefall*, this is departure control, what is your status?" The voice from the radio brought me back to reality, we were flying somewhere and maybe getting in the way, I hadn't had the chance to check for traffic since we had lifted off.

"Stand by, control, we have a systems problem," I replied.

"Computer, is there any traffic?" I asked, feeling a pang when I heard Myra's voice answer.

"Negative," she said. "We are in clear air." Suddenly her voice on the computer wasn't a cute joke any more. With a jolt, I realised that it was all I had left of her.

"We have another craft approaching, Dave," said Myra. "It's calling us."

"Is it the border patrol?"

"Negative, it's a private ship, no ID is available."

"It must be the Chenkos'," said Griff; clearly there were more than two men with Vlad.

"Can we outrun them?" *Freefall* had no guns or shielding and only light armour. Griff answered that question.

"I'm going nowhere," he growled. "We finish this today. Let's hear what they have to say."

Chapter 50

"But we have nothing to attack them with!" I reminded him.

"They don't know that, remember; this is an old Navy ship." Talk about bluffing! What did he think I would do, wave my fist at them?

The speaker burst into life.

"Vlad, Marik, are you okay? Have you got control? What sort of manoeuvre was that?" So that had been Marik, he had been part of this after all.

Griff shouted towards the microphone. "This is Griff; Vlad's dead," he said, "and Marik as well, there's nothing here for you any more."

"They're closing on us," Myra reported. "They have a missile lock."

There was silence; I could see them through the port, a small pleasure yacht, all black with an extravagantly curved hull. It would be fast and manoeuvrable. I could see an armament pack secured under each wing.

"Listen," Griff persisted, "Vlad's gone. If you were working for him because you had to; because he had some sort of a hold on you, then that's gone as well. So you have a choice."

There was silence. The other ship dropped astern out of view, into the perfect place to launch a missile straight into the exhaust. At that range they could hardly miss.

"Stand by for evasive manoeuvres," I called, knowing it was futile; they were closer than the *Moth* had been to the battery on Oonal, there would be no time for anything. I tensed my stomach muscles, ready for the end. Nothing happened.

"Yacht *Oblaya*, this is traffic control; warning, you are in proximity to commercial traffic, alter your heading immediately." The voice of the airspace controller filled the silence, would that be the last thing we heard?

"Where's the other ship now?" I asked. There was a pause before the computer spoke.

"It's heading into orbit," replied Myra's voice. "Full acceleration."

The ship shot past us and we rocked briefly in its wake, it was that close that the dampers couldn't cope. As they became a dot in the clear sky I let out the breath that I had been holding for several minutes.

"It looks like it's over then."

"We need to get somewhere and dispose of Vlad and Marik, and do something decent for Myra," said Griff, the ever sensible. "We can't land anywhere like this, if the customs turn up we're in deep trouble." He was right of course, no one would mourn Vlad or Marik but there would still be questions. I couldn't take the attention.

"We can go to Wishart anyway," I reasoned. "Let's drop the cargo like we're supposed to and then go check on Evan. We can empty the trash on the way."

"What about Myra?" asked Griff. "She's only just been back from her mother for a little while, don't you think we should tell her, she might want to have a say in where she rests?"

That was a fair point. "Do you know how to contact her?" He shook his head.

"Ria?" he asked.

"I don't know, honestly, she told me that she left her somewhere when she went into the retreat, her mother could be anywhere."

"I know exactly where Myra is supposed to go," I said.

Griff called traffic and said we had sorted out our engines, earning a rebuke, we would be probably face a fine and an engine inspection on our return but we would be clean by then. It would be a nuisance but no more. Griff probably knew someone in traffic anyway.

Between us we put Myra into the freezer. Vlad and Marik we dumped out of the lock as soon as we were clear of the system. The chair went with them, to drift around for eternity. But I removed the guns first; you never knew when they might come in handy. Then we had some cleaning up to do. I looked at the panel, I could smooth out the dent and repaint it, no one but me would ever know. I decided to leave it, for the time being at least.

I did turn Myra's voice off of the computer, using mode 101. I couldn't stand to hear her, knowing that she was in the freezer. Morrie had left the default voices in the system and I chose a male one for the time being, maybe I would put Myra back on when I felt a bit better. But I was glad that I had got the system when I had, at least I would always have her to listen to when I really needed it.

Ria was a comfort, I confided in her, cried on her shoulder and told her a lot about Myra and me, about our plans for the future. I told her about our last serious conversation just a few days ago, when she had spoken about wanting a child.

Ria's welled up at this point. "I didn't know she'd told you that," she said. "But I do know that she told me she had never considered the idea of children before she met you."

We delivered the cargo, picked up a few things and set off for the moon where we had found the wreckage of the *Orca*. I was going to leave Myra as close to her brother as I could.

We landed by the remains of the troopship and Griff and I suited up. Between us we carried Myra over to the wreck, it was just as we had left it when we had found Griff. He shouldn't have been able to help with one arm but he was determined and lifted his share. He looked at the wreck and shuddered at the memory. After we had laid Myra inside, I took the blasting charges we had brought and rigged them at the base of the mountains against which the hull rested. After retreating to *Freefall* I triggered them and the troopship vanished, buried beneath hundreds of tonnes of rubble. Dust hung over the site; it would take a while to settle.

Griff and Ria had been sobbing quietly on and off for most of the trip. I was barely holding it together. I knew it would have to come out. As the troopship vanished; the three of us had stood in the silent wheelhouse; in a circle; hugging and crying.

Eventually we had to go. As I lifted off, I felt release, Myra was at rest and I could come back and see her anytime. I would find Messinya and tell her, bring her here if she wanted, she could hear Myra's voice again in the computer, if she could bear it. Perhaps it would be time to turn her voice back on soon. But for now we had one more thing to do. And this had the potential to be difficult. Ria had run away from Evan and the farm, after promising to stay until Harly was up to speed. And Evan disapproved of Griff, hell he probably blamed him for Ria's departure. And of course I had brought Vlad to his door. So it was with a little trepidation that I approached the farm on Wishart.

I landed the *Freefall* by the barn that had been her home for so long and we all walked across to the house. It still had the same battered air as when I had first seen it; Ria seemed excited to be back, oblivious to the potential for conflict.

We found Evan around the back, tending to his chickens. "I heard you landing," he said in that slow style of his. "Reckoned I'd let you find your own way over. You're still with… him then, Ria? Sit yourselves down while I get us some tea." He cast disapproving glances at Griff; clearly he was even less impressed with him than he had been when he had had two arms. I was waiting for the explosion but it never came. Nor did the handshakes or hugs you might have expected at a reunion. The atmosphere was decidedly frosty and Ria faltered in her enthusiasm.

We all sat in silence, Ria made no effort to go and help him. "I can tell; he'll start on again about Griff," she said sadly, "then I'd get wild, we'll have to leave and we've been getting on okay up till now."

Based on what had happened since our arrival, I reckoned that the distance had helped their relationship, keeping them apart made it easier for them to get on.

Evan returned with tea and biscuits and poured. "So," he said at last, after we had sat for a while, "Ria sent me a message that you were coming. She told me that Vlad is dead, that she shot him." He looked at Griff, with a 'why didn't you protect her and shoot him yourself' sort of expression.

Griff stared straight back at him. "She did, and I'm proud of her." Evan muttered into his tea and turned to me.

"And I'm sorry to hear about your young lady," he said. "Terrible waste, that Vlad was evil, his men beat up Harly and he laughed while they did it, and I know it wasn't your intention to lead him here. And you've suffered enough without me adding to it." He waved his artificial hand around; it seemed to be working perfectly. "She fixed this for me," he said. "I liked her and I'm grateful, Ria says you buried her on a moon somewhere?"

"That's right, near to her brother." He thought for a while.

"That's good," he finally opined.

"And I'm sorry too," I continued, "that you got dragged into my problems. I thought that with Vlad in prison on Hulm everything would have been alright. You should never have been involved."

He shrugged. "Scum always floats. Is he the reason you only have one arm, Griff?"

"He is," Griff answered. "I know you don't like me too much, Mr Constable, but I'm looking after Ria the best I can. I hope that she's with me because she wants to be."

Ria leant across and held his one good hand. "Believe me, Father," she said with meaning, "I love you but there's nowhere else I'd rather be than with Griff, just as he is."

Things were starting to get cheesy when Harly arrived. He was middle-aged with a weather-beaten expression. His arm was in a sling. "Day all," he said, in a carbon copy of Evan's voice. "Nice to see you again, Miss Ria, perhaps you can finish showing me around, when you have a moment?" His delivery was deadpan and

I wondered what her reaction would be.

Just as she was about to speak, Harly's face cracked into a grin. "OK I admit it, I'm just teasing, you did fine, Evan talks about you a lot."

After that, the day got better. Harly seemed to have provided some sort of perspective on Evan's attitude and now that he was here, he was less grumpy. Maybe he could see and accept that Ria was happy. The beer made an appearance and we sat in the afternoon sunshine and swapped stories. Evan's sense of humour started to show through and helped by the alcohol we all relaxed.

He told us that the farm was doing well, apart from the loss of a few hogs to Vlad but he had already replaced them.

"It's a blessing really," said Evan, as we sat on his porch as the sun set. His barbeque was going and we were surrounded by empty beer bottles. "The hogs were due for slaughter anyhow," he said with a grin. "We've got enough bacon and sausage in the freezer for ages now, thanks to him."

Keep up with Richard Dee at www.richarddeescifi.co.uk

Myra is the prequel to *Freefall*

Dave Travise is an interplanetary trader with a past. Trying to forget, whilst being constantly reminded is no way to live, but sometimes letting go is just too painful. The ship is his past, so that's part of the problem.

So when excitement comes back into his life, in the shape of a dead girl and a stolen disc, his world turns upside down. Events take control of his life, and before he knows how, he's at the centre of a Galaxy-wide conspiracy, chasing the answers that explain the past and may hold the key to the future.

The story moves from the civilised centre to the edge of exploration. A cast of pirates, smugglers, and legendary explorers all play their part in a story that's older than us.

Here's a sample

As the night wore on I was getting more and more desperate, I had found news of three of the names on Griff's list, two were off-planet and the third was in lock-up for assault on a Guard. That meant that I only had one chance left. Wearily I trudged on down the brightly lit street.

Several drinks and bars later, I still hadn't found any news of her. Like the rest, this bartender professed never to have heard of Elana Vilde.

She was not the only woman on my list; when he sent it, I thought that Griff was still trying to find me a new Myra. His message said that Ria had suggested her as a very experienced mate, ex-captain of mine transports, demoted for a little misunderstanding with loading figures, but handy to have around in a tight spot.

As I nursed my drink in the noisy, smoke-laden atmosphere, I reflected on the Rim, and the people who worked it. You needed to be a special type of person to survive, unlike exploring the confines of a planet, out there was a whole big load of nothing, you might spend a lifetime in space, work yourself to death and no one would mourn your passing. Or you could make a name for yourself on your first day. And the work was physically very demanding. No wonder some people looked into the blackness and went crazy.

Someone slammed into my back and I turned, there appeared to be a fight developing and I had been hit by a flying miner, blood streaming from a cut on the side of his shaven skull. All miners had shaved skulls; it helped the helmets and ear protectors to fit snugly. And they had a reputation for fighting at the drop of a hat. Suddenly half the occupants of the bar were fighting the other half, chairs, bottles and glasses were flying and the noise had increased.

"Sorry, friend," he gasped. "More of them than I thought." As I turned back to my drink, I could see in what passed for a mirror behind the bar that there were three huge men advancing towards him, expectant looks on their faces.

"They seem to think it's my round," he explained. "You fancy giving me a hand?"

The request was strange, after all I didn't know him, but I had had just enough booze to feel invincible, and by the look of the bar, fighting was a regular occurrence. Besides which, I hadn't found who I was looking for, and I was starting to feel frustrated.

"Alright," I said. "Then it will be your round." He grinned and we turned to face the foe.

They were quick these three, and strong, the first picked up a wooden chair as he advanced and while I was looking at him his ally came at me from my left. I felt a huge fist explode against the side of my head and I reeled away, bouncing off the bar and scattering drinkers and furniture as I flailed for balance. My head was spinning and my thoughts seemed to have slowed down, so that I could hardly think of what day it was, never mind my next move.

He followed me and I tried to duck in anticipation of his next swing. This punch skimmed past my ear, but even the glancing blow was enough to make me see more bright lights.

I shook my head as I straightened up, he was stood in front of me, all stubble and broken teeth, but in his excitement he was unprepared for retaliation. Summoning up all my strength, I drove my fist into his stomach. I heard his breath whoosh out, and as he doubled over I raised my knee into his face. There was a satisfying crunch and he collapsed.

I felt my arms grabbed from behind and saw the third man advancing; looking over I could see that my new friend was down, there were pieces of chair scattered around his prone body.

I thought that I would be clobbered for sure, and the man raised his fist, preparing to punch me into orbit. My head throbbed and I still couldn't think straight. My arms were pinned tightly at my sides and I was surrounded by fighting drunks and shattered furniture. There was nowhere to go. He saw this and grinned.

A huge female figure appeared between us and waded in. My head was clearing and I remembered something that had been done to me once before; I kicked back with my boot and felt it rake the shin of the man holding me, he yelped and his arms briefly relaxed. With a wriggle and a lunge I was able to pull free.

He tried to hold on to me, but he was too slow, I grabbed one of the man's arms and pivoted on it, building up my momentum until I was in range, then I lashed out with a fist to his jaw. It felt like hitting a rock, only with less give, but he sank to his knees and slowly folded onto the floor.

"Thanks," I said to the woman, who was standing over the body of the third miner, "I needed that."

She grinned. "Not too much of a workout, I only hit him twice." Looking at the size of her arms; twice would be enough to stop most men, and probably many medium sized animals as well.

"Buy you a drink? I'm Dave."

"Cheers, Dave. I'm Elana, my friend behind the bar says you've been looking for me, and I had a message from Ria. I've been following you for a while, so what's it all about?"

Lightning Source UK Ltd.
Milton Keynes UK
UKOW01f2319030217
293568UK00001B/16/P